UNENDING LOVE

ALEX & KATLIN

KALYN COOPER

Unending Love

KaLyn Cooper

Cover Artist: Drue Hoffman

Editors: Trenda London, Rebecca Hodgkins

ISBN: 978-1-970145-17-5

Published 2021 by Black Swan Publishing, LLC

Copyright © Published 2020 by Black Swan Publishing, LLC

Printed in the United States of America

This is a work of fiction. The characters, incidents and dialogues in this book are of the author's imagination and are not to be construed as real. Any resemblance to actual events or persons, living or dead, is completely coincidental.

MESSAGE TO THE READER

Welcome to *Unending Love*, the seventh book in the **Black Swan series**. Although all my books are stand-alone, you may wish to read the entire series so you are familiar with all the characters.

If you are a fan of the **Black Swan series**, then you've seen Katlin and Alex from the very beginning. *Unending Love* concentrates on the tenuous relationship between them after she suffers a traumatic brain injury. Parts of *Unending Love* were written at the same time I wrote *Unrelenting Love*, but I decided to end the book when they committed to each other and write the other members of the Black Swan team. Look for more of Katlin and Alex's story in *Undefeated Love*.

Thank you for purchasing *Unending Love*. If you enjoy this book, consider purchasing the other books in the **Black Swan series** as well as the related **Guardian Security series**.

Always,
KaLyn Cooper

DEDICATION

*I dedicate this book to the men and women who spend time in
a military hospital.*

ACKNOWLEDGMENTS

I'd like to thank the Ladies of Black Swan Book Club who encourage me, make me laugh, and suggest names. A special thanks to Beverly Blank and Allison Utz.

Many thanks to my Beta reader, Teresa Christianson for catching several items I missed.

I couldn't have written this book without the help of my friend and fellow author Rachel Rivers. She shared her first-hand experiences with me so I could get the details of IVF accurate.

A sincere thank you to Drue Hoffman for my wonderful cover, Trenda London for her story guidance and insistence on changing the ending, and Rebecca Hodgkins for cleaning up my mistakes.

I want to thank my husband who was learning how to be retired, sequestered at home thanks to COVID-19, and ignored by me most of the time as I wrote this book.

My heartfelt thanks to all of you!

ABOUT THE BLACK SWAN SERIES

Rara avis in terris is Latin for "a rare bird in the lands." In the ancient world, it was believed that the landing of a single black swan created a change that would affect the entire world.

Fact: A woman can get a man alone within hours ...and kill him in seconds.

Fact: Men always underestimate beautiful women.

Fact: There are a lot of entities in our military that very few people know about.

Fact: Walter Reed National Military Medical Center has made amazing strides in Traumatic Brain Injuries.

CHAPTER 1

"Be safe, Kat." Alex Wolf put his heart and soul into the kiss, keeping it sweet and gentle. It could be weeks or months before he held his fiancée, Katlin Callahan, in his arms again. He refused to think about the possibility of her being hurt, or worse. He never knew how long she would be gone and since all her missions were top-secret, she couldn't tell him even if she knew.

Breaking the kiss, he took her hand and laid her palm on the middle of his broad chest. "You're taking my heart with you. Bring it back whole, and safe."

Katlin took his hand and pressed it between her breasts. The diamond ring he'd given her punched into his palm. She'd already taken it off her ring finger and secured it on the titanium chain where she wore it while on duty.

He loved the idea that his gift lay between her large rounded breasts, the exact spot his head had rested a few hours ago as he listened to her heartbeat slow down. They'd made love twice before she had to crawl out of bed and shower, where he'd had her once again. Then she shrugged into the black flight suit, morphing into Lady Hawk, team leader of the Ladies of Black Swan.

Two black unmarked SUVs pulled into the parking slots next to them.

Katlin let out a heavy sigh. "Time to go." She pulled him in tight, staring into his eyes. "I love you."

Five men poured from the newly arrived vehicles, loudly kidding each other as they brought their bags to the only door on that side of the faded green hangar.

"I love you, too." Alex briefly kissed her, then forced himself to pull away and open the vehicle door on his side. As he made his way to the back of the Guardian Security SUV, he reined in his emotions. Each time she left, it was harder and harder to say goodbye. Maybe someday he wouldn't have to make this trip to Marine Corps Base Quantico and let her fly away with his heart. Damn. He loved her.

As a former Marine Raider commanding officer, he understood her commitment to her country and the U.S. Navy as an active duty Lieutenant Commander. He accepted the fact that she and her team had been assigned to Section 7 of Homeland Security. He hated the control her boss had over her.

Fuck it. He had to be honest with himself. He hated Jack Ashworth, not just because he was Katlin's boss and could send her anywhere, anytime with minimal notice, but because the man controlled Alex's ability to be with Katlin.

Alex glanced toward the door where the men—who would be on this mission with her—gathered their gear. Katlin wasn't happy about this coed mission. Alex was a tiny bit jealous of the time she would spend with these men over the next few weeks, perhaps even months.

He had no doubt his woman would be faithful, as would

the other four women on her team. Each had found the love of a good man over the past two years. No. Alex was more concerned about how these men would treat Katlin and her team. More than once, she had referred to the male team leader as a misogynist. He hoped she didn't have to put up with too much of his shit.

Alex handed Katlin her bags then glanced around to see who was watching. He'd been through this drop-off procedure often enough that he knew he couldn't approach the hangar without the possibility of being shot by the armed Marine guard.

Pulling her into his arms, he gave her a quick peck before quickly releasing her. "Call me on your way back home. I'll get to D.C. as soon as I can." As the managing partner of Guardian Security, he could be at any of their ten locations spread across the United States.

"I'll try to contact you whenever I can." Katlin scowled as she looked at the men who were digging out official IDs for the second guard who showed up with a clipboard. "Johnathan is such a pain in the ass for protocol. He has no clue how deeply encrypted Lei Lu has made our computers.

"I'm not sure why they're even on this mission." She returned her gaze to Alex, then grinned. "Except Jack is so jealous that you and I are together." She wound her arms around his neck. "And I'm so madly in love with you it drives him fucking nuts." She kissed him, obviously not caring who saw her public display of affection. "That he wants to keep us apart as much as he possibly can, even if that includes a bullshit mission."

"Callahan," one of the men bellowed. "Quit fucking around and get over here. Little Johnny soldier won't let Will into the hangar."

Alex cringed at the man's insult. No Marine ever wanted

to be called a soldier. Soldiers were in the Army, just like sailors were in the Navy. Marines were…well…in the Marine Corps.

"Is that Jonathan?" Alex's eyebrows drew together.

"Oh, yeah." Katlin stepped out of his arms. "This is going to be so much fun. Not." She inhaled slowly and let out a deep breath. "This mission can't be over soon enough as far as I'm concerned. Love you."

A heavy duffel bag over each shoulder, she sauntered toward the hangar where her team was preparing their sleek black jet to fly to…wherever.

As he crawled behind the wheel of his company SUV, Alex pulled out his phone to check his secret Kat app. He smiled as he looked at the screen. A green dot pulsed on a map of the Washington D.C. area. When he homed in on the view, he could see that she was a hundred fifty feet away. Satisfied the phone application created by his computer genius to show Katlin's embedded tracking chip was working perfectly, Alex turned the key and headed out the Marine Base's front gate.

His phone rang as he merged onto Interstate 95. No phone call at one o'clock in the morning is ever good. The caller ID flashed on the screen, containing only the number with a southern California area code. It couldn't be too bad since it was only ten o'clock in California. He pressed the button on his steering wheel to answer. "Alex Wolf."

"Alejandro, I need your help," the woman said in staccato Spanish. "He…he's going to kill me."

The blast from his past hit him like stepping out of an air-conditioned house into a warm gust on the leading edge of a tropical storm. "Jae, slow down. Who is going to kill you?" He returned in the same language they had both spoken as children back in the seedier side of D.C.

Jael Jimena Martinez had been his first love in kindergarten; his first lust at twelve; his first kiss when they were thirteen; and his first virgin the day after her sixteenth birthday. They'd briefly reconnected in every way possible right after he'd purchased what was now Guardian Security Los Angeles Center.

"I don't know." Her voice shook on those three little words. "That's why I need you."

"Are you in a safe place, now?" Alex's anger wanted to explode at just the thought of someone hurting his beautiful friend.

"Yes. I'm staying with my friend, Payton." Then she quickly added, "A girlfriend."

"Good. Now tell me, where are you?" Since Jae's acting career skyrocketed a few years ago, she could be anywhere in the world. No matter where, though, he would go to her. He owed this woman his life.

"I'm in Irvine." She rattled off the address that Alex instantly memorized.

"I'm going to send a guard over there right—"

"No!" She interrupted. "Alejandro, I want you to come."

"Jae, take a deep breath. I'm coming but it will take me several hours to get there. In the meantime, I want you to be safe." Alex wasn't even sure he could catch a flight yet that night, but he was sure as hell going to try. For her, he would charter a fucking airplane.

"Oh, okay." She dragged in a shaky breath. "How soon do you think you can get here?"

"As soon as I make arrangements, I'll call you." He pulled off the exit toward Guardian Security D.C. Center. "In the meantime, what makes you think someone wants to kill you?" Jae had always been dramatic, which made her an excellent actress. It might turn out to be nothing to worry about, but he would go to her and soothe her worries.

"Because he's sending the fucking notes, pictures of me everywhere I go." Her voice was getting louder and shaking harder with every word. "He took a picture of me…naked… with Jon Michelson." She sucked in a breath. "We're… fucking. He scribbled over Jon's face, and across the whole picture wrote 'You are mine. Fuck him again and I'll kill you both.'" She was in tears, gasping in breaths to finish. "He tried to kill Jon this morning."

Alex pulled into the ground-level parking garage. So, he supposedly tried to kill her latest man. Fortunately, all of his centers had good relationships with the local police. It should be easy to get more details on the incident.

"Stay with me, Jae. I'm walking into my D.C. office and I need to talk to someone in the control room to get a man sent to your house." Alex got out of the SUV and headed into the stairwell.

"You're going to send someone to my house, too? As well as here?" She had a little more control of herself.

He needed to get his shit together. Why hadn't he thought about sending someone to her home and searching it? Unless she'd moved, again, Guardian controlled her security system.

"Yes, I intend to send somebody to both places." On the second floor, he strode into the control room. After giving the shift manager specific instructions for the Los Angeles office, he put the phone back to his ear as he took the elevator to his penthouse apartment.

"Jae, one of my men is going to call you as he pulls up outside your friend's house. Please let him in." Once in his apartment, Alex went straight to his computer to look for a West Coast flight. "Now, Jae, where are the notes and pictures this fucker has been sending you?"

"The latest one, with me and Jon…you know…should still be in the kitchen wastebasket." She hesitated a long few seconds before she confessed, "It's in pieces. I'm sorry. I tore it up."

"Understandable. At least you still have it." A thought flashed through Alex's mind. "Have you reported this guy to the police, yet?"

During her silence, Alex scanned the list of flights on the executive jet service his company used. If he hurried, he could make the three a.m. express to LAX. The four-hour flight was nonstop. He could be there before she woke up.

"No." Her quiet word interrupted his travel thoughts.

Realizing she answered his earlier question, he couldn't stop himself from blurting, "Why not?"

"Alex, I get threats almost every day." Her tone called him an idiot. "My PR staff handles all that. If it looks serious, they bump it up to Ivee. If she thinks I'm genuinely in danger, she talks to the security on the lot where we're filming." She sniffed. "But we won't be filming for at least a week. Maybe two. Jon got so banged up in the accident. If it was an accident."

Jon was obviously in the same movie as Jae. Alex would have time on the flight to check him out. In the meantime, he was relieved that her on-site security had been notified, but he had to clarify. "So, this Ivee person believes this is a viable threat and has notified the security chief on the set?"

"Hell, no! Ivee doesn't know anything about these pictures. I'd be so embarrassed if she, or anyone else, ever saw them. I'm completely naked." Jae screamed the last three words.

"Breathe with me, Jae. Suck in a deep breath, fill your lungs." Alex inhaled deeply as well. "Now, let it out slowly." He demonstrated two more times. "Feel better?"

"Yes. You always know how to calm me down." In a sultry voice, she added, "And rev me up. I'm looking forward to spending time with you again. I've missed you, Alejandro."

At hearing his childhood name, he realized they had changed to English at some point. "Jae, you know I go by Alex Wolf now, so when talking to my men be sure to use Alex. In public, I always called you JJ, just as you've asked. We aren't those scared little kids from the hood anymore."

"But in private, I will call you Alejandro." She purred. "Especially while I'm riding you and I scream your name while I—"

"There won't be any of that," he quickly interjected. "I'm engaged."

She giggled. "Engaged means you've promised to marry her, whoever the lucky bitch is. It doesn't mean you have to be monogamous. We can still have a little fun."

"Jael Jimena Martinez, you know me better than that." He hoped she heard the warning in his voice. If he had to fight off her advances, he would pass her on to one of his men and go to one of his other centers. He was too old to play her games…and Katlin still had monogamy fears. He wouldn't stray anyway. He loved her too much.

Changing the subject, Alex asked, "What makes you think this stalker tried to kill Jon?"

"Ten minutes after Jon dropped me off this morning, he was in a hit-and-run accident." Jae's voice sounded more in control. "He's banged up really bad, to the point that we have to stop shooting for at least two weeks. The promoters are having shit-fits because they can't shoot around him."

She rattled on about the movie as he efficiently repacked his bag. He had everything he needed at each of his ten locations, from black utilities to tuxedos, underwear to bathing suits. Alex had learned to always be prepared, but he always carried a few changes of clothes, comfortable shoes, and combat boots.

Tuning back in, he heard her say, "It looks like your man is beeping in. The caller ID says Guardian Security. Hold on while I check."

Thank Christ. She would be safe and he would be there soon.

"Yep. That was your guy." Relief and excitement were evident in her voice.

"Good. I'll be there when you wake up." Bag in hand, he headed for the door.

"Are you going to kiss me good morning?" She teased. "And wake me up the right way?"

"No. Engaged. Remember that. Try to get some sleep." He hung up on her before she could try to tempt him again. Her solicitations were already getting old.

CHAPTER 2

KATLIN CALLAHAN LEFT THE DOOR OPEN TO HER ASSIGNED suite at the newly renovated U.S. Embassy in Baghdad, Iraq, just as she'd done for the past week. It was an open invitation to join her should her teammates feel the need to talk…like usual.

Kicking off the three-inch stilettos on the way into her bedroom, she unfastened the custom-designed wide silver belt. Its wire edges could become a garrote and the large blue and white sapphire studded buckle hid her throwing stars. In one lithe move, she stripped out of the formal gown and rolled it into a tight ball before tossing it into her duffel bag. The navy-blue dress was one of her favorites but would definitely need dry cleaning after the night's activities.

She hadn't been arm candy in a Middle Eastern country in years and had forgotten that gentlemen of power in that area of the world loved their cigars. She hated the smell that her skin and hair absorbed. Unstrapping the thigh holster hidden all evening by the fluid movement of the dress, she took the small Kimber with her into the bathroom and turned on the shower. She always had a weapon within reach. Always.

Her soapy fingers ran over the titanium necklace holding her beautiful engagement ring. Sliding it through her index finger to look at it more closely, warmth filled Katlin at the thought of Alex. She was so lucky to have such a wonderful man. He'd personally selected the white diamonds on either side of the large blue diamond that had been a gift from her father to her mother.

She hoped her relationship with Alex would be as long and loving as her parents had shared for nearly thirty-five years before her mother was killed in a car accident. Her beloved father had joined her in heaven four years ago. She missed them both every day.

Chain still attached, she slid the engagement ring onto her left hand and admired it there. She never wore it while on a mission, but the moment they landed on U.S. soil, she always slipped it back where it belonged.

She wondered what Alex was doing. Before leaving, she'd memorized his schedule. As the managing partner of Guardian Security, the company they owned together, he traveled between the ten centers. Although he hated micromanagement, Alex made it a point to drop into each office every few weeks. That was, unless he and his Guardian Elite team were acting as backup for the Black Swans or on a covert mission for USSOCOM.

Given the time difference, Katlin decided to log onto her untraceable computer and shoot Alex an email before she fell asleep. She cherished the thought of waking up to a return message from him. Damn. She missed him.

Fifteen minutes later, her hair wrapped in a towel, wearing nothing but a cotton camisole with matching sleep shorts, she wandered back into the living room where her teammates already congregated. They, too, were dressed for bed, wineglasses already in hand. Katlin inwardly smiled.

This was her team being real. They were no longer performing as active duty military and agents of Homeland Security. These women were her friends.

"I don't know about you, but I need this." After handing Katlin a glass of her favorite Riesling, Grace released the towel holding her shoulder-length auburn hair and started brushing through the tangles. "I really hate cigar smoke. Thank goodness Griffin doesn't like them," she said, referring to her fiancé.

"Right there with you." She clinked glasses with her second-in-command then they filled empty seats on the couch.

"Tell me again, why the fuck are we even here?" Nita, the team's doctor and Katlin's sister-in-law, bit out. "I know we're trained agents and running backup for Jonathan's team, but in the week we've been here, I haven't picked up a single piece of good, reliable intel. We need to be outside of this Embassy talking to people. Doing what we do best…tracking down a terrorist. I am so over being attached to Josh's side."

"Yeah, me too." Tori poured more red wine into her glass. "And can I just state for the record that somebody needs to tell Kurt to lay off the aftershave and use more antiperspirant. That guy sweats like a double agent under CIA interrogation."

"Do you think he's a mole?" Katlin asked flatly. Intelligence agencies infiltrated each other on a regular basis. Since all the women in that room worked for Homeland Security, Kurt could be a spy from the CIA, the FBI, or from some other nation's version of an alphabet agency. Handlers had tried to flip her several times, unsuccessfully of course.

"No, I just think he needs more training." Tori took a sip before she continued. "Homeland doesn't offer, or require, the kind of interpersonal skills training we received at the

CIA. He's actually very awkward in social settings. He's much more comfortable in desert utilities and combat boots than a tuxedo."

After Katlin's team had successfully completed the All-Female Joint Service Special Operations School which trained them the same way as Navy SEALs, Army Special Forces, and Marine Raiders, they were then sent to the CIA for additional undercover training. Her team, the Ladies of Black Swan, were the most lethal women on the planet.

"I agree. I sat across from Kurt at the dinner and noticed he was always the last one to pick up a utensil and eat, yet often the first one finished," Lei Lu added. "I'll admit, when we sat down at the table tonight and there were seven forks, five knives, and two spoons flanking the dinner plate in addition to five more utensils above the plate, I got a little worried."

Katlin laughed. "I was wondering why we needed five glasses." She shrugged. "But we used every one of them."

Nita rolled her eyes. "How many different ways can they serve lamb? Oh, let's count the ways."

"Let's not." Lei Lu insisted. "But I really liked the way the chef cooked the *kibbeh*."

"It's pretty hard to fuck up ground meat with rice and spices," Nita noted. "Somebody needs to introduce the cook to chocolate. Now, don't get me wrong, I like fruit, but I'm over dates in every dessert. I've seriously thought about slipping over to the French Embassy for a Napoleon."

"Good Lord, don't even mention dates. I swear, they sneak them into every meal." Grace shook her head. "The oatmeal at breakfast has dates in it, the fruit at lunch had dates mixed in, and the biscuits at high tea had bits of them. Eating here at the embassy, you don't need a probiotic or a laxative. And Nita, I'll be more than happy to sneak over to the French Embassy with you, but it might be easier to get into the Swiss Embassy."

Katlin purposefully turned the conversation toward business. "Did anyone get any new intel tonight?" Although their primary mission was to back up Jonathan's team, they also had a responsibility to uncover new intelligence. The women were experts at divide-and-conquering a room filled with business executives, politicians, and their underlings. "I had to listen to Jonathan drivel on and on about all the wonderful things the United States is doing for Iraq. The fucking idiot doesn't realize that you learn so much more when you shut your mouth and listen. To hear him talk, you'd think he was on the embassy staff. I tried to get him to talk to some of the new prime minister's people, but he was more interested in swapping stories about problems in South American countries with the U.S. oil exec. When I tried to walk away from the bastard, he put his arm around me and pulled me in close as though he was about to get to the good information…which he never got around to asking."

"You and Jonathan are oil and vinegar. It's so obvious to anyone watching that the two of you are barely tolerant of each other." Lei Lu wasn't wrong. Noting so, she would have to step up her game if they were going to fool anyone.

"When I first came to Homeland Security, human resources divided the women up and assigned them to existing all-male teams." Katlin didn't believe she was telling them anything they didn't already know, but sometimes it was best to remind people of the past. "I was put on a team with Jonathan, but he wasn't a leader then. He's still a misogynistic asshole. That hasn't changed. He believes our role tonight is the extent of our abilities. We are to be beautiful women who hang on every word, making the man look good."

"Has the pompous ass come up with anything about the new Iranian-backed Hezbollah leader, yet?" Tori asked. "I overheard a conversation that none of the new government officials are welcome in the northern areas because that's still strongly controlled by the Islamic State, even though they don't have a new leader. Not new information, but confirmation of what we heard the other day."

"Fuck. We were told at our in-brief that there are certain streets right here in Baghdad that are controlled by the Shiites and we're supposed to stay the fuck away," Nita pointed out.

"I don't believe the right hand knows what the left hand is doing," Katlin surmised. "Since the Prime Minister has only been in office a few months, he hasn't gained control of the entire country, yet." She smiled. "But he will. He used to be the Intelligence Chief for the previous administration and before that he was in the Counterterrorism Service. He didn't hesitate to pull in U.S. resources."

"I'm just happy the Secretary of State has decided to take his happy ass back to the United States tomorrow morning." Tori voiced what was on everyone's mind.

"Hear, hear." Katlin raised her glass in a toast, and everyone followed suit. Although he'd arrived with his own bodyguards, and the State's version of special operators, the surprise visit had complicated their mission. No locals were going to openly speak of Shiite terrorists surrounded by that much heavy metal.

They heard deep male voices in the hallway. Jonathan's team was also billeted in the area, but they'd have to go out of their way to be at this end of the hall.

Tori, who was closest to the door, raised an eyebrow. Katlin nodded once and her friend gently closed the door. Not soon enough, though.

At the knock, Jonathan yelled through the crack. "Katlin, you still up?"

Tori stood and opened the door but did not invite the men in. "It's late, gentlemen. What do you need?"

The men gawked.

"If you're going have a pillow fight, can we watch?" Will asked as his gaze swept the room of scantily clad women.

"No," all five women said in disgust at the same time.

"We were enjoying a glass of wine before we were rudely interrupted." Katlin didn't get up, simply stared death daggers at the men crowding the doorway. "Was there a purpose to this late-night visit?"

Smugly, Jonathan stepped forward. "I got a line on the new Hezbollah leader. We are going to head up to Kirkuk and check it out." The shit-eating grin he gave her made her skin crawl. "We'll understand if you want to stay here rather than rough it for a few days. I could check with operations and see if there's a Four Seasons or Hilton Hotel anywhere close, but I wouldn't hold my breath."

Katlin seethed but held her tongue. She was quite sure she'd spent more time in a tent eating from an open fire or tiny cookstove than Jonathan. Secondly, where and when had he gotten this mysterious new lead? They had separated in opposite directions at the elevator, both supposedly headed to bed.

"That's got to be two-hundred and fifty miles north." Lei Lu reached for her computer which was never far away. She was the team's tech guru, a genius when it came to the keys.

"You jumping on Expedia to make hotel reservations?" Kyle chided. He used to be one of the good guys but had obviously been hanging around with Jonathan far too long.

Lei Lu looked up and smiled, "Did anybody leave anything back in Tikrit that we need to stop and pick up?"

She looked at Katlin. "Maybe we need to check on our handiwork?"

"Fuck. No." Nita couldn't keep the acid out of her voice. During a mission a few years ago, she'd been captured and tortured in that small Iraqi town.

"I wouldn't go within twenty-five miles of that place without a Geiger counter." Tori shuddered. "When we blew up that nuclear bomb-making facility, I'm positive it threw radioactive materials for miles."

"If I remember right," Katlin's near-photographic memory pulled up a map of the area. "There's a more direct route from here to there." As she thought about Baghdad, though, she suggested, "Check the route through the city first. To get to that main North-South highway, I think we have to go through the Shiite section."

Jonathan slashed her a condescending glance. "My contact gave me directions."

Katlin bolted to her feet. "You mean to tell me your contact isn't going with us?" How fucking dumb could this man be?

"No. He's got more important shit to do here in Baghdad." Jonathan's eyes raked over her braless and pantyless body.

Katlin didn't care. He could look all he wanted. He'd never be able to touch her or any woman in that room. She and her teammates would kill him the second he laid a sexual hand on their bodies. Each of them had a man at home, twice the alpha of any man in that doorway.

"What's this contact's name? I want to check him out before we jump into vehicles and caravan across the fucking desert for eight hours into bad guy country." Katlin would simply call her Uncle Tom, the Deputy Director of the CIA. He'd have an answer back to her within hours.

"No need." Kyle popped off. "I already ran him through Homeland's system, and he came back as reliable."

Katlin threw a glance at Lei Lu who immediately understood what she wanted. Backtracking Kyle's search would be completed before the men were in their rooms.

"Have you checked with the embassy quartermaster for food supply for our little jaunt?" Tori's forethought had the men shuffling their feet.

"Will," Jonathan ordered. "Get on that." The youngest member of his team disappeared from the huddle.

Tori stuck her head out the door. "Hey, Will. You might want to stop by transportation and see if they have an up-armored vehicle to escort us through the city."

"Good idea." The words echoed from down the hall.

This wasn't the first rodeo for the Ladies of Black Swan, but Jonathan's team seemed rather inexperienced. Not a good sign. Worse, they were not in charge. This was completely Jonathan's circus.

"How soon do you want to leave?" Katlin and her team could be ready and out the door within the hour.

"In the morning." Jonathan smiled at her as though he were dealing with a child. "We'll eat breakfast here at the embassy, then get started." His smile broadened. "Be sure to get a good night's sleep, ladies. You're going to need it. I hear the roads around here are rather rough. It's going to be a bumpy ride." He turned around and walked through his men who followed him down the hall.

Tori closed and locked the door. Every one of Katlin's teammates gazed at her as their jaws dropped. What a fucking stupid plan.

CHAPTER 3

"LOOK, CALLAHAN, I'M NO HAPPIER ABOUT HAVING YOU along interfering in my mission than you are to be here. I don't need a gaggle of females to watch out for and then have to worry about sexual harassment charges once we get stateside. We went through this coed team bullshit a few years ago and it didn't work out before, either. You'd just better remember that on this op, I'm in charge." Jonathan got into the driver's seat of the embassy SUV and slammed the steel-reinforced door.

Although she didn't want to be anywhere near Jonathan, they had to maintain their cover, so she slid into the seat directly behind him. "I was just pointing out that the route you selected is right through the middle of the Shiite-controlled part of Baghdad."

Katlin was over this pompous asshole. She was a heartbeat away from contacting Section 7 Operations Control Center and have a come-to-Jesus conversation with Jack. She'd talked to the Marine Captain of the Guard about the route suggested by Jonathan's mysterious informant. The head of embassy security said it was the most fucking stupid idea he'd ever seen.

But had that stopped Jonathan? Hell no. The new information just made him more insistent. Leaving in the middle of the day, practically advertising their route before they left, was one step away from suicide.

Everything about this felt wrong.

Or maybe it was just that she was so aggravated with Jonathan, and everything that man did and said rubbed her the wrong way. Besides, as Jonathan had so clearly pointed out, he was in charge of the operation, so Katlin and the Ladies of Black Swan had to do what he ordered.

When Kurt slid into the shotgun position, Tori crawled into the backseat next to Katlin. Jonathan started the vehicle.

Using the engine noise, Tori said just above a whisper, "This is such a clusterfuck. I have a feeling we'll be traveling for days looking for a ghost."

"Did I hear you say that this isn't the first coed team?" Kurt, the newest agent on the mission, asked.

"Not by a longshot." Jonathan pulled out into traffic, the other two SUVs right behind him. "When Katlin and Grace first came to Homeland, they tried to integrate women into existing teams. It didn't work, but Jack sure had a fucking good time when Katlin went undercover as his wife." He chuckled. "'Undercover' being the operative word." A second later, he added sarcastically, "Or, maybe 'fucking' should be the operative word. That's when Katlin started fucking her way into being a team leader."

Katlin shot out of her seat and wrapped her long, strong fingers around Jonathan's voice box. The SUV jerked suddenly at Jonathan's surprise but Katlin held tight. "Listen carefully, you little pin dick. I've never fucked my way into any job, and if you ever again infer that I did, I'll crush your voice box so you can't spew your venomous lies to anyone else." She applied more pressure, digging her short nails into the soft skin of Jonathan's neck.

She glanced toward Kurt. "To clarify, Jack Ashworth and I were posing as husband and wife while this asshat was backup. I did my job and slept in the same bed with Jack and acted as his wife all day for three weeks. Never, not once, did I allow Jack to touch me sexually or take the pretend relationship to a personal level."

But Jack had. He tried to rape her, and she fought him off. Very few people knew about that incident and she wasn't about to share it with Jonathan and Kurt.

"Have I made my point clear?" Katlin seethed into Jonathan's ear.

"Yes," he croaked out.

She immediately let go of his throat and sat back while he rubbed his neck and drove one-handed.

"I heard that you and Jack fucked like bunnies during the whole mission, and once he promised you your own team, you shut him off like the ice princess you're known to be." Jonathan's voice was still a little rough, but he managed to soak it in sarcasm.

"If you tell me who's spreading those lies, I'll go kill him." Katlin was serious.

Jonathan chuckled. "I'm pretty sure Jack's the one who brags about sleeping with you to anybody who will listen. He gets a hard-on every time you're around."

Katlin cringed. She wouldn't put it past Jack to be the source of those lies and she was well aware of his reaction to her presence. It sickened her.

"I guess I'll just have to kill Jack." That possibility was growing stronger and stronger as he continued to obsess about her.

Tori whacked Katlin's hip with the back of her hand in warning.

Kurt turned to gape at her from the front seat. "I should arrest you for threatening the life of the Director of Operations for Homeland Security."

"I might just let you do that if it means I get to leave this ridiculous manhunt." Katlin pasted on a smile. "I was just kidding. I wouldn't kill Jack. I would just shoot him. Maybe in the hip. He's been a pain in my ass ever since I came to work at Homeland Security. That way, I'd become a pain in his ass, too. Turnabout is fair play."

Out of the corner of her eye, Katlin watched Tori try to hold in her laughter.

When the caravan crossed the Tigris River, Katlin's whole body went on alert. They were getting close to the section controlled by the Shiites.

Katlin had to try one more time. "Are you sure I can't convince you to turn left and circle around this part of the city?"

"Fuck, no." Jonathan headed straight for Route 2 on city side streets. "My informant assured me that this was the quickest and easiest way." His lip pulled up in a sneer. "Are you afraid my team is going to kick yours out of that number one spot? Things didn't exactly go smoothly on your last mission. Your team almost got us into a war with Russia."

"You're just jealous that the Black Swans have a hundred percent success rate, knocking you out of that top slot... hmmm...ever since we completed our first mission." Katlin wasn't sure why she was poking the bear, but he seemed to deserve it.

As they turned the corner, the city seemed to change. Women were covered head to toe in traditional black abayas and niqabs, most with veils hiding their eyes. Although the majority of men wore a thaub, there were still a few in Western-style suits. All the colors seemed to be drained from the stores. Signs were in basic black and white with most windows covered.

It had been years since Katlin had been in this part of the city. She and the ladies of Black Swan had hidden under abayas, carrying their heavy military packs in the front, preferring to look like fat local women than to getting caught as American spies. After taking out their target in the northern provinces, they had to hide wherever they could as they escaped. She had been so glad to reach the Marine Corps base in Falluja. She doubted the base was still there because U.S. troops had been pulled out of Iraq several years before.

Right after that mission, she and Alex had reconnected.

Katlin looked at her watch and counted the time. It was five o'clock in the morning in Chicago where Alex would be just waking up. The green demon of jealousy flared as she thought about Aleta, the beautiful dark-skinned woman he'd taken as a lover for nearly two years before Katlin had reappeared back into his life.

She swept away the anxiety. Jack had planned to throw Alex and Aleta together again in front of Katlin. Her boss's plan had failed. Alex had explained to Aleta that he was in a monogamous relationship and would not be dating her ever again. Katlin trusted Alex. She was sure of his love.

Although he was expected to spend another few days in Chicago before moving on to Dallas, his schedule was fluid and changed depending on where he was needed. Until she was able to log into the Guardian Security computer system, she wasn't sure exactly where he was. He'd be working, that was certain. The man was a workaholic.

She'd sent him a sexy email before she'd gone to bed.

Perhaps when they stopped for the night, there'd be a message from him waiting for her.

They turned another corner onto what must've been a one-lane street. Their vehicles could barely fit between the parked cars on each side. Katlin hated tight spaces.

Every one of her senses seemed to burst alive.

Not a single person was walking down the sidewalk, but it was past prayer time.

Her heart beat faster as the SUV caravan crawled through another place where the cars on either side of the street had been parked too close together.

As she glanced out the window, she caught a glimpse of movement in the driver's side mirror. Leaning forward, she tried to identify what she was seeing as the vehicle bounced over the rough road surface.

On a rooftop behind them, a man in traditional white Arab dress had a green rocket-propelled grenade launcher on his shoulder.

"Incoming," Katlin yelled at the top of her lungs seconds before the car two feet from her exploded.

She bent forward, hiding her hands and face as a piece of the car bounced off the reinforced door and spun in the air before smacking the bulletproof window. Glass rained down on the back of her flak jacket. The percussion of the blast completely deafened her.

Her eyes closed, she thought she was dizzy until she realized it was the entire vehicle flipping in the air.

The side of her face felt as though someone had hit her with a baseball bat.

She fought to stay conscious. This was going to be a mess to clean up and she needed a clear mind to give orders.

Katlin's body slammed her spine into her seat then

bounced her shoulder and head into the door, smacking it hard.

The world started to close in around her. She couldn't seem to focus as her body rocked side to side, delayed a second behind the swaying of the SUV.

She had to force her eyes open.

Her team was in trouble and they would depend on her for orders.

But she couldn't open her eyes, no matter how much her brain willed them to do so.

Her heart beat so fast it hurt.

She tried to raise her left hand to touch the side of her head where it pounded, but her brain had disconnected there, also. Able to move her right hand, she swept away whatever was running into her left eye. Blood gushed over the left side of her face and dripped steadily off her nose. Scalp cuts bled like a bitch.

If only she could get her eyes to open, she could figure out how to get out of this vehicle. She'd worry about getting patched up later after her team took out the son of a bitch who shot the RPG at them.

As though completely exhausted, her right hand dropped down.

She finally cracked her lids open but couldn't seem to raise her head up. All she could do was stare at the blood that dripped off her right hand onto the black floor mats.

Good thing they're plastic. Blood is a bitch to get out of carpet.

Damn, Katlin. You don't have time to be thinking of silly things. Wake up.

I think I'll just take a little nap. Somebody else can deal with this mess.

Aware that she was not thinking clearly, Katlin tried to inhale deeply to clear her mind.

The scream she heard was hers.

Fuck. It hurt to breathe.

She just sipped in small breaths…until even that hurt.

If this was the way she was going to die, Katlin was ready.

As she did before every mission, she visited a local priest who performed Rights of Shriven. These were the Last Rights given in advance should she be killed on unholy ground. At the moment, Baghdad was about as unholy as her Catholic upbringing could imagine.

Her soul was ready to meet her heavenly father, but her heart was still with Alex. What would happen with him?

She gasped in a breath and cringed at the pain.

In her mind, she prayed to God that he would take care of Alex, help him find love again, and have a good life.

Believing that God would take care of Alex, she succumbed to the darkness and let it take her away from the pain.

CHAPTER 4

JACK ASHWORTH WALKED INTO HIS PRISTINE OFFICE AT exactly six forty-eight in the morning. Since it had been raining when he left his Georgetown home, he brought a light overcoat with him in case he had to go to The Hill or the White House. Although it didn't happen often, as Director of Operations for Homeland Security he occasionally had to report in-person. He certainly didn't need the coat while getting to work. His new Mercedes sedan was kept inside his garage, and at work, he had a reserved space close to the executive elevator.

After hanging the coat on the antique rack just inside the door, he strode to his desk and started all his equipment with a palm scan and code. Several screens lit up. He scanned his appointments for the day, quickly memorizing them before he looked at the world map that occupied the largest screen. Colored dots where he had agents blinked according to trouble priority. One glance at the large red pulsing circle in Iraq had him bolting out of his office.

Katlin was there. He had to make sure she was okay.

He blew into the Operations Center and froze. The room

was enveloped in controlled chaos. He'd been prepared to rant, ready to question everyone as to why he hadn't been notified but decided to watch and listen. An expanded view of Baghdad filled one screen. Live satellite streamed on another showing a wrecked black SUV lying on its driver's side. The carcass of a car smoldered twenty feet away, its bumper sticking out of a car's back window fifty feet down the street. A car door teetered on the roof of another. Windows had been smashed on most vehicles and pieces of the exploded car littered the street.

This didn't look like a car accident. It appeared to be a bombing.

And *his* Katlin was somewhere in the fracas.

He watched the live satellite feed, hoping to see her curvaceous body ordering homeland security team members through the rescue. He easily picked out Grace, thanks to her red hair. Jack was pretty sure that was Nita leaning over a male body stretched out on the ground. He recognized a few members of Jonathan's team who were attempting to extract people from the SUV.

"Her blood pressure is dropping," the technician at the biofeedback station announced without inflection. "Heart rate is down to forty-two beats per minute."

Panic swept over Jack. "Whose?" He demanded before he could stop himself.

"Lady Hawk," the tech replied.

No. No. She can't die. She's mine. Forever. We're supposed to have children. Grow old together. Jack strode across the room and stood at the command center.

"Fill me in," he ordered the operations manager on duty. He had to keep his cool, externally calm and professional, especially where Katlin was concerned. He'd finally convinced the agency shrink that he was no longer obsessed with her, finally ending his weekly sessions. Any tiny indication of his continued feelings toward her could get Jack fired.

The agency needed him; they just didn't always realize it. *They* being the Secretary and Deputy Secretary of Homeland Security, the idiot civilians appointed by whoever occupied the White House at the time. Jack had been in Covert Operations since the inception of the Department of Homeland Security's creation in November of 2002. He knew more secrets than he could ever use in his lifetime. With the right word dropped in the wrong place, he could start a war… or end one. At the moment, though, he needed more details on what was happening in Baghdad.

"One dead, one dying, one critical, several with concussions and cuts. Nita Banks is performing triage. We should have a complete report within minutes after they extracted Katlin Callahan from the wreckage." Robert's report was concise.

Jack scanned the screens and noticed one had grainy pictures. "We have two satellites feeding us video?"

The Operations Manager scowled. "Someone is streaming live feed." He pointed to a very young man in the far corner whose fingers flew over the keys. "We're trying to pinpoint the origin and destination now. It hasn't been a priority. I've been much more concerned about how exposed our two teams are and arranging their extraction."

Everything Robert had done was by the book.

"Who's dead?" Jack managed to ask the question now that he was sure that Katlin was still breathing.

"Jonathan Cummins. We're not sure if it was his proximity to the grenade or if he was hit by debris. The explosion was less than three feet from where he was sitting in the driver's seat according to initial reports."

Fuck. Jack hated to lose anyone under his command, but Jonathan had been with him for several years. He was friendlier with the team leader than any other agent. His mind immediately went to a list to replace the fallen man.

"Heart rate is at thirty-eight. Lady Harrier, do you have platelets ready?" The biotech asked.

"Not yet." Nita's voice came clearly through the background noise over the speakers in the room. "I'm working on Ben's gunshot wound. It was a through-and-through but I'm dealing with arterial bleeding. It looks like just a nick, but I don't want him to bleed out on the way home. Kyle's busy holding onto both ends of the artery at the moment. Besides, Will and Lady Kite still haven't gotten Lady Hawk out of the vehicle."

Jack's gaze shot to the photo of the mangled SUV. He had no idea how they were going to get her out of there.

"We've got action." The young blond guy who had been working on the video streaming excitedly yelled. "It sounded like someone busted through the door and gunned them all down. Still recording, but whatever, or whoever, was holding the phone camera, dropped it. It's now showing a close-up of a dark-brown-skinned man in Arabian style clothing with a large bullet hole in his head. He seems to be lying on the floor."

Robert clicked a few keys and the video filled four screens on the wall. He turned up the volume but heard nothing but soft footsteps. A light brown desert boot stepped onto the man's wrist and a large white hand picked up the phone a second before it went black.

"Director Ashworth, you have a video call coming in from CIA Deputy Director Tom Gillpatrick." A man with silver at his temples looked at Jack. "You want to take it here or in your office?"

Jack glanced around the room then decided Katlin's Uncle Tom wanted to know her condition. "I'll take it here, but I don't want him to see anything behind me."

"Over here, then, please." The man pulled back an office chair.

As Jack sat down, Tom Gillpatrick's face appeared on the small computer-style screen in front of him.

"You're welcome," Gillpatrick said by way of greeting. "Tell me, honestly, how is she?"

It took Jack a few seconds to catch up. "Were you able to trace the video feed to where it was being sent?"

"Yes. That end has also been handled. We happened to have a few members of our SOG in the area." Gillpatrick referred to the CIA's Special Operations Group. They recruited the best of the best from the Navy SEALs and Army Special Forces. Those men were certifiably crazy. Jack wondered who they'd been chasing in Baghdad.

"Jack, don't fuck with me. Is she okay?" Concern penetrated each word.

He stared at Tom Gillpatrick's picture on the screen, debating what to tell him. Jack was equally as anxious for news. He glanced at the wall of screens and watched Will and Lady Kite carry Katlin over to Nita as the team doctor pulled bloody gloves off her hands.

Not wanting to share any more than he had to, Jack asked, "Tell me what you know, and I'll add what I can to it."

"Katlin gave me the name of Jonathan's contact who thought he had the lead on the new Hezbollah leader. We've been running the man's name through everything we have and can't find anything on him. He's a ghost. Even our local assets connected directly to the Islamic State have never heard of him." Gillpatrick was telling Jack so much more than he knew.

Out of the corner of his eye, Robert waved his tablet. He'd find out who the fuck this lying piece of shit was, and he'd be dead as soon as Jack could assign an assassin.

Nobody tried to kill his woman.

"We're taking a deeper look at him, too," Jack admitted. With the flick of his finger, the tech at the bio station put Katlin's vitals onto the corner of his screen. "It took them a while, but they finally got Katlin out of the damaged vehicle. Nita is triaging her now. I can tell you that her vitals are improving. As soon as everyone is stabilized, they are heading straight to the airport. I want them all back on U.S. soil as soon as possible and the fastest way to do that is on the Black Swan jet. I just hope someone is healthy enough to fly it home."

Tom Gillpatrick grinned. "I have a few people in the area who could get them back here."

"That's the fastest bird within two hundred miles." Jack returned his grin. "Those ladies aren't going to let anyone fly their plane but them."

"You're right. Keep me posted as to Katlin's condition. DD CIA out." Gillpatrick's picture disappeared from the screen, but Jack didn't move or speak until he received the all-clear. It was a commonly used trick to turn off the camera yet leave the connection open. It was always surprising what people would say when they didn't think the other party was watching or listening.

"Mr. Director, you're clear."

Jack's phone buzzed a unique pattern which was Mrs. Ward's way of telling him that he was needed back in his office immediately. She was a wonderful secretary. Someone higher up the food chain was hunting him, so he'd better leave.

"I want an hourly update on this team." What he really wanted was to know how Katlin was doing.

Five hours later, Jack was back in the Operations Center. The Black Swan jet was screaming through the sky. They were more than halfway home on what should have been a thirteen-hour flight.

"Operations, we need fuel and a fast turn," Grace said from the cockpit. "Flying at this speed, we're burning through it."

"Working on it," a tech called out.

"I need to talk to a neurologist, immediately," Nita said in her controlled professional voice. She continued giving the latest update as she went from patient to patient at forty-thousand feet in the air.

Jack glanced toward Robert. "Find me the best neurologist in the system. I want him here by the time they land."

"The Army's chief of neurology is at Fort Hood in Texas." Robert had been impressive all day during this crisis, often anticipating Jack's needs before he even asked. "He's been in surgery for the past three hours, but his staff has orders to have him call me as soon as he comes out."

"Control, get him on the line as soon as you can. Nita, how bad is she?" Jack said, ignoring all the other wounded on the plane.

"I don't know," Nita said quietly. "Her brain is swelling, she's bleeding from every hole in her head, and she never regained consciousness."

"Are the others stabilized? Can they make it to D.C.?" Jack asked, more because he was expected to, not that he was really interested in anyone but Katlin.

"Kurt should be operated on immediately. He took a lot of shrapnel from the bomb. Time could make a lot of difference in his recovery," Nita explained. "Tori has dozens of cuts and gashes from the broken glass, as well as a concussion. I've got butterfly bandages holding them together but she's going to need a plastic surgeon."

"Already done," Robert reassured him. "She's in-flight from Miami, now."

Good. Tori Denton was a truly beautiful woman, just not his type. She'd been one of the highest-paid teenage models and had grown more gorgeous with age. Jack would hate to see her smooth latte skin marred by this incident.

They were still five hours out, but Jack sent a reminder to human resources about Jonathan's body. They would handle everything, although Jack would be expected at the funeral. Ben, Kurt, Tori, and Katlin would be immediately transported to Walter Reed National Military Medical Center. Nita would most likely go with them. That only left Kyle, Will, Lei Lu, and Grace.

Jack didn't want anybody to contact Alex Wolf. Engaged wasn't considered immediate family and he wasn't active duty military or high in the government to be allowed in the facility to see Katlin. Jack would take care of her and see to all her needs. He would take her to his home so she could recuperate. She would be so grateful to him for helping her in her time of need that she would never leave him.

With his plans set, he needed to keep Lei Lu and Grace quarantined, at least for the first few days. Maybe a week. He'd have to play that by ear. Under the auspices of a deep debrief due to the severity of the accident and loss of life, he would insist that they stay within the confines of the Homeland Security offices…without contact with the outside world.

Jack grinned as he left the Operations Center with new purpose.

CHAPTER 5

ALEX LEANED BACK IN THE BUTTER-SOFT SEATS OF THE
production company's Learjet flying from Puerto Vallarta,
Mexico to Los Angeles. His job was done. It had taken a
week, but they'd finally captured JJ's stalker. The man was
currently sitting in a Mexican jail, a hell Alex wouldn't wish
on anyone—except that guy.

Jae had taken the bed in the back to get her beauty rest
and a spa treatment, in case any paparazzi were waiting at the
airport when they landed. She wanted to look her best.
Supposedly, she'd been stressed during the entire week they'd
spent at the private beach resort flushing out her stalker.

The only thing Alex ever saw her do was check her social
media, lay naked in the sun, and consume alcohol-saturated
fruity drinks. Oh, and paw at him while taking selfies. They'd
agreed before leaving L.A. that Alex would appear to be her
new boyfriend, making him the stalker's new target.

The plan worked, but Alex was nervous that Katlin would
see his picture all over social media with JJ before he had an
opportunity to explain to her that it was just the job. Several

of the photos looked extremely intimate, but he never touched Jae in any sexual way the entire time.

All Alex needed was a few minutes to explain it to her. She knew he was nothing like her first husband, Tyler Malone, who honestly believed there was a line-of-sight clause on his wedding vows. Unless Katlin was next to him, the man didn't know how to keep his cock inside his pants.

They had texted and emailed several times while she was gone but hadn't spoken. He told her he was headed to Mexico on a job trying to catch a stalker. He just hadn't mentioned the client. He doubted that Katlin even knew that he and JJ had grown up together, or that they'd dated a few years before. Unfortunately, the paparazzi was well aware of his past with JJ and they'd made references to their reconnection multiple times.

It would be okay. It had to be. He loved Katlin and she loved him. They were going to be married. When, he had no idea. He needed to lock Katlin down on that soon.

They needed to set a date. She needed to plan a wedding. Although Alex's first wedding was quick and inexpensive, Katlin's had been the total opposite. She and her mother had spent nearly a year planning everything, from renting guesthouses to transportation to the United States Naval Academy Chapel, then on to the reception venue. Her wedding to Ty was as orchestrated—and perfect—as possible.

If she wanted the big white dress and full Catholic Mass again, Alex would be sure she got it.

Glancing around the airplane cabin where his men slept, Alex decided it was safe for him to check the special app on his phone. Sliding in earbuds, he opened the program custom-made by his computer guru. A map of the spinning world began to hone in on her location, finding her unique tracking signal. It placed her over the Atlantic Ocean.

She was headed home.

Excitement filled him. He would see her soon.

He clicked on the sound and listened to her heartbeat, the way he did every night as he fell asleep. It was his way of keeping her close. Her heartbeat was very slow which usually meant she was either sleeping or meditating.

Immediately, he speed-dialed her. He desperately wanted to hear her voice, and did, the recorded one. Alex hated leaving voicemail, but it was a good place to start with his explanation. Maybe they were between satellite signals.

Before he tried again, he booked his flight from L.A. to Washington D.C.. She would definitely beat him home, but he would be there as soon as he could.

Over the next several hours, Alex tried, and failed, to get in touch with Katlin.

While waiting in the private terminal for his flight to D.C., Alex's phone vibrated in his side pocket. Deep in conversation with a Fortune 100 CEO, he almost ignored the call. At the last second, he checked the caller ID.

GRACE flashed on the screen.

Fuck.

He swiped the answer icon and stood. "I'm very sorry. I need to take this." He stepped away and stared out the windows, seeing nothing, concentrating on her words.

"Alex," Grace said in a whisper before he could even say hello. "Don't say anything. Just listen. Katlin is being taken to Walter Reed Hospital in D.C. She's hurt…bad. Brain injury. RPG exploded next to the car on her side. I'm in the cockpit and being watched. I'll call you again as soon as I can, but that may be a while. We're all on lockdown."

"Lieutenant Hall." Alex heard a stern male voice in the

background. "Are you finished with all your shutdown procedures? We need to leave. Now."

The connection ended.

Alex couldn't breathe.

He'd seen by her tracker that Katlin was moving toward the U.S.A. and anxiously waited for her usual call. As he saw her get closer, he was disappointed that she hadn't called yet, but he thought she might be the pilot on that leg, not that it'd stopped her in the past.

Alex had never considered that she *couldn't* call him. That she wasn't physically able to call.

Bad. Grace had said she was bad. Fuck, no. He couldn't lose her. He had so many plans for them.

He had to get to Washington D.C.. He would go straight to the hospital.

CHAPTER 6

"Can you please tell me what room Katlin Callahan is in?" Alex asked the elderly woman in the pink smock behind the Information Desk.

"One-minute, young man," she replied in an aged, gravelly voice. Using one finger and staring at the keyboard, the white-haired woman typed in each letter. "I'm sorry, we don't have a Katlin Callahan here. Let me try one more time. How do you spell that?"

As Alex spoke every letter clearly, it was followed by a keyboard click.

"No, sir, no Katlin Callahan. You might want to try another hospital. There are several in this area." She patted his hand resting on the tall counter. "Have you tried her cell phone?"

Oh hell yes. He wanted so bad to tell this woman that she needed to keep looking. "Maybe she's under another name," he suggested. Kat had so many AKAs and he didn't know half of them. "She was brought in a few hours ago with a head injury."

"You should try the Emergency Room. She may still be there," the elderly woman offered.

"Thank you," was all Alex said as he stepped away and dialed his D.C. center. His quest had started in the ER since that's where they'd initially taken her.

"Brett," he ordered his computer guru, "I need you to get into the records at Walter Reed Hospital and find Katlin. They admitted her earlier today."

"No need, sir. Lei Lu texted me on her throwaway phone. Katlin was immediately admitted to the Intensive Care Unit. They put her under L. Hawk."

Thank God for Brett. He amended his thought. Thank God for Lei Lu.

With this new information, Alex was able to get Katlin's room number and the complicated directions to that wing.

Pasting on one of his lady-killer smiles, Alex approached the Adult Intensive Care Unit nurses' desk. Several women jumped up to talk to him as he laid his left hand on the high counter, assuring that they saw no gold wedding band. He flirted with several of them as he introduced himself as Alex Wolf, the owner of Guardian Security, and gave each of them his business card.

Alex knew that only immediate family members could see a patient in ICU and he didn't know who had medical power of attorney for Kat. Most likely their attorney and high school friend, Barry, was in charge of medical decisions for her if she was incapacitated. It could take hours before that paperwork was processed through the system.

Deciding to keep it close to the truth, Alex said conspiratorially, "We all know L Hawk is not her real name. Katlin's family is not able to come so they asked me to check on her and report back to them. I'm an old family friend. Her attorney is faxing the paperwork to the hospital today." He certainly hoped the last was true.

"Oh, but her husband was here just a little while ago," a perky redhead offered.

"That's impossible, she's not married," Alex retorted. "What did he look like? Katlin's life may be in danger."

The red-headed nurse widened her eyes. "He told us he was her husband, so we let him in to see her."

"What did he look like," Alex insisted.

The short brunette stepped up to the counter. "He was tall, about your height, and very handsome, distinguished."

"He was dressed very well, like a senator, and acted like he was in charge," the redhead added.

"About forty, but he looks younger," a second brunette nurse called over her shoulder but didn't leave her computer.

"You've just described her boss, Jack. He's not her husband. He only wishes he was." Several nurses stared at Alex and drew in a breath between clenched teeth.

"It's okay, ladies. He won't harm her, but others might. I may talk with your security force and put a bodyguard on her," Alex said. "Please, what can you tell me about her condition?"

At that moment, a very tired physician in blue scrubs walked up to the desk and grabbed a thick notebook.

The cute little redhead said, "Alex, this is Doctor Tobias, her neurologist. Doctor, this is Alex Wolf. He needs to update the family of Ms. Hawk."

Alex held out his hand. "Can we talk privately somewhere, perhaps in Katlin's room so I can get a look at her to assure her family of her condition?" The doctor looked at the nursing desk and all heads bobbed in approval.

"This way." The mid-fifties doctor with greying temples pointed toward the inner unit where beds were separated only by curtains, all facing the Nursing Center. Several nurses walked around the six patients, checking liquid drips and monitors, always talking with the patients, using their names. He walked beyond the open area to a glass-enclosed room where a nurse was sitting beside Katlin, holding her hand and reading the Washington Post to her.

Looking at his business card, Dr. Tobias said, "Mr. Wolf, this is highly unusual, but nothing about this case is normal so I'm just going with it." The doctor stared at him for a long moment, but Alex couldn't take his eyes off Kat.

Her face was swollen on the right side. The mottled red splotches made her blond eyebrows and eyelashes stand out, like they'd done for a week after she'd gotten badly sunburned at the beach when they were in high school. Tiny little gashes speckled her beautiful face; larger ones were delicately stitched with minute thread.

Alex's heart seized. He couldn't breathe. Behind his eyes, a burning sensation grew to a blazing bonfire, but he fought back tears.

"You know her, don't you?" It was more of a statement than a question.

"Yes, very well. How is Kat?" Alex said as he walked over and took her un-bandaged hand. The other arm lay atop the sheets, wrapped in gauze from her shoulder to her fingertips.

"Nurse, give us a minute."

"Certainly, doctor," she said on her way out the private-room door.

"Is that her real name, Kat?" the doctor asked.

"Yes. If you're taking care of her, you deserve to know a few things about her. Let's start with what you know, and I'll fill in some of the blanks," Alex offered.

"I was ordered to leave all my patients and incoming

neurology residents at Fort Hood, immediately board a private jet, and take care of this woman. She must be important."

"She is to me," Alex admitted.

"Do you know what happened to her?"

"I was told an RPG, a rocket-propelled grenade, impacted near her side of a car. I was told she has a head injury and that she was here. That's it," Alex explained.

"You were told more than I was. Who is she? Everyone on the plane called her Lady Hawk and that's what she's registered here as, but that's obviously not her name." The doctor hesitated then continued. "It helps a patient recover more quickly when they are referred to by their given name. We have the nurses talk to the patients constantly as though they were awake. It also helps them remember more."

"She's Navy Lieutenant Commander Katlin Callahan. She's temporarily assigned to Homeland Security. One of the best in the world at what she does. You must be, too. That's why you're here." He tore his eyes from her and glanced up at the tired doctor who stood a little taller at the compliment. His gaze led to where Alex's hand held Katlin's, his thumb rubbing over the back in a very gentle manner.

"Please, doctor, tell me what you know," Alex said in a quiet voice.

"She has a TBI, a moderate closed traumatic brain injury, which means that her brain has swollen inside her skull with no external punctures or skull fragments inside. That's good. The medic who was there—"

"Nita," Alex interrupted. "Lady Harrier, they probably called her."

"Yes, Lady Harrier, was very good. She really knows a lot for a medic. Is she a Physician's Assistant or something?"

Alex shook his head. "No. She's actually a doctor, of sorts. Long story."

"I'd like to hear the rest of that story sometime." Dr. Tobias continued, "The hospital plane they were on had the latest in imaging equipment, so she began treatment immediately. I was really surprised when she was able to send x-rays to me while I was flying here. She did a great job."

"I'll thank her when I see her," Alex said.

"That gave her, did you say her name is Katlin?"

"Yes, Katlin Callahan."

"It gave Katlin a much better chance of recovery," the doctor said. Alex's eyes flew up to his. "But we've got a long way to go."

In that professional doctor's voice that Alex had come to hate while in Marine Special Operations, Dr. Tobias began a speech that sounded like he'd given it hundreds of times before. "Head injuries can be classified into mild, moderate, and severe categories. The Department of Defense uses the three criteria of the Glasgow Coma Scale; resuscitation, duration of post-traumatic amnesia, and loss of consciousness. Katlin is at Moderate. We have to closely monitor her intracranial pressure and control all her body functions to keep it within tolerance. It's a delicate balance of heart rate, blood pressure, and respiration." Doctor Tobias looked at Alex with that 'are you still with me?' face.

"I understand." He had understood everything so far. Alex just hoped it didn't get too much more complicated.

"Lady Harrier did an amazing job under her circumstances. She was able to keep a good oxygen flow and position her head for optimal cerebral blood flow through the vessels in her neck. So far, Katlin hasn't had any seizures, which is wonderful. She is a very healthy young woman and that will help in her recovery."

"Is she in a coma?" Alex asked tentatively.

"Yes, a chemically-induced one with sedatives, analgesics, and paralytic agents. The body is incredible. Give it what it needs to work, along with time, and it will often heal itself. Keeping her still will help it work faster and lessen the chance of a secondary injury. Any movement of the brain could cause additional damage. I'll be looking for hemorrhaging blood vessels and seek to control bleeding."

"She's going to be okay then?" Alex said with hope in his voice.

"No, she will never be the same," Dr. Tobias said, regret in his voice.

A spear drove straight through Alex's soul. His Kat would never be the same woman he'd fallen in love with. How bad was she going to be?

The doctor continued, "A TBI causes cognitive deficits that can include impaired attention, disrupted insight, judgment, and thought. She will have reduced processing speed, distractibility, and deficits in executive functions such as abstract reasoning, planning, problem-solving, and multitasking. Always, there is memory loss. People who have suffered a TBI may also have difficulty with understanding or producing spoken or written language, or with more subtle aspects of communication such as body language."

Alex was crushed. But he controlled his voice as he asked, "When will we know the extent of the damage?"

"When we wake her up. But that won't be until her cerebral swelling is significantly reduced. We are a long way from there," the doctor explained.

"What can I do for her? How can I help her?" Alex's throat was so tight he could hardly speak, but he had to know the answers. "What do you need to do your job better?"

"What I need is sleep right now. I've been on my feet for nineteen hours." Dr. Tobias gave him a small grin.

"Did they give you a room at the BOQ? Would you rather stay in a house nearby? We have several safe houses in D.C.." Alex's offer didn't seem to register with the doctor. He just looked at Alex and glanced at his business card again. Sudden enlightenment hit the exhausted doctor.

"Actually, I live in D.C. As the Army's Chief of Neurology, I was greeting the new neuro residents at Fort Hood when I was ordered to come here. I could use a ride home though."

"Done. Now, what can I do for Kat?" Alex asked again.

"Well, her husband said he'd be back tonight to be with her…" the doctor started but Alex interrupted.

"He's not her husband," Alex snapped. "He's her boss."

"Where's her husband?" The doctor innocently asked.

"Arlington National Cemetery." Alex wasn't going to lie.

"Oh, and how are you related to her?" The doctor's question was a good one.

"She's my…friend….my business partner….and my fiancée." Alex didn't want to add 'my lover' because that wasn't any of the doctor's business.

"Your partner, in the same line of work?" The doctor seemed to think that they were both undercover federal agents.

"Something like that. If I told you, it would be one more piece of knowledge that could get you killed," Alex lied, remembering Katlin's line to the Marine Lieutenant Colonel during the bomb threat on Black Swan.

"Spend time with her, talk to her as if she were awake. Let her know that she is now safe. When we start to bring her out of the coma, she might think she's still back in the bombed car and thrash around. We want to bring her up slowly and gently. But we are weeks away from that."

"Doctor Tobias, is there anything you need to do your job better? I want her to have the best care available. We have resources." Alex left it at that.

"Walter Reed is the best place for her right now. We wrote the book on shock wave head trauma and update it with every patient who returns from the war. Katlin's scars tell me she's seen a lot of action."

"We all have, sir, and as you know, not all the scars are on the outside." That was all Alex would say.

The attending nurse broke into the men's conversation. "Doctor, she's getting over-stimulated. Perhaps the young man would like to come back in an hour or two. We usually only allow ten minutes."

"We should go, Alex," Doctor Tobias said, laying a hand on Alex's arm. His rock-hard muscles lying just beneath his pressed dress shirt automatically flexed. The doctor immediately noticed and removed his hand.

Alex bent down and kissed Katlin on the lips, but she did not respond. He whispered to her, "Come back to me, Kat." He slowly released her fingers. Rolling his lips in, he felt the greasy lip balm they used to keep her lips from drying out. As he walked away, he took slow deep breaths, re-grouping his thoughts.

"If you are ready to leave now, I can give you a ride home or I can send a car for you later," Alex offered.

Dr. Tobias stopped in the hallway. "Let me grab my bag and I'll meet you at the main hospital entrance. What are you driving?"

"A black Mercedes SUV with the gray Guardian logo on the side." He'd had the D.C. office bring him a vehicle so he could head straight to the hospital.

The doc raised one eyebrow. "You obviously work for a better branch of government than I do."

Alex chuckled. "I own the company. Well, Kat and I do. I only work for the government when it suits me. I'll meet you out front in just a few minutes." Alex left to get the car.

During the ride to Dr. Tobias' College Park home, Alex spoke very little, silently trying to process everything he'd seen and learned.

Dr. Tobias finally broke the silence. "I know it's a lot to absorb and digest and I apologize for my abrupt bedside manner. Treating a patient, sight unseen while she's traveling at five-hundred miles an hour, forty-thousand feet in the air, was a new experience and not exactly a welcome one. More than once, I was given the 'need to know' line. You told me more in ten minutes than I learned since I boarded a jet in Texas."

"Homeland Security is very secretive, and Katlin is one of their best-kept secrets." It was the truth. "They are very protective of everything and everyone connected to them."

Changing the subject, Alex asked, "May I see her anytime, even outside normal visiting hours? Dr. Tobias, please understand, my schedule has unusual hours sometimes and I often have to travel with very little notice."

"Certainly. I'll make that happen tomorrow. She needs to make connections even while she's unconscious. The brain continues to work and process information from other senses even though the eyes are closed and the body is resting. Talking to her and holding her hand are important. You probably didn't notice but her heart rate increased when you entered the room. She smelled you. It increased even more as you spoke to me. You missed it, but it spiked when you kissed her. She knew you were there."

His words gave Alex hope. Kat had known he was there.

"Is that what the nurse meant when she said Kat was becoming over-stimulated?"

"Yes. A prolonged increase in heart rate can cause an imbalance in the Cushing's triad—heart rate, blood pressure, and respiration—which can raise intracranial pressure. We want to stay away from that right now," the doctor explained. He then asked, "Does she have a roommate or a best friend?"

"That would be me," Alex said quietly. "She's also very close to her team. I'm not sure if they're available right now. The Agency put them on lockdown. I was hoping Nita was going to stay with her at the hospital, and Tori was injured in the same accident."

"Do you mean Victoria Denton?"

Alex had to think a minute. He wasn't sure he'd ever heard her last name. It would soon change to Hernandez if Marcus ever got around to proposing. "Yes. I believe so."

"I examined her for a concussion, which she has, by the way." Dr. Tobias gave him the next few driving directions. "She's in for overnight observation, which basically means the nurses have to wake her up every hour and check her memory. She's scheduled for a follow-up tomorrow with the plastic surgeon. Depending on how well she does tonight and her test results, I'd planned to release her to light duty sometime in the afternoon. I could allow her to go visit Lieutenant Commander Callahan before she leaves."

Alex smiled. "I'm sure they'd both like that."

"In that case, I'll leave permission for her to visit when it's convenient." The doctor was quiet for a moment before he asked, "Is Katlin's family nearby?"

"Her parents are dead but her brother lives in the area." Alex wondered if anyone had contacted Daniel, but then remembered that he was married to Nita. Of course, she would call and tell him…if she could. He wondered if she too was sequestered.

Thinking about family, Alex added, "Her uncle is a Monsignor at the Pentagon. I'll call him. There is another person, Top Cooper, who should be on the visiting list. He's known her since she was four years old."

"What about this guy who claimed to be her husband? What's his story?" Dr. Tobias asked. "Her heart rate was sky high the whole time he was in the room. The nurse asked him to leave."

Anger rose like an erupting volcano from deep within Alex. Jack had upset her, putting her in danger. Tamping down his hatred, he managed to say, "Jack is her boss but wants to be a lot more."

"Do you think she subconsciously blames him for her condition?" The doctor brought up a good question, but Alex didn't think that was the reason her heart rate increased.

"No, she hates the man on a personal level. I don't know the whole story but it's ugly. You should try to keep him away from her." He debated before telling the doctor more, then decided he needed to know. "Her lawyer has a restraining order already written but Katlin had put it on hold since he'd been keeping his distance."

"Her boss mentioned that her life may be in danger and he didn't want anyone visiting her without notifying him first."

Alex sneered. "Jack probably didn't want me visiting her."

"Is there a chance that someone is trying to kill her?"

"I really don't know for sure, but I intend to put a bodyguard on her," *if nothing more than to keep Jack away* he thought to himself. "Someone tried to kill her whole team a few years ago but I think they eliminated that threat. You should keep her registered under L. Hawk or even change her name every few days. I suggest a passcode for visitors. Her hospitalization should be top-secret." He could only hope that would be enough to keep her safe.

"I'll take care of it," the tired doctor said, dialing his cell phone. "What do you want as the passcode?"

"Smith Mountain Lake. I'll tell everyone who should have it." Alex pulled into the driveway of a two-story white colonial. "Thank you, Dr. Tobias." He pulled out another business card.

"I already have your card," the doctor said.

"Not one of these," Alex said, handing him a different card with his cell phone number and emergency numbers on it. "Call me anytime. Don't hesitate. Put me in your speed dial. Things happen fast and we can react very quickly. If there is anything that you need to take care of her, it's yours for the asking."

As the doctor got out of the SUV, Alex looked at the house again and asked, "Doctor, do you have a security system for your home?"

"No, are you going to try to sell me one?" he asked, looking at the Guardian Security card.

"Information is dangerous, and it can get you killed. You, sir, have a lot of information." Alex hoped the man took his warning to heart.

The doctor looked at his house, then back to Alex. "Do you think I need one?"

"Definitely. I'll send over a crew within an hour. No charge. I know all too well about military salaries."

"I can't do that." The doctor shook his head. "Governmental rules. I'll pay you for the system."

"If anything happened to you or your family because of Kat, she'd never forgive herself or me," Alex admitted. "Expect several men in Guardian uniforms with guns within an hour. If you haven't been to the range lately, I'll take you to our private range. You do have a gun, don't you?"

A look of fright passed over the doctor's face as he began to realize his situation. With hesitation, the doctor said, "Yes, but do you really think it's that serious?"

"Yes, as serious as Kat's head injury. My men will be here within an hour. Call me if you need anything." Alex backed out of the driveway and headed to the D.C. Center, already talking with the manager on duty.

Alex had a mental list, and next up was assuring the right man was making Kat's medical decisions since she couldn't.

"Barry, does Katlin have a living will?" Alex asked his CFO and high school friend.

"Well, hello to you too, Alex. Thank you, I'm fine," the man in Miami replied jokingly. Then, as though Alex's request caught up with him, he became serious. "Yes, why the fuck do you want to know?"

"Kat has a brain injury and is in a chemically-induced coma at Walter Reed ICU." Alex barely got the explanation out through the constriction in his throat.

"Fuck me. How bad is it?" The concern in Barry's voice was too pronounced to be ignored. Katlin was his friend, too. He was her personal attorney as well as the lawyer for their company.

"Bad. I just left the hospital and had a long talk with her neurologist." Alex swallowed hard. "Are you her designated executor? You might have to start making serious decisions in the next few days."

There was a hesitation before Barry answered, "No, Alex, you're her executor."

Surprised, Alex asked, "When did she decide that?"

"She signed the paperwork the night we had supper at the University Club. That's why you couldn't sign as a witness."

That shook Alex even more. Katlin had entrusted her life to him only days after they met in the Miami apartment. "What do I need to do?"

"I'll fax a copy to the hospital and one to Guardian in D.C. If they give you any problems, I'll fly up and we'll see them in court." Barry let out a heavy breath. "Are you expecting problems?"

"Only from her boss." There was going to be blowback once Jack realized that Alex had control over what happened —and didn't happen—to Katlin.

"Did you know that Katlin had me draw up a restraining order against Jack about two years ago? She told me to hang on to it until she needed it," Barry said in his best attorney's voice.

"Yeah. She told me about it." And threatened to sign it every time Jack pissed her off. Alex drove into the underground parking garage at Guardian Security D.C. Center. "Thanks for taking care of us. I'll call you as soon as I know more."

"You'd better. My secretary is already faxing documents. Please tell me her fucking boss is not on the approved list for visitors." The smile in Barry's voice was obvious.

"Jack Ashworth is not on the approved visitors' list," Alex repeated as he headed into his D.C. office. "But you are if you want to come and see her."

"It would take something this serious to get me to go to Washington D.C.." Barry then added, "Take care of our girl."

"Always." As Alex hung up, he promised that he would take care of her, no matter what.

CHAPTER 7

"WHAT DO YOU MEAN I'M NOT APPROVED TO SEE HER?" JACK screamed at the very young redhead behind the ICU nurses' desk.

"Sir, you are not on the list of approved visitors so I cannot allow you to see Ms. Hawk," she tried to diplomatically explain. "Do you by chance know the password for today? I can let you see her if you know the password."

Jack looked at the determined woman who didn't look as though she was able to legally drink, say nothing about being a specialized nurse, and decided it was too late for charm, so he tried legal bullshit. "Who created the approved visitors' list? As her husband, I left specific instructions yesterday."

Red hair shook side to side. "Mr. Ashworth, we know you're not Ms. Hawk's husband. The executor of her living will, Mr. Alex Wolf, presented the paperwork yesterday. He is now in charge of her health and well-being."

Anger roiled in Jack's stomach as his breakfast flipped over and over. He had no idea that Katlin had designated fucking Wolf. All Homeland Security agents were required to keep such legal paperwork on file with human resources, but Katlin and her team were only temporarily assigned to Section 7. Since the women were active-duty, the military maintained such documents.

Fuck. He hadn't taken the time to hunt them down. He'd assumed that her brother, Daniel, was designated to make decisions if she couldn't. He'd planned to use Nita as a bargaining unit since as soon as she left the hospital she, too, was put into lockdown at his Homeland Security offices. He hadn't allowed her to go home and see her husband or her adopted brats.

Glancing around, he saw only the nurses behind their tall circular desk. He just needed a minute to assure himself that she was still comatose, yet well taken care of, and to check the room for any kind of video feed. He was in the spy business. Tapping into her video loop would be so easy for his men.

He charged into the patient area.

As he approached Katlin's room, the child nurse on his heels yelled, "Stop him. He is not permitted in here."

The six-foot-three overly muscled Guardian bodyguard on duty stepped in front of him and drew his Glock, pointing it at Jack's heart. Recognition was written all over the man's face.

"Stop right there, Jack. I *will* shoot you. You are far from being my favorite person right now." The man's southern drawl was exceedingly thick.

It took Jack only a minute to figure out that he was face to face with Parker "Griffin" Mitchell…a true idiot in Jack's mind. Who would be foolish enough to give up a promising political career to become a Navy SEAL? This former

Georgia football player, that's who. Both his father and grandfather had been embedded in politics all their lives. Griffin, as he preferred to be called, would easily have been elected. His gold trident would've assured his win. Instead, he worked for that damned Alex Wolf.

Jack would have to check his records. He thought Griffin Mitchell ran the Miami office for Guardian Security Inc. What the hell was this man doing standing in the ICU at Walter Reed Medical Center? Jack tuned back into the rantings of Grace Hall's fiancé.

"...Alex will give me a bonus for putting a bullet into you, then I'll enjoy spending every dime of it on Grace. With you no longer in charge, she'll be set free from your bullshit quarantine."

Jack looked into the hazel eyes of the committed man in front of him and knew he would be shot if he stepped one more foot forward. Instead, he inched backward.

Griffin smiled, a thin white slash in a very handsome face.

"You're smarter than I gave you credit." Griffin didn't move and the gun didn't waver. "I was looking forward to that bonus and the pleasure of shooting you."

"I've denied you the pleasures of Grace and I can continue to do that," Jack taunted as he watched the flicker in Griffin's eyes, but the gun held steady. "We can make a deal. Just let me see Katlin for two minutes and I'll release Grace from lockdown. You could be having dinner with her tonight and sleeping in a warm, no, make that hot, bed tonight. I know exactly how long it's been since you touched her. Since you ran your hands over that beautiful body of hers. I even know when you last pushed into her until she shook with pleasure."

Griffin growled.

Good. He was getting to him.

"You could have that tonight if you let me see Katlin. Just for two minutes. That's all I ask, and Grace will be yours."

"I should shoot you and do the world a favor, you manipulating sonofabitch." Griffin's eyes narrowed. "You are not allowed to be in here. You are not permitted to see Katlin. Turn around and walk away. Don't bother coming back. When she recovers, she'll decide when she wants to see you."

Jack looked past Griffin into the glass-enclosed room and saw Katlin, tubes and monitors surrounding her, recording every function. He had watched her tracker on his computer desktop for hours as her heart beat steadily. In the far upper corner of her room, Jack saw what he was looking for, a small hospital camera. He'd have his men tap into the Walter Reed video so he could see her anytime he chose.

"Very well, I'll leave. But tell that bastard Wolf he hasn't won. This is a small battle and I will get to see her. Too bad about Grace, though. The women will stay on lockdown. You'll think about this moment tonight as you crawl into a cold lonely bed, I guarantee it," Jack said, smiling back at the bodyguard before he turned and left the ICU, already on the phone to Operational Control and Tech.

His team could tap into any video feed anywhere in the world. The fact that Walter Reed was a military facility made it easier. He could drop in on his woman anytime he wanted, via video. Someday, he would take care of Alex Wolf once and for all.

As he passed the nursing station, Jack smiled inwardly as he recognized the floating nurse's face. She was being well-paid to oversee Katlin's special care.

Next order of business was to get Wolf out of that room

and away from his Katlin. Thinking of her, he checked his schedule. He had to meet with the department psychologist in five days. He could honestly tell the man that he had been banned from seeing her in the hospital. Lies buried within the truth. He was an expert.

Forty minutes later, Jack walked past his secretary's empty desk. Glancing at his watch, he realized it was lunchtime. Closing the door as he passed through, he didn't hear a click. He glanced over his shoulder to see Nikkole Chernakov slither through the crack before turning around— giving him ample opportunity to look at her perfectly sculpted ass—and locking the door.

Jack hated this woman. But he discovered that she was still useful as a Katlin stand-in. She was the one who had reported him to the Assistant Secretary of Homeland Security and the reason that he had spent nearly a year visiting the agency psychologist.

She was also the reason he could live out his fantasies. He couldn't have Katlin Callahan—yet—but he could have Nikkole Katrina "Kat" Chernakov anytime he wanted and she would do anything he wanted. She'd died her hair blond, underwent plastic surgery, and become the submissive woman he wanted in his bed. He couldn't stand having this fake Katlin in his life, though. He didn't trust the manipulative bitch.

"What do you want?" Jack didn't bother to hide the disdain in his voice.

She prowled her way to his desk, slowly unbuttoning the silky light blue blouse until the ample breasts he'd paid for were exposed. "You haven't called me in what seems like forever."

She scooped her breasts out of the lacy blue bra and ran her fingertips around the areola before she rolled her nipples between her thumbs and forefingers. As the small dark raspberries hardened, so did his cock.

Her wicked smile made him throb with every heartbeat. He started to stroke himself through custom-tailored slacks. He knew her games. "What do you want, Nikkole?"

She lifted the pencil skirt, exposing long, toned legs in three-inch stilettos.

Fuck. She'd bleached her pubic hair blond.

Jack licked his lips.

She ran her fingers through the neatly trimmed strip of hair that matched the recent dye job that fell below her shoulders. "You like it don't you." It was a statement. Not a question.

"Nice touch," he said through clenched teeth.

She gave him two rows of bright white teeth. "I thought you'd like it. It's the way she keeps hers."

Heat rushed through his whole body. She had seen Katlin's patch. Of course, she had. All the women showered together after the recent physical fitness test. The thought of Katlin naked in the shower, soapy water running over her body…

Jack unzipped his pants, freeing his weeping cock, and stroked it.

Nikkole licked her red-painted lips. "I'll take care of that for you. I know just the way you like it."

"I know you can, and I might let you." His whole body went as hard as his cock. Why was she here? Now?

When she reached out to touch him, he grabbed her wrist. "First, you're going to tell me what you really want." He looked down her body. Luscious breasts exposed, her navy-blue skirt around her waist with nothing on below that except her fuck-me heels.

She ran her fingers through her folds then painted his lips with her wetness.

Jack couldn't stop himself. His tongue slid out, lapping up her essence.

"The Black Swan team is short one woman. You know I'm ready. I want that position."

"Never." Jack scoffed. She had to be fucking kidding. "They're a tight team. Those women would never follow you."

She moved in closer, rubbing her bare breasts against his chest. "Just put me on the team. I'll prove to them, and you, that I'm a valuable asset." She kissed him, her tongue pushing into his mouth in the same rhythm as she stroked his cock. Breaking the kiss, she kneeled in front of him.

Looking down at the top of her head as she took him deep in her mouth, he imagined it was Katlin, just like he always did. His hips started to rock. She pulled all the way to the end, leaving only the crown in her mouth before releasing it.

"What do you say, Jack? Temporarily assigned me to the Black Swan team, just until *she* comes back." She gave the underside of his cock a lick from base to tip then swirled her tongue around the head before lapping up his prerelease.

Fuck. He regretted teaching her how he liked it best. She peered hopefully up at him through special blue contacts that made her eyes look exactly like Katlin's.

Katlin. Who was lying unconscious in a hospital bed. The woman on her knees in front of him was not her.

Jack pulled her to standing, twisted her around, and pushed her face down onto his desk. Opening a side drawer, he grabbed a condom and quickly sheathed himself. At this angle, beautiful ass in the air, long blond hair splayed over his desk, he could once again pretend she was Katlin.

As soon as he came, he pulled out and headed for his

private bathroom hoping she'd be gone by the time he took care of everything.

To his disappointment, she was sitting in his chair, knees spread, and high heels hooked on the edge of his desk. She was stroking herself, hips rocking, close to coming. "Jack, finish me off." Her eyes met his. "Please."

He couldn't refuse those blue-within-blue eyes. He picked her up out of his chair and set her on his desk. As he sat down in the warm seat, he rolled toward her. Her unique scent, which mentally he had attached to Katlin, filled his nose. His gaze fixed on her fingers as she stroked her swollen clit.

With the back of his hand, he swiped her away. Soaking his fingers in her juices, he shoved two into her channel and circled the bud of nerves with his thumb. She came instantly, hips jerking, those precious sounds filling his office. Jack closed his eyes pretending that he had just finger-fucked Katlin. He ran his fingers under his nose. Eyes still closed, he licked every drop from his hand.

When he was able to force his eyes open, the blue contacts covering Katrina's brown eyes met his gaze.

"So, what do you say, Jack?" Her eyes searched his. "Temporarily assign me to the Black Swan team. Cycling newer members through established teams is not an unusual practice."

He needed to wash this bitch off every inch of him. He needed a shower. Jack stood and headed for his bathroom, again, then turned toward the office door. He held the knob as she pulled her skirt down and rebuttoned her blouse. She reached for him, but he knew she wanted a kiss.

He opened the door. "I'll take your recommendation under advisement, Agent Chernakov."

As Nikkole left, she passed Mrs. Ward coming in. His assistant handed him a stack of messages. "Please call

General Lyon first. He wants the rest of the Black Swans at the National Training Center immediately to work with Black Swan Team 2."

The smile he gave his fifty-something assistant was joyous. "Thank you, Mrs. Ward. I'll do that." Nikkole problem solved.

CHAPTER 8

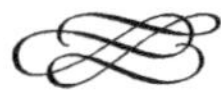

Same yellow tile flecked with gray.

Same beige walls.

Same white ceiling tiles.

Same fucking hard seats covered by one inch of foam and gray plastic.

It was day four and there was no change in Katlin.

Alex had just returned to the waiting room from his allotted ten minutes sitting at her side, holding her soft limp hand in his, listening to the rhythm of beeps. As instructed, he talked to her as though she were awake. He told her about personnel changes he was considering, who he wanted to promote, where he wanted to expand the company next, and always how much he missed her. He never left without telling her exactly how much he loved her.

Back in the ICU waiting room, he opened his personal computer. He'd been using his cell phone as a secure hotspot, placing it on the window ledge to get better coverage than that offered by the hospital. Most often he was the only one in the barren room during the day. Some of the other patients would get company during evening visitor hours, but they were long gone by nine o'clock, just like tonight. Thanks to Dr. Tobias, Alex could come and go anytime day or night.

The same arrangement had been made for her brother, Daniel. His CIA hours were just as erratic as Alex's, the difference being his soon-to-be brother-in-law also had two small children. Often arriving well after normal visiting hours, when his two little ones were tucked away in bed and safe with their nanny, Daniel would make the long drive to the other side of D.C. to see his sister.

Alex made sure someone stood guard duty twenty-four hours a day even though Jack hadn't attempted to see her again.

Alex just didn't trust that man.

"Alex, I'm going to lunch." The cute little redhead with freckles across her nose and cheeks smiled at him through the open door. "You can go in a bit early if you'd like. I'll come get you when I return."

Thirty whole minutes with Katlin.

Stuffing his computer into his briefcase and cell phone into a side pocket of his cargo pants, he wasted no time in getting to her room. Nathaniel stood guard.

"I'll be here for the next thirty minutes, or until Nurse Kramer returns. Why don't you go take a break?"

"Thank you, sir." Nathaniel beamed ear to ear. "Maybe I'll just happen to have lunch with Nancy." He then corrected himself. "I mean, Nurse Kramer."

Alex smiled at the anxious younger man. "She is cute." He slapped the man on the shoulder. "Good luck with that."

"Hey, babe, I'm back," he announced as he set his briefcase on the floor next to the guest chair and kissed her dry lips. He automatically picked up the lip balm and spread it over her usually soft lips. He noticed her heartbeat increased slightly, just as it had every time he entered.

At least she knows it's me and I'm here.

"Top Cooper will be back from his vacation tomorrow. He and Gina are headed straight here. That gnarly old Marine loves you, you know." Alex took her hand and wove their fingers together. "He tried to come back as soon as he heard about your accident, but I insisted he stay and enjoy his first vacation in years. Gina couldn't remember when they'd been alone together for more than forty-eight hours."

Out of the corner of his eye, Alex caught a glimpse of the camera. He'd known from the first minute entering the room that it was there. Not for the first time, he wondered who was watching and listening. He knew the men and women at the nurses' station watched each patient carefully but only turned on the volume when a patient became restless. They were all so kind to Alex and his men. Most of the single women were a little flirtatious, but nothing his men weren't used to handling, one way or the other.

When the door opened to Katlin's room, Alex expected to see Nancy declaring it was time for him to leave. Instead, Daniel Callahan stepped quietly into the room.

"They said I could come in, but I can only have a few minutes." Daniel walked over and stood beside Alex's chair.

Unwilling to give up his connection to Katlin, Alex remained seated.

"Any change?" Daniel queried.

After releasing a heavy sigh, Alex quietly admitted, "No." Wanting to change the subject, he asked, "I take it Jack-ass hasn't released the Black Swans yet."

Daniel smiled. "They're supposed to be able to come home for half a day tomorrow...then they're leaving for training in Nevada. I actually think it was orchestrated by Aunt Ava pressuring General Lyon to get our women away from Jack's lockdown."

Alex chuckled at how well-connected the Callahan family was to others in the military as well as the government. "I love how you call newly promoted Marine Corps Major General Ava Standish, Aunt Ava. Is she still dating your Uncle Tom? I wasn't about to ask him when he and your Uncle Francis were here yesterday."

It was Daniel's turn to chuckle. "They've been dating for years. I have no idea why they've never married. I'm constantly surprised that their relationship has never gone public, but they seem to be able to keep it private. I guess that's the way they prefer."

"So, you were finally able to talk to Nita?" Alex wondered if Griffin had spoken with Grace yet. It was unlike his friend not to share such good news, but they hadn't talked in a few hours.

"No." Disappointment filled Daniel's single word.

"Then how—" Alex started to ask.

"Somehow Lei Lu finagled access to a computer and sent an encrypted, very short email to Henry telling him the plan and instructing him to pass the word."

Katlin stirred and machines beeped faster.

"Talk to her," Alex instructed. "Touch her."

"Hey, baby sis. It's me, Daniel." He gave her bicep a small squeeze and the beeping immediately slowed.

"Any chance her team will be able to stop by on their way out of town?" Alex knew how tight the women were and how much they would want to see Katlin before leaving.

"I doubt it." Daniel shook his head. "Jack keeps a close eye on them and for some reason, he doesn't want them seeing Katlin in this condition. He'll be watching their trackers to be sure they make it to the airplane and lift off on time."

Alex wasn't sure if every field agent for Homeland

Security had a tracker embedded in their carotid artery, or if it was something new the military was testing on its special operators, but each member of the Black Swan team had one. Once he'd been given access to her tracker, he had gone to sleep every night listening to her heartbeat.

The door opened softly behind them. "Gentlemen, it's time." Nancy smiled at both of them. "I'm sorry, but all of her vitals are elevating. We're going to be adjusting her meds and putting her back into a deep sleep for the rest of the night. You both look like you could use some sleep, too. I'm strongly suggesting you go home." She reached out and touched both men's forearms. "I have all your numbers and I'm on duty until seven tomorrow morning. I'll call you if there's any change whatsoever, but don't expect to hear from me, especially since we're putting her down deep. She needs to heal and only time can do that."

Daniel slapped Alex on the shoulder. "I've got time for a beer. How about you?"

"That's the best idea I've heard in days." Grabbing his briefcase, Alex and Daniel left the hospital once Nathaniel was back at his post.

Alex had lived his life based on ten minutes every hour for nearly a week. Lack of sleep and worry were taking their toll, so when Top Cooper arrived at the hospital on the fifth day, Gina convinced him to return to Guardian Security and sleep. Since she'd been an ICU nurse for nearly twenty years, and knowing that Katlin was in good hands, he took her advice.

Alex hadn't realized how physically and mentally exhausted he was until he lay down on the soft sheets in his penthouse bedroom and fell asleep with all of his clothes on.

Nearly six hours later, Alex emerged from the best shower he'd had in days. Dressed in his Guardian uniform of a black polo shirt with gray guardian logo and khaki cargo pants, he decided to take a few minutes and check his email.

Fuck. Fuck. Fuck.

The Internal Revenue Service was investigating the San Francisco Center claiming that the company he'd bought out had been money-laundering for the Chinese. Since he was now the owner as well as the managing partner, they were requiring his presence.

The next day!

He immediately hopped on the phone to the center manager who knew nothing about it but received the same email while they were talking. The attachment included a list of files they expected ready for them when they arrived in the morning.

Alex had no choice. He had to fly as soon as possible to San Francisco.

An hour later, his packed bag in the Guardian vehicle, Alex trotted to the ICU. He'd texted Dr. Tobias asking him to meet there.

"I have to go out of town for a few days," he told the neurologist. "You have all my numbers. I expect you to call me immediately if anything changes." He glanced into Katlin's room. "How is she doing, really?"

"As well as can be expected, maybe even a little better than we had hoped."

Hope. Alex grabbed on to that single word and pressed it against his heart.

"She seems to be rising from the deep state we keep her in more often than I would like. It's as if she is fighting to wake up," Dr. Tobias explained.

"Is that a bad thing?" Alex wondered aloud.

"Not really, but I don't often see that in a moderate TBI. That'll happen in a mild TBI quite often because they recover faster than initial indications." The doctor's clarification gave Alex even more optimism. "I'll run some tests on her today to check the swelling and brain functions."

"Will you please call me with the results?" Alex asked.

"Of course," Dr. Tobias assured him.

"While I'm gone, Top Cooper will be in to visit her more and some of my men may stop in. Daniel will be here, of course. If the Ladies from her team come, they should get in immediately, no matter what time." Alex was trying to cover all the bases before he had to leave.

"Not a problem." Dr. Tobias held Alex's gaze. "How long do you expect to be gone if, I may ask?

"I'm hoping I'll only be a few days on the West Coast." Alex was really hoping he could wrap things up in a day and turn them over to his center manager.

"Good, Katlin seems to react well to your visits."

He was helping her get better, faster. Alex couldn't hold in the smile. It fell immediately when his phone buzzed. He needed to go.

"Please call me when you get the test results." As Alex left, he overheard Dr. Tobias ordering several tests. Since she was in ICU, some of the tests would take place during the night when X-ray and EEG were not busy with outpatients. Almost every department at Walter Reed operated 24/7.

Without asking permission, Alex stepped into the glassed private room and took Katlin's hand. "I love you, babe. I won't be able to see you for a few days, but you will be my first stop as soon as we touch down in D.C.." He brushed his lips over hers. "Come back to me, Kat."

CHAPTER 9

DANIEL PULLED THE GUARDIAN SUV TO AN UNLIT BACK entrance of Walter Reed Medical Center. "Lei Lu, are you sure this is going to work?"

She patted his shoulder on her way out of the vehicle. "The light's out, isn't it? I told you I'm damn good."

"Honey, check the tracker app that Alex's computer geek created." Nita kept her hand on Daniel's forearm as he pulled up the application on his phone. Sure enough, it showed her on her way toward Marine Corps Base Quantico. He didn't care how the hell she did it, Daniel was just thankful that Lei Lu, and some guy named Brett at Alex's office, were fucking computer geniuses. The tracker diversion program worked.

Nita bent over the console and kissed him. "Thank you for doing this for all of us. We'll be out in just a few minutes." She was the last one out of the vehicle.

Ten minutes later, his beautiful wife stomped to the SUV. It seemed as though all four women were talking at the same time. The doors slammed as Lei Lu, Tori, Grace, and Nita filled the seats.

Daniel couldn't make hide nor hair of anything they were

saying. Maybe they hadn't been able to get in to see Katlin. Had her condition changed? Was his sister all right?

"Whoa. Silence. One at a time." He held his wife's gaze. He knew what he wanted to say but his throat tightened. Swallowing, he finally managed to croak, "Is Katlin okay?"

"She is at the moment, but she won't be by morning," Nita declared.

The back of Daniel's eyes burned. Even though he and Katlin were born eight years apart, raised separately, he'd quickly gotten over his childhood resentment and truly, deeply loved his sister. He unbuckled his seatbelt. He needed to see her for himself, especially if this might be the last time.

Nita grabbed his arm. "No, honey, you've got it wrong. She's not going to die. It's much worse than that."

Daniel's jaw dropped as he stared at his wife. He couldn't think of anything that would be worse than dying.

"Jack is planning to impregnate her tomorrow morning." Nita held his gaze.

"I'll kill that motherfucking sonofabitch." Daniel's fist pounded the steering wheel. "What's he going to do? Go in there and rape her?" Daniel reached for his phone. He'd simply call Alex and make sure that the bodyguard didn't let Jack anywhere near her.

"In vitro fertilization," Nita explained.

"Uhm, Daniel, we need to get a move on. The hospital rent-a-cop in the truck just turned the corner," Tori announced from the back seat. "We should have been gone from here two minutes ago."

Daniel pulled out and headed for Quantico, Virginia. "From the beginning."

"You already know that I tapped into the medical center's security program and set things on a loop to cover our trail," Lei Lu began.

"Yeah, I got that." Daniel was thankful for the minimal traffic as he headed toward the Interstate 495 Beltway.

Nita picked up the story. "On our way in, we passed the doctors' lounge, so I borrowed a white jacket."

"She actually borrowed it," Grace interjected. "She returned it on her way out."

"Well, I'm so glad you didn't steal it. I don't know how you would've explained to Jack that you needed bail money for stealing from the Walter Reed hospital in Maryland when you were in Quantico, Virginia."

Nita smacked his bicep. He was being a dick and deserved it. She continued, "While the others were going through identification at the nurse's station, I grabbed Katlin's chart. I couldn't figure out why they were giving her pre-pregnancy drugs. Sure, in her condition she couldn't take the pill like we all do every day. But these medications are designed to help a woman get pregnant, not prevent conception."

Daniel was glad his wife was so damned smart. How had he ever gotten so lucky as to marry this brilliant woman? He reached over and squeezed her thigh. A thigh he had caressed, kissed, and licked three hours before, bringing his wife to a screaming orgasm. Thank goodness their children were deep sleepers and the nanny hadn't returned yet. The look she gave him said she was remembering the same thing.

"I'm with you. Continue," he insisted.

"Being Katlin's brother, I doubt you know this, but about four years ago it was determined that her ovaries weren't functioning properly."

Daniel wasn't sure he wanted to know this about his sister.

Nita continued, "She was told that she could never have children, but they could harvest a few eggs and maybe she could do in vitro fertilization later. She went through the procedure, but somehow her eggs disappeared."

"You have any idea how much an egg from a blond-haired, blue-eyed, Mensa member with a bang-up body like your sister's is worth?" Tori asked from the back seat.

"Are we talking designer babies?" Was that a real thing? He thought that was just science fiction.

"I can show you on this website that her eggs would sell for close to fifty-thousand dollars each. Possibly as high as one-hundred thousand dollars." Lei Lu's face glowed from her computer screen in his rearview mirror.

"Holy fuck. I had no idea," Daniel admitted.

"Jack somehow found Katlin's eggs…and fertilized them with his sperm." Nita shook her head. "I saw the DNA matches. They're her eggs."

"Now ruined by damn Jack so Katlin will never have a chance to have a baby." All eyes flew to Grace as she slapped her hand over her mouth. The preacher's daughter never swore, yet she'd been so emotional about Katlin's situation that the word slipped out.

"Katlin is scheduled for implantation at seven a.m. with prep to begin at six," Nita announced.

"That bastard knows Katlin would never abort a baby, even if it was his," Daniel stated, fuming deep inside. "Unconscious was the only way he'd ever get her pregnant. She'll be tied to him for the rest of her life. Just what he wanted."

Nita continued. "From what I could tell, someone named Dr. James Greer has ordered her pumped full of folic acids, progesterone, and steroids preparing her body for the IVF."

"I've got him." Lee Lu spoke from the middle of the backseat. "He's a highly respected infertility expert."

"I can only imagine what lies Jack told him," Tori added.

"I'll bet this is why Jack wouldn't let us anywhere near Katlin. He knew you would look at her chart and know what he was doing." Grace shook her head. "That man belongs in h-e-double hockey sticks."

"That's why we were on lockdown. That sonofabitch!" Tori said through clenched teeth.

"And why we're getting shipped out tonight," Grace noted.

"So, what are we going to do?" Lei Lu asked. "If we're not in the air soon, Jack is going to know something is up."

Nita looked at her husband. "You're not going to let Jack do this to your sister, right?"

"Fuck no." Daniel thought for a few minutes. "I wonder if Jack had anything to do with Alex's last-minute trip to San Francisco."

"Alex being out-of-town can work to our advantage, and his." Grace met his eyes in the rearview mirror. He'd never thought of her as a tactician. "I suggest we start with calling Top Cooper. If you want, I'll call Griffin and ask him to stay in town an extra few hours."

"I can forward my security video program to Brett," Lei Lu offered. "Covering your tracks is child's play for him. You can thank him while you're at it. He helped me with the satellite end of the tracker distraction program."

Forty-five minutes later, a basic plan in place, Daniel kissed Nita goodbye. "I love you. Fly safe. The kids and I will video call you tomorrow night at bedtime." He gave her another quick peck. "I'm so glad we will at least be in the same country, even though we're not in the same time zone."

"Me, too." The security lights outside the dull green hangar reflected in her wet eyes. "I didn't have hardly any time with the kids, or you." She blinked and looked away. When her gaze returned it was filled with anger and determination. "I hate fucking Jack Ashworth. If things don't change soon, I'm going to think twice about taking my next promotion and the additional years that go with it."

Daniel never thought he'd hear those words from his wife. The military had always been her dream. He wondered if she'd actually leave the service. It was her decision, though.

He pulled her in for one last kiss. "Don't think about it now. Your emotions will get in the way. You need a clear head for big decisions like that." He gave her a quick peck on the lips." Now, go play nice with Black Swan Team Two." Hands on her shoulders, he turned her toward the door.

Leaning over her shoulder he whispered in her ear, "I love you."

She started to walk away. Looking back, she gave him the smile that was reserved just for him. "I don't know what I'd do without you, Daniel Callahan. I love you."

Since this wasn't his first time taking the Ladies of Black Swan to the hangar at Marine Corps Base Quantico, he knew he was not allowed to linger. As he backed out of the parking space and headed toward the front gate, he speed-dialed Top Cooper. "You think we ought to call Alex and let him know what's going on?"

"Nope. This way he has complete plausible deniability. He's on the West Coast. The less he knows, the better." Top was right. Time was of the essence. A clean, tactical strike in and out, using the fewest men possible, was the best idea.

Since Daniel had visited Katlin several times, he was too recognizable to the nurses to handle the inside job himself. He was relegated to being the driver. As soon as he was sure his sister was safe and settled, he would head to work…as though he hadn't kidnapped a federal agent at dawn.

"Don't worry, Daniel, we've got this," Top said with confidence.

"I'll meet you at Walter Reed in a few hours." Daniel glanced at his watch. At least he'd get a few hours' sleep as long as one of the kids didn't wake him up. Thank God they had a wonderful nanny.

At five-thirty, as the first streaks of dawn replaced street lights, Daniel pulled into the now-familiar hospital complex with Rick and Doug from Guardian Security in the back seat. Riding shotgun was Rafe Silva, who lived next door to Katlin in the condo off DuPont circle and also worked for Guardian. He handed Daniel a communications earbud.

"We're not tied into the operations center." Rafe explained, "We can talk to each other, Top Cooper, and Brett. Are there any last-minute questions?"

"No, sir," the two in the backseat said in unison.

"Brett, we're in place and ready to roll." Rafe glanced around the cab one last time.

"Taking control of cameras now." The words came through Daniel's earbud. "You're a go. I repeat, you have a go."

Daniel blinked and the Guardian SUV was empty.

"Turning on cameras now." Brett's voice was loud and clear. "Daniel, can you tell me if you have images?"

Grabbing the specialized Guardian tablet, he nervously fumbled turning it on. Several squares filled the handheld screen with amazing color and clarity. Guardian had the best fucking toys. If Daniel was ever going to turn in his CIA agency badge, he wanted to go to work for the company owned by his sister and future brother-in-law.

"I'm seeing everything, everywhere." Rafe was walking around outside of the emergency room entrance. The two Guardian men passed through the double doors with

Operating Rooms, No Admittance written in bold letters. One square seemed more like a picture because nothing moved outside the door labeled Morgue. In another square, Daniel watched Top Cooper's wife, Gina, test half-a-dozen monitors surrounding a hospital bed.

Once Rick and Doug were dressed in scrubs, disposable booties, and surgical hair covers, they started to leave the lounge. As if they knew exactly what they were doing, they stepped into the pre-op area, sifted through clipboards, and grabbed one.

"We lucked out. We have her transfer paperwork." Doug waved the clipboard so it was visible to the camera.

"Taking her out of ICU just got easy," Rick said as they headed to ICU.

From his parking place in the second row, Daniel was about to say something when an ambulance pulled up to the back door of the morgue. He glanced at the tablet and realized it was Rafe driving the *borrowed* emergency vehicle.

Perfect. They were ahead of schedule.

"We're here to pick up," Rick made a show of looking at the clipboard, "Ms. L. Hawk."

Without looking up at the pretend orderly from the desk where she was busily writing, she held up her hand. In less than ten seconds, she'd signed the paper and pointed. Weekend shift change made everything so easy.

The two men deftly pushed a transport bed into Katlin's glassed room and expertly lifted her onto the new gurney. Doug unhooked the bags from the polls and placed them on the bed while Rick unclipped the heart monitor leads but left the patches. They would need those.

No one concerned themselves with the process, to Daniel's relief. As they passed the nurse's desk, Rick paused and lied smoothly. "The anesthesiologist asked me to grab her file. He wants to double-check the allergies."

As soon as the ICU doors closed behind them, one of the men announced, "We have the package."

The two carefully maneuvered the bed down the hallway to the elevators, got off on the second floor, and went down another hallway to a different set of elevators to the morgue. Rick grabbed a white sheet and Doug snagged a toe tag from the empty morgue. Once tagged, they tucked her into the sheet and headed to the back door.

With the engine running, Rafe opened the ambulance doors. They quickly loaded Katlin, taking special care by holding her head so as not to jar it. Rick hopped into the back with her. Without sirens or lights, the ambulance pulled away from the hospital.

Still dressed appropriately for the operating room, Doug headed back into the hospital. He went directly to the surgical techs who prepared all the equipment and trays for each operation. "Hey, do you have the trays ready for the IVF in OR eight?"

The tech, who didn't look old enough to drink, smiled broadly at him. "I just finished." She handed Doug a large stainless-steel tray. "The fertilized eggs are over there next to their shipping cooler. They started the thawing process last night." She giggled and pointed. "Those timers are counting down the viability of the embryos. The sex is on the label."

When he turned his back on the young tech, he spoke quietly into his comm. "I was supposed to take the tray and put all the items away as though they'd been used. What the hell am I supposed to do with the embryos?"

"Bring them," Daniel and Top Cooper said at the same time.

An hour later at the Tysons Corner safe house, Daniel

backed the white van into the extra-long garage. Transferring Katlin at the large acute care facility had been ingenious. Rafe had pulled the ambulance to the doors on the north side where patients were usually received. Rick had ditched the toe tag and pulled the sheet off Katlin's face.

Leaving the ambulance running, they'd wheeled her down the hall, turning toward the east entrance where Daniel had been waiting. The covert transfer took forty-two seconds.

Somebody would eventually notify the private ambulance company and some poor clerk would search for hours looking for the work order so she could bill the insurance company.

Rafe, Rick, and Daniel carefully extracted the gurney and carried her into the house, not allowing her head to jiggle. Top Cooper opened the door and they wove their way through the kitchen and dining room, down the hall to the master bedroom they'd transformed into a private hospital room.

Gina held Katlin's head while the four men moved her onto the new hospital bed. Then she took over as the charge nurse she'd been for over twenty years.

Daniel glanced at his watch. "Time for me to go." He would show up for work at the usual time as though nothing had happened. The CIA had taught him to lie easily, so if Jack Ashworth questioned him, a circumstance he'd love, Katlin would be protected. Even if tortured, he would never reveal her whereabouts.

Once again surrounded by beeping machines, bags on poles sending life-sustaining liquid into her body, Daniel stepped to his sister's bed and took her hand. "How's she doing, Gina?"

"Very well, all things considered." The woman pushing fifty with silver strands sprinkled through short-cropped dark brown hair gave him a reassuring smile. "We'll know a lot more after Dr. Tobias gets here. Isn't that right, Katlin?" Gina patted the unmoving body as though she were awake.

Daniel bent down and gave his sister a kiss on the forehead. "I love you, sis. I'll see you soon." He smiled as he heard the beeping increase. She knew he was there.

He felt bad that he couldn't return to this place. Jack was sure to place a tale on Daniel knowing how close he and Katlin had become. He'd already arranged with Top Cooper for daily updates via disposable cell phones. Jack wouldn't hesitate to tap their phones if he thought it could lead them to Katlin.

He headed out of the room but couldn't resist looking one more time. Gina jabbered to Katlin as she checked all the IV lines and equipment.

They'd done the right thing.

Katlin was safe.

Jack couldn't get to her there.

CHAPTER 10

JACK ARRIVED AT WALTER REED MEDICAL CENTER TEN minutes to seven and strode to the in-patient operating rooms as directed by Dr. James Greer who would perform Katlin's in vitro fertilization. Everything Jack had ever wanted in life was about to come true. Katlin would be his wife. They would share a child. Maybe two or three. But damn it to hell, the next ones would be conceived the natural way.

His cock grew hard at the thought of making love to her every night for the rest of his life. His mind looped back to those few brief weeks they'd been undercover together. Those had been the happiest days of his life. He loved coming home to a sexy wife, a hot meal she'd cooked in their kitchen, eating at the beautiful table she'd set, then competing against the intelligent woman as they watched Jeopardy while devouring another delicious dessert. Damn, the woman could cook.

The first step in his future was about to take place in the operating room down the hall. He would be a father in forty weeks. The doctor had advised him that it would be better to implant several embryos, thus increasing the chance of impregnation. He didn't care if she had a boy or girl, so he'd asked the fertilization clinic to send both.

As an Ashworth, his father and grandfather would prefer a son to carry on the name. He'd love a little boy. He would do so much more with his son than his father had done with him. His boy wouldn't have to be perfect all the time. His son would be allowed to play in the sandbox and get dirty. He'd never be rushed to the hospital if he fell off the swing and scraped his knees and palms. And he'd never be trotted out at a dinner party in a custom-made child's three-piece suit and quizzed on current events to prove that his parents had spawned a genius.

Nor would his son—*his* son!—be raised by nannies. Jack chuckled to himself. Katlin would never tolerate that. She would resign her commission as soon as possible so she could take it easy during the pregnancy. He would allow only the best care for her. He'd already started researching obstetricians and the best delivery hospitals.

Suddenly the image of a smiling blonde toddler romping through fresh-cut grass toward him filled his mind. They could have a daughter. He grinned. The image of a chubby-cheeked blonde baby with Katlin's unique blue eyes sucking at her bare breast filled his heart.

And his cock.

According to the pregnancy books he'd read, one of the first indications of her pregnancy would be enlarged and sensitive breasts. Katlin was already well-endowed. Countless times he'd stroked himself to ecstasy thinking of holding her large breasts in his hands as he took her from behind. His grin grew to a full smile as his cock began to throb.

The first step to his future was only minutes away.

He had perfectly orchestrated this coup, right down to

paying the floating nurse thousands to give Katlin her pre-procedure injections and forgetting to chart them. The tear he had mustered when he first approached Dr. Greer had been masterful. His wife was catatonic. They'd both wanted a baby to the point that she had undergone egg extraction and fertility treatments, and he'd already given his sperm. Their babies were waiting. She would recover, but she was primed for inception. It had to be now, or they may never have the children they so sought.

He'd sold it and Dr. Green had bought it.

Jack paced the waiting room like an expectant father. He hoped Dr. Greer would come out and speak with him before the procedure, but he'd been warned there might not be time given the full surgery schedule at Walter Reed Medical Center.

Once again, Jack debated when he'd tell Katlin she was carrying his baby, maybe even twins since she would have several embryos implanted within the hour. He considered letting her believe that she was carrying Wolf's baby but rejected that idea. The sooner she moved beyond her Latino lover and into the reality that it was Jack's babies, the sooner they would be married. He would tell her the moment she woke from her coma.

He wanted her now. His. Forever. The thought of her sleeping with Wolf, especially while carrying his child, sickened him. No. As soon as she regained consciousness, he would tell her.

On second thought, he would assure the eggs were securely planted and got a good start on life before telling Katlin that they were connected forever. She would want to be with her child's father. She'd want to be with him. Forever. She would love him, he was sure. The babies would insure that.

Several people had come and gone from the operating room waiting area.

When the hell had it gotten to be eight o'clock? The procedure should have been completed over half an hour ago.

He went to find someone in charge.

In the hall, a panic-stricken Dr. Greer rushed toward Jack.

Oh, no. Something had gone wrong and Katlin…he couldn't even bear to think the thought. She had to be okay.

"We're trying to find out what happened," the doctor dressed in blue scrubs started to explain.

A Navy commander stepped up beside the doctor. "Director Ashworth, we're doing everything we can. Nothing like this has ever happened here before."

Satisfaction that at least they knew who he was in his importance in the United States government. Then the other half of his sentence slapped him in the heart.

"Exactly what happened?" Years of running high tension operations clicked in. *Define the problem.*

"Your wife is missing," the commander reported succinctly.

Jack felt like he'd been kicked in the solar plexus. He had to force himself to suck in a breath of air.

"Katlin's missing?" Jack choked out.

"I've got security looking for her now," the commander quickly interjected.

"What the hell happened? My wife is in a coma. She didn't get up and walk out of the hospital," Jack allowed his voice to raise with the demand.

"This is my Chief of Security," the commander announced as an armed man walked up to them. "Please tell Director Ashworth what you know."

"Sir, this is highly unusual, but it seems that your wife is temporarily missing. We know that two orderlies took her from her room just before six this morning, as ordered. She never arrived at the pre-op room. My men are checking the video feed now, frame by frame, but hundreds of cameras need to be viewed."

Jack stared at the security officer. "Send a copy of everything you've got to Homeland Security Operations Center. My men do this for a living. They can scan video faster than anyone else on the earth." When the man didn't move or pick up a communications device to transfer the information, Jack yelled, "Move."

"Yes, sir." The man sprinted down the hall.

Katlin was a highly trained special operator. She had enemies. If any of them had found out she was incapacitated, several governments would pay millions for her, dead or alive. Most of the Black Swan team's assassinations had been attributed to Navy SEALs, Army Special Forces, or other special operators in the area. Even though the women had been careful to cover their tracks, rumors ran rampant around the world of a special team of women assassins. That had been part of the reason he'd had her registered under L. Hawk.

The clock was ticking. How long had she been gone? Once she was found, could they still proceed with the IVF? And where were his babies?

Jack knew the fragility of the fertilized eggs. Frozen several years ago, thawed so his sperm could fertilize them, then watched carefully as several had divided multiple times, growing his babies in a petri dish before refreezing. He knew there was a very slim window of opportunity. "You do have the fertilized eggs, right?"

Dr. Greer looked away. Without meeting Jack's eyes, he said, "I've been told the tray is missing also."

"What the hell is going on?" Jack burst out. "First, my

wife goes missing and now my babies are gone?" Thinking more rationally, he suggested, "Did someone move the procedure to another room? Maybe she's already prepped and waiting for you in some other operating room."

"No, sir," the commander said. "That was our first thought. We've checked every operating and pre-op room and she is not there."

Jack flipped open his phone and called Control. He knew where every agent was at any given minute. "Check Lady Hawk's tracker. Where is she?"

"Yes, sir." The click of keys could be heard through the line. "Director Ashworth, her tracker indicates she's still in the intensive care unit. It hasn't moved."

"She's still in ICU!" Jack took off running, phone in hand.

Her room was empty.

"Double-check the coordinates," he demanded.

"Sending you a screenshot now," the nervous tech replied.

Jack stared at the picture on his phone. Her red dot pulsed as though it were in the room where she'd been since returning from Baghdad. He knew there was no way in hell she could have removed the tracker. It was embedded in her artery.

"Call IT and have them check the program. Are her vitals reading normal?"

"Yes, sir. No change. They're coming through loud and clear. I just notified IT and they're checking now." The tech sounded more confident. "The department director will contact you with updates."

Jack scowled. They'd better unfuck this, now. With every minute that passed, the chance for the future he'd dreamed of was slipping through his fingers.

He questioned the nurses who explained that she had

already been taken down for the procedure when they came on duty.

Within an hour, Jack brought in every agent in D.C. and borrowed a few from the F.B.I. under the auspice that a Federal agent might have been kidnapped. With pictures in hand, they searched every room in the hospital.

No Katlin.

No one had seen her since the two men in scrubs wheeled her out of the ICU. The security video showed her in her room one minute and gone from every frame after that.

Katlin had disappeared.

Her fertilized eggs were gone.

Jack was furious.

Defeated.

This time.

Thank God, there were more unfertilized eggs.

Even though several countries around the world may want to capture and torture the assassin of a particular target Katlin and her team of Black Swans had eliminated, Jack didn't believe anyone knew their true identity.

The only other person who may want her removed from the hospital was Alexander Wolf.

Jack pulled out his phone and found the number.

"Where the fuck is she?" Jack hissed when Alex answered the phone.

CHAPTER 11

"Who the fuck is this?" Alex slurred, still drowsy from sleep as he rolled onto his back in the San Francisco Guardian apartment. "And why are you calling me at five in the morning?"

"Jack Ashworth. As if you didn't know." The fucker's shouting didn't help Alex wake up.

"What the hell do you want?" Why the hell would Katlin's boss call him at this hour of the morning?

"Where did you take her?" Ashworth seethed.

"Who? Where is who?" Alex asked as he took deep breaths to bring his brain up to the awakened state of his body.

"Katlin, she's gone."

A cold shot of adrenaline hit Alex's brain. Fully awake now, he said, "Jack, slow down, what the fuck are you talking about?"

"As if you don't know. Katlin is missing from the hospital. She is gone. Disappeared." Each word was punctuated with a hiss.

"Jack, I'm in San Francisco. I've been here for two days.

You just woke me up from a sound sleep and are accusing me of exactly what?" Alex had no idea what the hell Ashworth was rambling on about. He did get the point, though, that Katlin was somehow involved.

"Did you, or did you not, remove Katlin from Walter Reed Hospital?" The strain was evident in Ashworth's voice. The man was truly worried.

"I haven't a clue what you are talking about. Are you telling me Kat is gone?" Alex's brain kicked into gear. "Have you searched the whole hospital? She was having a lot of tests these past two days and they had to take her out to other departments. Have you checked there?"

"Lobo, I'm an expert at finding people, especially those in hiding. Agents have checked every room in this hospital. She's gone. Where did you take her?" Ashworth's accusations were beyond annoying.

While the man continued to rant, Alex flipped to check Katlin's tracker. She was in her ICU room. When he flipped to his video app, her room was empty.

Now, more worried than pissed at Jack, Alex insisted, "I don't have her. Who would have kidnapped her?" Alex was out of bed and grabbing clothes and throwing them into his go-bag. If he couldn't find a flight with the executive service they used, he'd charter a plane to get him back to D.C. He had to find Katlin, and Ashworth already had hours of searching on him.

"I don't know. We haven't seen any activity that would indicate a threat to Katlin or her team. The Ladies flew out last night and Katlin was sleeping in her room at that time. I checked on her myself before going to bed."

That was information Alex didn't have before. Obviously, the Agency had also tapped into the hospital's video feed and Jack was watching her, too. Alex briefly wondered if Jack had watched as he held Kat's hand and listened as he talked to her several times a day. Had Jack watched as Alex kissed Kat goodbye every time he left the room? Nothing he could do about that now. "Jack, who would want her captive? Who could handle a comatose woman? Who could get her out of the hospital without being seen?"

"I don't know, but damn it, I intend to find out." Jack hissed out a breath. "If I find out you have her, I'll—"

"You'll what?" Alex interrupted. There was absolutely nothing that Jack Ashworth could do to him. On the other hand, Alex had already proven that he could kill Jack anytime he wanted.

The line went dead.

Alex shook his head and began to piece the puzzle together. He knew who could pull this off—the Ladies. But they were in the air before the kidnap. His men could do it too, especially with Brett's skills. He punched his speed dial.

"I'm glad you called," Top said to Alex. "You need to get back to D.C. immediately. Katlin has been kidnapped."

"Do we have a ransom notice?" Alex asked logically.

"No, sir, and I don't believe we will." Top Cooper sounded cocky. Did his D.C. manager know where she was? The cranky old Marine loved Katlin like a daughter. If he knew she was missing, he'd already have called in every resource to help find her.

"Do you know where she is, Top?" Alex didn't have time to play games.

"You need to get back here so we can figure this whole thing out, Mr. Wolf."

Alex noted the avoidance of his question but realized that Top wanted him back in D.C. immediately. The *Mr. Wolf* was another indication.

"Can you book me on the next flight? I need a shower.

Call Griffin and send him to the San Francisco Center to handle things here."

"Want to talk to him? He's standing right beside me." Top said nonchalantly.

Why the hell was Griffin still there? After saying goodbye to Grace, he usually caught the redeye to Miami so he could be there when his office opened in the morning.

"Why are you in D.C.?" Alex asked his Miami manager.

"Because this is where Grace was last night, and today is my day off. Turned out to be a good thing I was here. I was heading back to Miami in a few hours, though. You should get here as soon as you can." Griffin had thrown another clue at him.

Again, noting what wasn't said, Alex saw puzzle pieces begin to connect. "Trade places with me," Alex said. "You come to San Francisco and deal with the IRS here. I'm headed to D.C. to find Katlin."

"That shouldn't be a problem," Griffin said, but Alex wasn't sure which statement Griffin was responding to, or both. "Have you ever thought about putting a scrambling system on our phones? In this day and age, it might be a good idea."

"Of course, I've thought about it. Do you think we need it?" Alex asked, following the subtext.

"Definitely, sir." Griffin had given him all the confirmation needed.

So, the lines are probably bugged, and the Agency is listening to this conversation. That could explain a lot, Alex thought.

"Griffin, head to San Francisco immediately unless we have a situation in Miami that we need to discuss in person. If so, wait for me in D.C. and take a later flight," Alex suggested.

"I'll pick you up at the airport with Top. A multi-center managers' meeting might be needed," Griffin said. "See you in a few hours."

The next voice he heard was Top's. "I think that's a great idea. We'll pick you up at Regan National. Shower fast, you have a flight to catch." Alex headed for the shower as the text with his flight information beeped on his phone.

Six excruciating hours later, Alex strode out the glass doors of the small terminal for private planes. Go-bag in hand, he trotted to the pickup island where he jumped into the front seat of the black Guardian SUV.

"Do you know where she is?" Alex asked as soon as the door was shut. He had waited too long for any information on his fiancée. Being thousands of miles away from her was bad enough, especially since she wasn't conscious to speak to him the way they always would if they were in the same country. He missed her in ways he couldn't describe. The ten-minute intervals with her non-responding body weren't enough. He needed her to wake up. Talk to him. Tell him that she still loved him.

Top pulled out, headed toward the GW Parkway, checking his side mirrors. Griffin used an electronic device in his right hand and placed his left index finger over his lips. He began pointing it all over Alex's body.

Alex gave his best friend a side glance. Did Griffin really believe that Alex was bugged? And by whom?

Loud beeping filled the vehicle as the device pointed at Alex's jacket. What the fuck? The beeps increased in speed as Griffin carefully unfolded the black windbreaker. On the sleeve was a small black dot that blended into the material. Who had tagged him with a micro transmitter? And when?

Griffin carefully removed the sticky dot and stuck it to a

piece of paper before throwing it out the window. After sweeping Alex one more time, he announced, "We're good."

Alex silently vowed to carry the small bug detector everywhere he went. If he had to guess which alphabet agency was spying on him, his money would be on Homeland Security. Specifically, Jack.

"Yes, we know where she is, but we can't go there right now. We're being followed." Top looked in his rear-view mirror. "Yep. Dark blue Nissan two cars back."

Alex was more concerned about Kat than the tail they'd picked up. "Is she okay? What the hell happened? Who kidnapped her?" Alex wanted answers. Now.

Top took a deep breath and let it out slowly. "She's the same as when you left four days ago. You're really going to hate this part, but we had to get her out of the hospital before six this morning." Top changed lanes and checked his rearview mirror again. "Jack had her scheduled for an IVF implantation…with his babies."

Alex sat there, stunned. He couldn't say anything. It was too much to process all at once.

The thought of Kat pregnant warmed his heart. She would love that. She wanted children. But, she couldn't get pregnant. Her body didn't produce eggs. Or so she'd been told.

In vitro fertilization. She could get pregnant. They could have a baby.

Jack was trying to make her pregnant, with his baby.

Anger swelled from the deepest part of Alex. He was so furious with Jack.

But his men didn't let that happen.

Thankfulness overwhelmed Alex. He had the best men in the world. His wonderful men had risked imprisonment to kidnap Kat. They had saved her from a lifetime of being tied to a madman, because Jack Ashworth was most certainly insane to have tried this.

"I'll kill that fucking bastard." Alex chuckled. "If Katlin doesn't kill him first." But she'd have to wake up and be the Katlin she'd been before the explosion. No one knew when, and if, that could happen.

The other men nervously chuckled in agreement.

"How the fuck did Ashworth think he was going to get away with…" Alex couldn't even say the words.

"Did you know that Katlin had her eggs stolen several years ago and they were supposedly lost?" Top changed lanes without signaling and slid off the exit with mere feet to spare.

"Yes." The single word was all Alex could squeeze out through his tight throat. She had told him about it soon after they had reconnected.

"Obviously, Jack knew right where they were because he had them fertilized with his sperm." Top Cooper wound his way through busy traffic.

Alex didn't want to think about that fucking asshole jacking off and then it being used on Katlin's future babies. Children that he and the woman he loved should be having. Suddenly, he wondered if there were more. If they could find her eggs, hopefully still unfertilized, then he and Katlin would have a chance to have children of their own. The thought of her belly rounded with his baby, a child suckling on her breasts, gave him hope.

"Then fucking Jack had Katlin pumped full of progesterone in preparation for the procedure that was scheduled for seven this morning," Top's words brought him out of his dreams for a future he'd never thought possible. "Alex, we had to get her out of there." HIs barely restrained fury filled the vehicle.

"I can't thank you enough. I will always be indebted to

you." Alex managed to say. "Who figured this out? I looked at her chart every day and never saw this coming."

"Nita found it last night," Griffin explained. "We helped the Ladies sneak into the hospital before their flight. She read the chart and saw the procedure order then checked Katlin's meds."

Alex sent a small prayer heavenward thanking God for Nita.

"How did you get her out?" Alex wasn't sure he really wanted to know. On the other hand, he might need to know how many laws they broke to figure out how much bail money he needed to come up with to keep his men out of jail.

Top and Griffin took turns telling the story of their early morning kidnapping. Or was it a rescue?

"Brett created a computer program to fool the satellite feed on their trackers." Top shook his head. "That man is a genius. He had already taken control of the hospital cameras for you, so it was easy to cover their movements this morning. While Rafe stole an ambulance—"

"Borrowed," Alex interjected. "Terminology here is the difference between weeks and months in prison."

Both men chuckled and agreed with the grunts.

"Two of our men dressed as operating room orderlies." Griffin quickly added, "In borrowed scrubs, and wheeled her from her room in ICU as though they were taking her for the operating room. They loaded her into the ambulance at the morgue dock and Rafe and one of the guys took off. The whole operation went fast and easy. Our other man ran back in and stole the tray that they were supposed to use on Katlin, and Daniel picked him up out back."

Top picked up the story from there. "Gina, you've met my wife, used to work in ICU but now does home health care, so she ordered a bed and all the equipment we needed through the company she works for. We created a fictitious patient so if Jack starts looking, he'll find a really sick old lady in Lorton. Gina is taking care of Katlin in our Tysons Corner safe house."

Alex let out his breath. Katlin was safe and in good hands.

"I called Dr. Tobias and told him that Katlin's life had been threatened and we thought the leak was at the Agency, so we moved her. He agreed not to reveal her location to anyone. He came over this afternoon to check on her. She's doing as well as can be expected." Top gave him a sympathetic glance.

"Thank you!" Alex said, slowly regaining his composure. "That sonofabitch! He's so desperate to have her that he'd make her pregnant with his baby while she was in a coma. I could kill him."

"You won't have to," Griffin said. "Katlin will. As soon as she wakes up, he's a dead man walking."

"By the way, while you were in the air, Jack had the D.C. Center searched. Every room." Top slowly shook his head side to side. "The Metro Police and his suits showed up with a search warrant about three hours ago. They weren't allowed to touch or take anything, just search rooms, looking for Katlin."

"I think they were surprised at how many apartments we have." Griffin grinned. "Jack walked around personally checking every inch of the penthouse."

"Good," Alex said, "That keeps my story legitimate." Thinking about that, Alex opened his phone and hit redial on Jack's number.

"Have you found my fiancée yet?" Alex pressed. "I just got in and I'm headed to our D.C. Center. What have you done to find her?"

"Lobo, Wolf, whatever the fuck you're calling yourself

these days," Jack said, probably identifying the caller to the others in the room. "I searched your offices."

"That was a waste of time and manpower that you should have used elsewhere. I told you I didn't take Kat. What are you doing to find her?" Alex was hoping Jack would reveal something. Anything.

"I don't report to you, Lobo. We'll find her. She's a valuable agent of Homeland Security. Whoever took her will face federal charges for kidnapping." With that intended warning, Jack disconnected.

To the men in the car, Alex said with a grin, "That went well. I hope I was convincing that I didn't know where she was."

Griffin suggested, "We should probably do our own search to keep up the facade that we're hunting for her, too. That might keep Jack from looking at us too closely. I'm sure he put that tail on you, so getting you over to see Katlin may be tricky."

Alex smiled as he said, "We can do tricky." He was already planning disguises and ways of getting to see Kat within the next few hours.

THE DOOR SQUEAKED OPEN AS ALEX AND TOP STEPPED INTO the kitchen at the safe house. They had driven a rental car into the windowless garage and closed the overhead door with the remote control before exiting. Alex was sure they hadn't been followed. He'd taken neighborhood streets, winding his way from downtown D.C. to Tysons Corner.

"Hi, Alex," Gina said as she hugged him, then her husband. "She's doing very well. I think she wants to wake up. Dr. Tobias should be here in a few minutes. He was going to stop on his way home from running errands. Do you want some coffee or a beer?"

"I'd love a beer, but I'll get it. May I get you something, too?" Alex offered, opening the refrigerator.

"No thank you. My replacement should be here soon and then we'll head home," Gina replied. "I made beef stew. I didn't know how long you'd stay or if you had eaten."

"You don't need to cook, Gina. You're here to take care of Kat." Alex popped the cap off the long neck from a local microbrewery.

"This is our supper, too," Gina said with a smile. "At least half of this is coming home with us."

Top pulled his wife into his arms and placed a smacking kiss on her lips. "You are such a good wife. I think I'll keep you."

Gina smacked his ass. "You should be damn glad I keep you." She went on tiptoes and kissed him. "I'm glad you're here."

Dr. Tobias didn't bother knocking, he simply let himself in using the key they had made for him. "Good evening," he said to everyone gathered in the living room. "I'll just go and check on Katlin."

Alex followed the doctor into the master bedroom and watched as he listened to her lungs and heart, checked the monitors, and examined Katlin.

"What did the tests conclude, Dr. Tobias?" Alex asked, stepping to the bed and taking her warm hand.

"Katlin's intracranial swelling has decreased significantly. We may be able to bring her out of the coma within the next few days. Will you be available?" The doctor glanced at the heart monitor. "She should see you when she wakes up. It'll make it easier on her."

"If you need me, I'll be here," Alex said firmly. Then he decided to just ask the question, "Did you know about the IVF procedure scheduled for this morning?"

The doctor looked at Alex as though he didn't understand the words. "What are you talking about? I didn't schedule any kind of procedure."

Alex picked up the large medical notebook and turned to the IVF order before handing it to Dr. Tobias.

The doctor scanned the page then looked at Alex pointing to a timestamp. "This was added after I left the hospital last night. I would never approve of such a thing. Not only is it unethical but it can be dangerous for Katlin. A fetus saps the body of so many nutrients and increases the mother's heart rate. It would make the Cushing's Triad even more difficult to balance. I would have taken this physician to the board over this."

"That's why Katlin is here now." Alex nodded toward the book in Dr. Tobias's hands. Glancing around the room he asked, "Do you have everything you need here to take care of her?"

"Yes," the doctor said, taking inventory of the equipment. He stopped and looked at Alex for a long moment before he said, "The IVF wasn't from you, was it." A statement, not a question.

"No, it was Jack Ashworth's orders…and his babies." Just saying the words made Alex's stomach roil. What almost happened to his precious Katlin was beyond rational. Once again, he was so thankful for the wonderful men who worked for him. And, of course, Daniel.

Alex glanced at Katlin. And the brilliant women who worked with her.

"He's insane!" the doctor spurt out.

"Likely. He's powerful and gets what he wants, except Katlin." Alex leaned down and kissed her on the lips. "She's mine, and I'll never let her go."

"Thank you for saving her," Dr. Tobias said. "Jack is also obviously smart. Today was my day off and you were still on the West Coast. Neither of us would have known until it was too late. Let me assure you, Alex, once I found out what had been done to her, I would have ordered an abortion."

Alex looked at the doctor and said with dismay, "I couldn't have let you do that. Katlin is a devout Catholic and as her executor, I must do what she would want. She would never want an abortion." Looking at Katlin, Alex added, "I'm so very glad that she is here now and neither of us has to make that decision."

"Agreed." Moving on, Dr. Tobias announced, "I'm going to order a decrease in her medication to begin the process of bringing her out of the coma. I think she can wake up in the next three days."

Alex stroked the back of her hand before he raised his gaze to meet the doctor's. "Say it. I know you're debating on telling me something. I'd rather have all the information available to make informed decisions."

The doctor nodded once. "Alex, she will never be the same. You have to prepare yourself for that. She will have memory loss. She may not even recognize you or anyone else. She will be slow to process thoughts and words. It will be a long journey back to what may never be a normal life. You need to be ready for that and decide if you're going to be there to help her through what could be years of therapy. She'll need occupational, physical, and probably speech therapy." The doctor looked down at their joined hands. "It will never be the life you two had planned, assuming that you had planned a life together."

Alex couldn't imagine a life without Katlin—but that was the woman he knew before the explosion. The Katlin who would wake up in three days might be a totally different woman.

She may not even recognize him, know how much he cared for her. She might not know that he loved her. Would she remember that she was his best friend? What if she had forgotten everything? The years. The tears. The fears. Everything that they had shared might have been wiped out of her memory.

When they had gotten engaged, it had been a promise for a long-term commitment. Forever. But they had never actually planned that life together. There were no wedding plans in place. No house they would call a home. There hadn't been time, or so they told each other. They had just found each other again and hadn't been in any hurry to move beyond what they had. Because of her job, and the black ops he occasionally took, they'd agreed to live every day as though it were the last. They both understood the reality of their situation. Tomorrow was never guaranteed.

"Thank you, doctor," Alex managed to say around the tightness in his throat. "Please let me know what I need to do to help her wake up."

"Talk to her as though she were awake. You can remind her of things you've done in the past, but once she wakes up, you must let her regain her memories on her own. You can invite family and friends to come visit her, as long as they abide by those rules." He smiled as he glanced at the heart monitor. "She knows you're here." Checking his watch, the doctor announced, "I need to get home to supper. I'm looking forward to spending the evening with my family." The doctor waved as he left the room.

Alex heard him talking for a few minutes with Gina and Top Cooper before he heard the front door open and close.

"I made up the bed in the room across the hall in case you decided you wanted to stay here," Gina said as soon as they walked in.

Alex hadn't given a thought as to where he'd sleep that night. His entire focus had been on reaching Katlin. He glanced at the sitting room attached to the master bedroom where two rocker recliners faced a fireplace with the television above it. He could sleep in that chair. He'd be close to Katlin, able to keep an eye on her. Then he noticed the bag of knitting and the purse next to the other chair in the room. *That must be where the nurses relax,* he thought.

When Alex didn't respond, Gina added, "It's a very lovely room. It has its own attached bathroom. All the bedrooms in this gorgeous house do." She smiled broadly. "This whole house is beautiful. I wish we'd been able to afford this neighborhood when Jimmy retired."

Alex raised his gaze to the loving couple in their mid-fifties. "Your name is Jim?" Alex raised an eyebrow. He'd only ever known the man as Top, referring to the nickname of his former military rank.

The older man scowled. "No. It's Jimmy." He threw his arm around his wife. "Gina is the only person who's allowed to call me that. Everyone, and that includes you, calls me Top."

Changing the subject, Alex gave Gina what he hoped was a thankful smile. "I really appreciate you preparing the bedroom for me. I can work from here just as easily as I can from the office at Guardian. I really don't want to leave Katlin."

For the first time, he glanced around the house. It was quite beautiful. In the setting sun, he could see a large backyard with forty-foot-tall deciduous trees. The property line seemed to be defined by large holly bushes whose sharp pointy leaves would deter any intruders.

Alex knew this was just one of many safe houses that his company owned. Well, technically, Katlin owned them, and Guardian Security rented them from her. Alex had always been surprised at how many times alphabet agencies inside the Beltway called in need of a safe house.

"How many bedrooms does this house have?" Alex wondered aloud.

"This one has six bedrooms and six baths." Top smiled, leaning over and kissing his wife. "Sweetie, even though Alex pays me well, we still couldn't afford this house now and sure as hell couldn't have afforded it five years ago on an enlisted Marine's retirement. This house is worth about a million and a half, even though it's fifteen years old."

"Katlin remodeled it a few years ago." Gina replaced one of the small bags dripping down the tube into Katlin's arm. "Have you seen that kitchen? She had all the old crappy cabinets replaced with sleek white ones of solid wood and added new stainless-steel appliances. The black and white granite countertops look just amazing with the black, gray, and white subway tiles she used in the backsplash. She has a remarkable eye for color and design."

Alex wondered if Katlin would still have that talent in a few days when she woke. He tuned out Gina as she raved on about the house that would be perfect for her and Top Cooper; the gorgeous patio for entertaining, large backyard for their grandchildren to play, and finished basement where her husband could create his man cave.

The alarm system beeped.

"That must be Karen." Gina looked at Alex. "I hired her and two other nurses to care for Katlin. We're pulling twelve-hour shifts. And before you ask, yes, Jimmy vetted each one of them. I worked with all three of them when I was the charge nurse in the ICU. I negotiated a fair price for their time."

"I don't give a fuck about the money." Alex looked at the beautiful woman in the bed. "I trust you, Gina."

"Thank you." She turned and left the room to open the door for her replacement.

"While they handle the shift change, why don't you go get settled in the room across the hall," Top suggested. "I think both you and the nurses would be more comfortable if you didn't sleep in this room. Our D.C. Center cook has stocked the refrigerator and will have lunch and supper delivered to you." The cook at the D.C. Guardian Center was one of the best, in addition to being a wonderful woman. Secretly, he was glad he wasn't expected to prepare anything beyond microwaved meals and sandwiches.

"There's an office that looks more like a library down the hall on the right, just before you get to the living room. Operations Control has this place covered five by five." Top Cooper seemed to have everything in place. "If you don't leave here, Jack's spies can't follow you. If by chance he discovers this place, the house on the other side of the back fence is one of ours, too." Top chuckled. "Katlin always wondered if we ought to dig a tunnel between the two."

"Not a bad idea." Alex wondered how they could do it without having to pull a city permit. He also liked the idea of staying put. He truly did not want to leave Katlin's side. "What are we doing to 'find' my fiancée?"

Top grinned. "Brett is having a field day supposedly tracing her bank accounts— not the real ones, of course—and leaving a trail that a blind man could follow. He's also placed inquiries with Guardian Security contacts around the world. No real names are being used and the descriptions are relatively generic. I also sent a few men to question people at the hospital."

"How did that work out?" Alex didn't want his men to become a nuisance, especially since the hard-working men and women had already been questioned several times by different alphabet agencies.

Top's grin broadened to a full-on smile. "Nathaniel got a date with that cute little freckle-faced nurse."

Alex grinned. "I like Nancy. I hope that works out for them."

Gina stepped into the room and introduced Alex to her nighttime replacement. After eating some beef stew he checked on Katlin, sitting with her for thirty minutes before he found the library, settling in to work. He took a break every hour, checking on the woman he loved, stretching his legs, determining exit strategies. At one point he strolled around the block and entered the other safe house, just so he was familiar with the layout.

Before going to bed, Alex visited Katlin once again, giving the nurse a lunch break. He talked to her about the escape house in his now-familiar one-way conversation. In the morning, he jogged the neighborhood after kissing her, touching her, and checking all the constantly recording machines. Breakfast with Katlin, a chat with Gina, work broken up with visits to the woman he loved more than life, lunch with Kat, more work, and more visits, was his life for the next two days.

Each evening, Dr. Tobias stopped in and checked on Katlin, adjusted her medicine regiment, and warned Alex that she wouldn't be the same woman upon waking.

On Alex's third night in the safe house, the doctor announced, "We'll bring her out of the coma tomorrow morning. We have to be prepared to put her back under, though, if she starts fighting."

"What do you mean put her back under?" Alex hadn't heard that possibility mentioned before.

Gina put her hand on Alex's forearm. "Quite often when someone awakes from a long-term coma, in their mind they are still in the midst of the accident. They have no concept of the amount of time that has passed. In Katlin's mind, she may believe she is still in Iraq and under fire. Her initial response may be to defend herself and her team. It's not unusual for a TBI patient to wake up swinging."

Dr. Tobias chuckled. "I've had more than one black eye from an awakening soldier. Trying to hold them down, or restrain them to the bed, just makes it worse. Our research has shown the best way to wake up a TBI patient is to do so slowly, talking to them the entire time. A familiar voice is even better."

"I'll be here." Alex would do whatever he must in order to make things easier for Katlin.

"Then I'll see you in the morning."

After Dr. Tobias left, Gina hugged Alex. "I've been through this several times." She glanced at Katlin's still body on the hospital bed. "She'll do just fine. And so will you."

Later, when the night nurse took her lunch, leaving Alex alone with Kat, he crawled onto the hospital bed and lay next to her. He desperately needed to be close to her.

Alex had been to Mass more often since Katlin returned to his life than he had at any other time, except when he was a child. As he slid his arms around her, he silently prayed that she would miraculously be all right, that God would send her back to him whole.

We've just found each other again. Please, don't take her from me. I can't lose her. We've been through so much together. Lost those three years. I pray it is your wish for us to be together. In the name of the Father, Son, and Holy Ghost, amen. He crossed himself and cuddled into the most important woman in the world.

"Come back to me, Kat, all of you," he whispered into her ear, then kissed her an inch below. She sucked in a quick breath, not the slow steady breathing he had heard for days. It shocked him. He sat up and stared at her, but the breaths were slow and steady.

Maybe he was imagining it. He kissed her neck and distinctly heard another quick breath. Maybe it was a sign. He hugged her tightly and soon his breathing matched hers as the physical and emotional exhaustion of the past weeks caught up to him. He fell into a deep sleep.

When the night nurse returned, Alex's eyes popped open. She smiled as she saw the two of them together on the bed. After glancing at the monitors, she covered them with a blanket. "Sleep there. It's good for both of you."

More thankful than he could believe, Alex let out a long breath, releasing all his pent-up tension. He fell into a deep sleep; the best he'd had since the last time they shared a bed. On some level, Alex was aware of the night nurse performing her duties. Mostly, he was aware of the warm woman tucked in beside him.

At six-thirty the next morning, Alex was immediately awakened by the opening of the front door. Gina and Top were talking but were shushed by the night nurse. Dr. Tobias followed them in and announced, "Let's wake her up."

The nurse on duty giggled. "You'll have to wake up Alex first. He slept with Katlin last night."

Alex gave Katlin one last squeeze and was rolling off the bed as the four of them entered.

"No, stay there," the doctor ordered. "It would be very normal for Katlin to wake up with you in bed with her, right?"

"Yes," Alex replied. As often as possible.

"I'm going to reduce the medication now, making her wake up." The doctor adjusted her IV line. "Talk to her, Alex. Tell her who you are. She might start fighting as she awakes, thinking that she's still in the bombed car, so be prepared. You need to tell her that she's all right. Reassure her that she is safe now."

Dr. Tobias swept his gaze over everyone in the room. "I want all of you to prepare yourself for the fact that she might not remember you. Even if she does, she might not remember occurrences from your past together. Let her regain her memories on her own. If you happen to mention something that you did together, or that happened to the two of you, don't be surprised if she doesn't remember it. Don't tell her about it. Tell her that when she remembers it, you'll have a good laugh together."

Katlin stirred, then gasped in a breath. Her whole body writhed, but not as though she was fighting. It seemed more like stretching. Alex placed his palm on her cheek and said, "It's time to wake up, Kat."

"Un, uh," she croaked and tried to roll over. Alex pulled her gently toward him.

"She's going to rely on her core personality to guide her," the doctor pointed out as Katlin continued to awaken. "From what you've told me about her, she's friendly but doesn't trust easily. Most likely, that distrust will be even more prevalent. There may be other parts of her personality that she's suppressed that you may see now. These are all normal responses from a TBI patient."

"Come on, sleepyhead, time to wake up." Alex ran his thumb over her lips, slippery with the balm.

Katlin took even deeper breaths and began to open her eyes.

Alex could practically feel Kat's gaze scrape over him, but her head never moved.

She quartered the room with her gaze, taking in everything, saying nothing. It was a survival technique taught to special operators. Many could pretend to still be unconscious yet crack their eyelids to assess their surroundings. Katlin's eyes were wide open.

"Welcome back," the doctor spoke first. "Do you know who you are?"

"U.S. Navy Lieutenant Commander Katlin Callahan." Her voice was so gravelly they could hardly understand her.

"May I give her some ice chips?" Gina offered.

Katlin nodded her head. "Please," She said in a whisper.

Gina raised the bed slightly and spooned the ice into her mouth. "This should help with the dryness."

Katlin's eyes continued to dart around the room.

"Do you recognize anyone in this room?" Dr. Tobias asked her.

She smiled as she looked at Alex the way she did every morning when they slept together, lovingly, and contentedly.

"Alex." Her voice was hoarse from lack of use.

She knew him.

She. Knew. His. Name!

"Yes, Kat, I'm here." Peering into her beautiful blue-on-blue eyes, he ran the back of his finger over her soft cheek.

She pinched her eyebrows together as though thinking hard. "Why is everybody in our bedroom?"

Could it be a miracle?

Could she have returned to him whole?

Dare he hope?

CHAPTER 13

"It's time to wake up, Kat."

The voice was so far away it didn't seem real.

The situation she was in was real, though.

Her team was in trouble.

Every muscle in Katlin's body hurt, especially her head. Her ears were ringing from the explosion.

Man on the roof.

RPG.

Her team.

Katlin had to get to her team.

She had to protect her team members.

Where were the others?

She reached for the weapon in her thigh holster but her whole body screamed in pain.

Glancing around the upended SUV, she couldn't see anyone. Everything was a glare of white.

She was in the backseat, behind Jonathan. Tori was to her side. She should be able to reach out and find Tori.

Nothing. What the hell happened to Tori?

Leaning forward, she blindly tried to find the front seat. Fucking hell, her head hurt.

"It's time to wake up, Kat."

Alex? He wasn't on this op. She must have misunderstood.

The bad guys were trying to get her out of the crashed SUV.

"No. No." She pulled away from them. She couldn't let them take her.

Where the fuck was her gun?

"Come on, sleepyhead."

She wasn't sleeping.

Was she?

Had she had another nightmare? *Oh, God please make the nightmare stop*, she prayed. Sometimes, she couldn't force herself awake from some of the nightmares. She tried to wake up, but her brain would just suck her back into the madness.

No. No. She had to wake up. She didn't want to be pinned in an SUV with bad guys reaching for her. Trying to grab her. She couldn't find her fucking gun.

"It's me, Alex....I've got you, babe."

Alex had her?

"Time to wake up." Repeated in her head.

Alex was calling her. It was his voice. She was sure of it.

She had to make her way back to him. Alex held her heart. He was her life. He was her future. He was... everything. She loved him.

Forcing in a deep breath, she tried to clear her head.

Almost there.

"Time to wake up, Kat."

She breathed in deeper. Wakefulness shoved the nightmare away.

She felt Alex's warm body next to hers.

But was it Alex?

She didn't dare move in case it wasn't.

Molten brown eyes flecked with gold met hers when she finally forced her lids up. His dark brown hair was down to his shoulders once again. She recognized the hard planes of his face, the overnight scruff of his beard, and the soft lips that had kissed every inch of her body.

Yes. It really was Alex.

Wasn't it? Or had her nightmare morphed into a good dream?

She felt as though she were awake, but nothing felt right.

Digging her nails into her palm, she quartered the room looking for bad guys.

A man in his late forties, maybe early fifties, stood next to the tubes that ran from bags on hooks into her hand. They obviously didn't want to kill her because they could've done so at any time.

Near the back of the room stood a familiar man with graying hair and a very fit body. She knew him. He was…a Marine, but he was in civilian clothes. What the hell was his name? The woman beside him was Gina.

Top Cooper—that's his name! Top Cooper. His wife, Gina, is standing beside him. As her gaze continued through the last two quarters, she discovered the room was empty…and not the one she usually shared with Alex.

Had Alex and Top Cooper rescued her?

"Welcome back," the older man said. "Do you know who you are?"

"U.S. Navy Lieutenant Commander Katlin Callahan." She could barely get out her whole name. Her mouth was so dry. Even her throat felt sandy.

"May I give her some ice chips?" Gina was a godsend.

"Please," she managed to say but it sounded like a

whisper even to her. Had she slept with her mouth open? Had she snored? How embarrassing if all these people had been there while she was sleeping. She'd have to apologize to Alex later for the nightmare and thank him properly for pulling her from her mental madness.

Gina raised the bed and spooned ice slivers into her mouth which nearly melted on contact. Bliss. Katlin tried to pick up her arms, but they were just too heavy. For now, she'd let Gina feed her.

"Do you recognize anyone in this room?" Katlin noticed that the man asking questions kept his hands on the drip control of her IV.

Would he knock her out with some kind of drug if she didn't answer his questions correctly? What if she didn't know the answer? Would he give her some kind of truth serum? Maybe that's what was in the bag hanging from the pole.

She scanned the room one more time looking for video equipment. Maybe somebody was watching this interrogation from a remote point.

But everyone in the room seemed so casual around him, but Katlin wasn't sure of the man's threat level.

Okay. Maybe she was just being paranoid.

"Katlin, did you understand the question?" Although the man's voice was gentle, it was still insistent.

Fuck. She'd better answer him.

"Top Cooper and his wife Gina." Katlin watched the middle-aged couple beam with pride.

Her gaze returned to Alex's. "And this is Alex." It was a damn good thing nobody asked her his last name because she didn't know it. "You're here."

"Yes, Kat, I'm here." His gaze held hers as he ran the back of his finger over her cheek, smiling as though they hadn't seen each other in months. But they had, hadn't they? Katlin tried to remember when the last time she and Alex had been together.

Nothing. She simply couldn't remember. Perhaps her brain was still tired. She needed to roll over and go back to sleep, or start working on her first, followed immediately by her second, cup of coffee. Maybe then her brain would start working and she could remember when she and Alex had seen each other last.

She was happy that Alex was there, but she wondered why everyone was in the room with them. She gathered as much moisture from her surprisingly still dry mouth as possible and swallowed. "Why is everybody in our bedroom?"

Alex laughed. "Where else would I be?"

Where else would he be? The question threw her. All of a sudden, she couldn't think of where else he might be. She thought very hard and couldn't come up with a single other place that Alex could be. Should be.

He worked. Didn't he? He must. "At work?" She asked tentatively.

"I couldn't leave you." Alex leaned over and kissed her lips. She felt weird kissing in front of other people.

"That explains your presence, and I'm not really concerned why the Coopers are here, but what I really want to know is who the fuck is he?" Katlin pointed to the oldest man in the room.

The man nodded his head. "Katlin, I'm Dr. Brian Tobias, your neurologist."

For the first time, Katlin realized they were not in the penthouse apartment. She glanced around the room. Nothing looked familiar except Alex, Gina, and Top Cooper.

Alex gave her a quick kiss then slid off the bed standing next to her.

"Stick out your tongue," the doctor ordered as he moved to the other side of her bed.

She couldn't feel any stitches on her tongue, but her mouth was sure as hell dry. She complied, sticking it out as far as she could. "May I have more ice slivers?"

Gina picked up the glass and fed her another spoonful.

"Now wiggle your toes." Dr. Tobias lifted the sheet off her feet.

She got it. He was testing her. Complying, she watched her toes move up and down.

"Without turning your head, follow my finger with just your eyes." The physician moved his finger in all directions including making a circle.

With a nod to Gina, she placed a rubberized cap over Katlin's head and attached wires from a machine to the metal nodes. "This is a small portable EEG. We need to take a look at your brain waves."

Over the next ten minutes, the neurologist gave her a thorough examination, testing her involuntary reflexes while asking her the year, the president, where she was born, the names of her family members, and a litany of other innocuous questions.

"Look, I'm over this," Katlin snapped. Anger poured from every cell in her body. "It's my turn to ask the fucking questions." As soon as the words were out of her mouth, she was appalled at her behavior. She wasn't like that. Immediately contrite, she apologized. "I'm so sorry. I have no idea what came over me. But I do have questions."

Dr. Tobias patted her hand. "It's completely understandable. The inconsistent behavior is common after a TBI. It may last several days or even weeks."

TBI. What was that? She should know that abbreviation but couldn't seem to pull the words together and connect them to the letters.

The doctor gave her a small smile. For a second it looked almost condescending and Katlin's anger flared. Then she realized it was just his way.

"You've had a moderate, closed, traumatic brain injury. That means that your brain was jarred around and swelled inside your skull. The good news is that there were no external punctures and we haven't seen any fragments floating around inside." His face scrunched up.

Was he mad at her? Had she done something wrong? A paranoid fear raced through her. Katlin glanced around the room. Gina and Top stared at her expectantly. Alex had a hopeful smile pasted on. He was nervous. Maybe even scared.

"Do you remember what happened to you?" The doctor's question forced her focus to return to him.

"When?" Popped out of her mouth.

"What is the last thing you remember?" the doctor said slowly.

Anger flashed. She was not some child with a learning disability. She clearly understood English. Her memory was simply blank in places. A second look around the room and Katlin felt like she was overreacting. She should simply answer his question.

She had to think hard. She remembered sitting around the bedroom, she thought it was hers, talking with a bunch of women. She focused on their faces. She knew them all very well. They were her team members. But where? Were they on a mission or were they at her place?

"I'm not sure," she admitted. "But I remember sitting around with my team." As she said the words, she recalled a group of men coming to their door. Although she could see their faces clearly, she felt the annoyance they'd caused. As her gaze drifted to Alex, she instantly knew he hadn't been there.

"I think we were on a mission, maybe with some men?" She shook her head. "Beyond that, I'm not sure of anything."

The doctor patted her hand once again. "Amnesia surrounding the trauma is not unusual." He glanced at the others before returning his gaze to her. "Don't worry about it. Many accident victims don't remember the few minutes before, during, or after. It may come back or be lost forever."

Accident. The word bounced around in her mind. Her vision blurred. The roar of the SUV's huge engine filled her ears. She felt her body rock side to side.

A flash streaked across in front of her.

She threw her arm up to protect her eyes. Cringing, she waited for the explosion to her right.

Silence.

Katlin opened her eyes and felt like an idiot. Everyone in the room stared at her. She lowered her arm.

Dr. Tobias patted her hand. "Flashbacks are not uncommon with a TBI either."

The double negative took Katlin a few minutes to unravel. Her mind had just relived the situation which the doctor had called an accident.

"I remember." She gleefully smiled. A memory had returned. "I'd never call an RPG an accident. I'm quite sure they shot at us on purpose which makes it the antithesis of an accident," Katlin replied.

Everyone in the room stared at her, again. Dr. Tobias looked at the other three people.

"She was speaking Arabic," Alex said in English as he

took her hand in his. Looking down at her, he asked in English, "How many languages do you speak fluently?"

She replied in perfect Spanish, "Five languages, twelve dialects but it's rude for us to speak in Spanish when others might not know that language. Does Gina speak Spanish, Top?" Katlin said as she looked at the man she'd known nearly all her life. Exactly how long she wasn't sure, but she knew she had a familial love for him. He wasn't her brother, though.

Fear of the unknown shot through Katlin once again. She was sure she had a brother but couldn't picture him. Was he blond like her? Did he have red hair? She felt sure she was of Irish heritage.

"No, but she knows a little Japanese," Top answered in Spanish, redirecting her thoughts.

Katlin looked at Gina and said in Japanese, "Thank you so very much for the wonderful care you've given me these last four days."

At Dr. Tobias's raised eyebrows, Katlin translated.

"How long have you been here?" The doctor asked.

"Four days, maybe five?" Katlin wasn't sure, nor could she say how she knew that. "I think that's what you, Gina, told me."

Gina smiled. "Yes, every day I would give you a count. Today is day five. But you were in the hospital for a week before they brought you here."

Katlin looked around the bedroom. "Where am I?"

"You're in one of the Tysons Corner safe houses." Top's smile was sincere. "We brought you straight from the hospital here."

Katlin's gaze slowly swept the room. It was very nice. The blue-gray walls were just a shade beyond institutional yet warm and homey. The hospital bed obviously didn't belong there. She wondered where her king-size bed was. Had they taken it out to make room for this one? As she stared at the furniture, it didn't look familiar.

"Is this my house?" She finally asked.

Top chuckled. "Yes. And no."

Now Katlin was more confused than ever.

"You own this house," Alex explained as his thumb rubbed over the back of her hand. "And several others. They are contracted to Guardian Security for use as safe houses."

He stared at her as though waiting for a reaction.

She had none.

Okay, so she owned a bunch of houses, but she'd asked if this was her home. At least that's what she'd meant.

"I don't think you've ever lived in this house." Top answered her question.

"If I don't live here, then why didn't you take me to my house?" Seemed like a reasonable question to her, but she wondered when everyone else in the room exchanged a worried glance.

Had something happened to her home?

All of a sudden, Katlin caught a whiff of coffee. She was never a morning person, barely coherent until she had a second cup. Obviously, her brain needed to be caffeinated. "May I have a cup of coffee?"

"Only a little," Dr. Tobias said. "We want to watch your blood pressure."

"Pardon my lack of manners." Gina's gaze swept the others. "Who else wants coffee?" Orders taken, she disappeared from the room.

Now, what were they talking about before her body demanded coffee? She couldn't remember. No one else seemed to be anxious to return to that conversation so Katlin asked, "Alex, is Griffin still in San Francisco? How's the audit going?"

Alex's gaze whipped to her. "How did you know about the audit? You were unconscious when all that happened," Alex said to Katlin before turning his head toward Dr. Tobias, "How can she know those things?"

Well, hell. How did *I know about the audit if I was unconscious? Am I psychic now?*

Dr. Tobias smiled at her but addressed Alex. "I told you before, the body is amazing. Now you know why we talk to the patients as if they're awake. Obviously, you talked to her about San Francisco."

"Did you?" Kat insisted.

Alex nodded, his smile so broad and happy as though she were a good child who had performed a difficult task. She guessed she had.

Katlin couldn't understand why she could remember some things while she'd been unconscious, yet she couldn't remember what her brother looked like. She couldn't picture him as a child or as an adult.

Did she have a sister? No. Not exactly. She had sisters of the heart not of blood. Nita, with her dark curly hair and pleasant, yet not distinct, facial features came clearly into view. She was married to Katlin's brother. What the hell was his name? Nita and…nothing.

Bella and Simon. They had two little kids. Katlin loved her niece and nephew. She could picture the little ones, but not her brother.

Nita was on her team.

"Oh my God. My team. What happened to my team?" Her last memory of them was in the hotel-like room. Had they all been killed? Why weren't they in the room? Were they in other rooms with nurses caring for them?

Why wasn't anyone answering her questions?

"What the hell happened to my team?" She was screaming, anger spewing each word.

Alex wiped his thumb across her cheek. She hadn't realized she was crying, again. "Your team is fine. They're on a training mission."

Even as relief washed over her, Katlin continued to cry. She was so frustrated that she couldn't remember. When she got herself under control, she wiped away her tears, wondering if they'd ever stop. "I apologize for lashing out. It's frightening not knowing if your best friends are alive or…" Her throat had swollen so tight she couldn't even say the words.

Dr. Tobias jumped in. "There's a strong possibility that most of your memories will return within the next few weeks." Patting her hand, he continued, "You need to accept the fact that not all your memories will come back."

Katlin burst into tears. Her head pounded. "I can't remember my brother. I know I have one, but I can't remember what he looks like." She gasped for breath, crying her eyes out, once again. She placed her fist over her heart. "I know I love him. I just don't know what he looks like." She couldn't control her breathing or tears. She also couldn't remember bawling like this ever before.

Alex took her into his arms and rubbed his big hand up and down her back. "It'll be okay. You're safe now. I've got you." He kissed her temple. "It'll come back. If Dr. Tobias thinks it would be okay, I'm sure we can call him, and he'll be here within the hour."

"What if I don't recognize him when he walks in?" She huffed in a breath. "He'll hate me forever. I'm his sister. I'm expected to know what he looks like." The thought of her brother hating her brought on more tears.

Part of Katlin's brain screamed, *Where the hell are all these emotions coming from? This isn't like you. You don't cry. Ever.*

As she tried to pull herself together, she concluded that she now cried. Probably a side effect from the TBI.

"Besides this horrendous mood swing, what else can I expect?" She asked Dr. Tobias.

"To be pissed as hell at Jack Ashworth." Top whispered from the back of the room.

Hatred ripped through Katlin at the mention of the man's name. Expensive popped into her mind followed by a deep-seated loathing. Images rapidly blinked on and immediately shut off. A nearly bare desk. Perfectly coiffed hair graying at the temples. Expensive conservative clothes. His face too close to hers as though he was going to kiss her.

"I hate that man. What did he do to me this time?" Katlin's gaze bounced from Top to Alex. She wasn't sure why she'd added the words *this time*. They were just there. Maybe that's why she hated him, because he'd hurt her in the past. She needed to get her mouth under control.

Both men then looked to Dr. Tobias.

"She asked why she was here and not at her home. I don't approve of lying to a patient in her condition. It just confuses them once they discover the truth." Dr. Tobias spoke as though Katlin wasn't in the room. That kind of pissed her off, but since he'd all but insisted they tell her the truth, she decided she'd let the slight pass.

"We're not changing her memories." Top pointed out. "It happened to her while she was unconscious."

"Agreed." Dr. Tobias nodded.

Alex squeezed her hand and slowly sucked in a deep breath. "Jack tried to impregnate you."

Katlin bolted upright in the bed. "That fucking bastard tried to rape me, again?"

All three men's eyes grew wide. "Again?" They said in unison.

Katlin slapped her hand over her mouth. Well, that secret was out.

Maybe Dr. Tobias had given her truth serum. She couldn't seem to keep her mouth shut.

"We can talk about that another time. Besides, I don't remember much about it." Katlin hoped her lie was convincing. "Tell me, what did Jack do now?" She needed them to answer the question, although she was quite sure she wasn't going to like the answer.

"No. Not the way you'd think." Alex said through clenched teeth. "IVF. He...he..." Alex swallowed hard. "found your eggs and...he fertilized them."

Top stepped next to Alex. "We kidnapped you from the hospital just before the procedure." He glanced at Alex before returning his gaze to her. "Technically, we're federal fugitives because we kidnapped you. Jack is turning the world upside down looking for you." He slapped Alex on the shoulder. "That's why he hasn't left the house. We were too afraid Jack's men would follow Alex back here."

They had saved her from a fate worse than death and were now wanted men, all because they loved her.

"Thank you." She looked between the three men standing around her bed. Tears poured from her eyes. "If...if he'd..." Katlin didn't know what she would've done if Jack had succeeded.

Her eyes went to Top's and held.

"Thank you." The words came from the bottom of her heart.

Katlin's gaze slid to Alex. Had it been his baby, though,

she had no doubt she would've done everything in her power to deliver them a healthy baby.

Once again, Jack had fucked up her future with Alex.

He would pay for his diabolical plan. She would cut off his balls, figuratively if not literally.

CHAPTER 14

Two days later, Alex watched as Dr. Tobias made notes in Katlin's chart. "To start, I'm putting you on six weeks of medical leave. I want to see you every other day for the next two weeks." He sat down on the edge of the bed and dedicated his entire attention to Katlin. "I know your type. You won't like what I have to say, but these are doctor's orders. I want you to take it easy. Keep in mind that anything strenuous—like running five miles, working out in the gym with weights, or God forbid, sparring—increases your heart rate which increases your blood pressure. That same blood that flows through your heart, strengthening it, goes all the way around your body and flows over the top of the brain that you just hurt. Walk first. Then maybe I'll let you run."

The doctor patted her hand and gave her what he probably thought was a reassuring smile but looked more like a grimace. "Before your injury, you were in peak physical condition. I know you want to return to that point, but it's going to take time. It took you years to get there so don't expect that level of conditioning in weeks. Your body has had a traumatic injury. Although you seem to have bounced back quickly, you are far from out of the woods. It's not unusual for you to discover areas that don't return as quickly as you hope."

"Like what?" Katlin asked hesitantly.

"Given the brain areas of greatest trauma, I'm most concerned about executive functions. Your physical body seems to be responding as normal. We're not sure, and it's far too early to predict, how you're going to react in emergencies. You were responsible for making life-and-death decisions based on limited information with only seconds to decide. Your brain in those areas still must heal before we can accurately test them."

Dr. Tobias stood and looked at Alex. "Is her cell phone here?"

After opening a nightstand dresser, he handed Katlin her phone.

"I want you to call your boss. Tell him what happened and where you've been. Tell him I've put you on six weeks medical leave and I may extend that to up to six months before you have to face a medical board." Dr. Tobias nodded at the phone in Katlin's hand.

Suddenly Alex realized what the doctor had done. She would have to use several different parts of her brain to accomplish everything he asked of her, including remembering three things. Smart. He was testing her executive functions, establishing a baseline.

Katlin stared at the phone in her hand.

She continued to stare at it.

Alex slid a glance toward the doctor who was covertly looking at his watch. He was timing how long it was taking her to make a decision.

Katlin giggled. "You told me to call my boss. I have several of them including the president of the United States, but I don't have his phone number. Legally, I'm a lieutenant commander in the United States Navy but I don't really have anyone in the Navy that I report to. And, here again, I'm pretty sure the… head man…" She glanced at Alex as though for help.

Alex wasn't sure if he should give her the name she sought. He slid his glance to Dr. Tobias who nodded affirmatively.

"Babe, are you talking about the Chief of Naval Operations?"

Her whole face lit up. "Yes, the CNO. He wouldn't take my call even if I knew how to get hold of him. The closest person I have to as a military boss is Army General…" She snapped her fingers. "With the squeaky chair. General Lyon. He's the commanding officer of USSOCOM. But, I'm temporarily assigned to Homeland Security, and that would mean I need to call Jack Ashworth, the fucking sonofabitch who tried to plant his baby in my comatose body."

Katlin rolled her lips in as she looked away. A few seconds later her gaze returned to Dr. Tobias. "I'm not sure I can address him respectfully, yet, as someone should speak to their boss. Forgive me, but I haven't had enough time to decide how I want to deal with him."

"I don't think you should call Jack." Alex squeezed her hand. "I think you should let Barry Howell talk to him." Alex shifted his glance to Dr. Tobias. "Barry is our attorney, both corporate and personal. Kat had him draft a restraining order against Jack."

"I agree, talking with him might put her under too much emotional stress."

Katlin let out a long, slow breath, dropping her shoulders as though she was relieved. She shrugged. "I know I probably just failed my first test, but I'm going to call General Lyon."

Alex was so damned proud of his woman that he couldn't continue to simply hold her hand. He cupped her face gently in his hands and kissed the woman he loved. He'd spent the last two days watching Katlin eat small meals, bringing her bodily functions back online.

She'd been like a puppy. Eat and sleep. Gina had worked with her doing isometrics in bed. Every movement seemed to be tiring, but that morning she'd gotten out of bed and made it to the bathroom on her own. Tiny steps, but steps in the right direction.

"General Lyon seems to be the appropriate person for you to call." At Dr. Tobias's words, Alex stepped back. Both men watched as Katlin dialed the standard ten digits, listened, then dialed an additional series of numbers.

Dr. Tobias seemed pleased as he added another note to her thick file.

"Excellent." The doctor said just above a whisper.

Katlin's eyes lifted to meet the physician's. He smiled. "Are your ears still ringing?"

She smiled and lifted the cell phone. "No. But the phone is."

"Please put the call on speaker," the doctor requested.

Within a few minutes, she was connected to General Lyon. "How's the weather?"

"I wouldn't know, I'm—" she paused then rolled her eyes. "The skies are blue, and the sun is shining."

Dr. Tobias shot a glance at Alex.

Before he could ask, Alex leaned over and quietly whispered, "Code phrase for her physical condition and if she's under duress."

The doctor made a note of that. Alex didn't hide the fact that he read over the doctor's shoulder. Katlin did not respond correctly at first but in less than ten seconds gave the correct answer.

"Sir, I have you on speakerphone. I'm with Alex Wolf and Dr. Tobias."

"It's good to hear from you, Lieutenant Commander Callahan. Alex, I'm glad she's with you. Dr. Tobias, I know that you were her neurologist while she was at Walter Reed. I assume you've continued her care." An ear-piercing squeal came across the line. Both Katlin and Alex winced, but Dr. Tobias covered his ears. "Are you able to tell me where you are?"

"Not exactly, sir. Somewhere in Tysons Corner. I was taken to a safe house after Jack Ashworth attempted to impregnate me while I was still in a coma." Her voice shook but she visibly held herself together.

The squeal of the chair was immediately followed by boots hitting a tile floor. "Lieutenant Commander Callahan, please repeat. I don't believe I heard you correctly."

Katlin cleared her throat. Her eyes met Alex's and held them as she squeezed his hand. "I was rescued by Guardian Security men minutes before an in vitro fertilization procedure was to take place on my unconscious body." Tears started to roll down her face. "He was going to put his babies inside me."

Katlin burst into tears.

"Alex!" The general bellowed. "What the fuck happened?"

"You obviously know that she was in Walter Reed with a TBI." Alex began.

"Of course, I do. Fast forward to when somebody kidnapped one of my special operators."

Alex wasn't sure he should mention the Black Swan team visiting Katlin the night they left town, so he bypassed that information. "When my men were informed that an IVF was to be performed on Kat in the morning, they put together a rescue mission."

"Thank Christ."

"They brought her to this safe house. They needed to keep her hidden until the viability of the embryos had expired."

"Goddamn sick motherfucker." A loud slap on wood filled the air of the bedroom. "I don't even know where to start with this." The sound of heavy boots faded then returned. "Since Ashworth isn't military, I can't bring him up on UCMJ violations. I need to talk to our JAG officers. The military assigned her to Homeland Security so maybe there's something we can do for her. Maybe I can start an investigation into that slimy fucker."

The general must have sat down by the small squeal that pierced the ears of everyone in the Virginia bedroom. "This could ruin the JAFSOS program. Her team was doing a stellar job for Homeland. I hate to yank them away from the agency. Hell. I'm not sure I can. Those decisions were made at the highest levels. POTUS had to sign off on it."

There was a long pause before the general continued, "Is there even proof that Jack Ashworth was behind the IVF?"

"Yes, sir." Alex picked up Katlin's file and double-checked. "Jack Ashworth signed the release form and I'm quoting here 'allowing the planned in-vitro fertilization of their children into his wife, Katlin Callahan, to move forward as planned.' There is verification here that the eggs were from Katlin and the sperm from Jack Ashworth."

General Lyon growled. "This makes me fucking sick." After a second, he asked, "Lieutenant Commander Callahan, did you ever consent to this IVF?"

"Hell, no, sir." She shifted in the bed. "I'm now beginning to wonder if he stole my eggs. Several years ago they were harvested after I'd had reproductive problems." She scoffed. "Back in the days when I thought I might want to have Tyler Malone's baby." She swallowed audibly. "While I was in JAFSOS, they went missing, supposedly stolen and sold on the black market."

"Sometimes even I'm surprised at the depravity of humanity," the general admitted. "Katlin, I'm sorry that happened to you. Hopefully, we'll be able to find the rest of your eggs so you can use them as intended."

"Actually, General Lyon, my men were able to find her eggs and retrieve them from the fertility center where they were being stored. They've been moved to a more secure location." Pride shone through Alex's voice.

"Thank Christ you got all the rest of them."

"Yes, sir." At least Alex hoped so. They couldn't find any records of the original egg harvest so they had no idea how many eggs they were looking for.

"I've got to leave in a minute. Shit's gone bad in North Africa." The general's chair squeaked. "Lieutenant Commander Callahan, you are no longer designated AWOL. I want you to compile every indiscretion by Jack Ashworth. You know what's needed. Dr. Tobias, how long will Lieutenant Commander Callahan be on medical leave?"

"A minimum of six weeks. If I need to extend it up to six months, she'll let you know, but I'll file the appropriate paperwork up my command which will send it to yours."

"Lieutenant Commander Callahan, I expect you to follow the doctor's orders and keep me apprised of any changes. Before you can return to duty under my command, you'll have to pass the special operators physical fitness test and be examined by one of our psychiatrists in addition to Dr. Tobias's release. Any one of those doctors has the right to refer you to a medical board that can medically retire you. When you accepted the rank of Lieutenant Commander a few months ago, you signed an additional commitment to the Navy. Your expertise is invaluable. Even though you might not be physically able to return to the field, I'll find a place for you here. You have a great deal to offer special operations command. USSOCOM—"

"Sir, before you go, may I ask a favor?" Katlin interjected before he could sign off.

"You can ask, but you know me well enough that you might not get the answer you want." There was a distinct warning in the general's voice.

"Sir, would it be possible for my teammates to call me? I know they're on a training mission, but—"

"Granted. USSOCOM out." The line went dead.

"Dr. Tobias, as soon as possible I'd like to leave the safe house and move to Guardian Security. They have excellent physical fitness equipment and it's the safest place I can possibly be." She glanced around. "I don't believe I need this equipment any longer so it can be returned and made available for someone else who truly needs it. I can also come to the hospital to meet with you so you won't need to make house calls any longer."

Yes! Although the safe house was beautiful, Alex really needed to be in his own apartment and facility. Working in the home library was certainly quiet, but he had so much more at his fingertips at his office. Then it dawned on him. Katlin had stayed in the Guardian penthouse before they got back together because it made her feel safe. Was she feeling insecure in the Tysons Corner house? Maybe once she was in familiar surroundings her memory would return faster.

"I'm fine with those arrangements." Dr. Tobias packed his things. "Alex, do you have a gaming console?"

"I'm male. Of course I do." He smiled proudly. "I actually have several."

"Good. I'd like Katlin to play as many video games as she can. Especially the 3D ones." The doctor glanced up at Alex. "Card games, too." He directed his attention to Katlin. "Poker will help you identify visual cues. Games like gin rummy will help you pay attention and remember. All these games will help you develop efficient scanning, problem identification, and judgment skills. Besides, they're fun."

He picked up his bag. "I'll see you in my office in two days." On his way out the door, he spoke with Gina, but Alex couldn't hear his words.

"We've never played video games together," Alex pointed out. "And I can't ever remember playing cards with you. If you get into a poker game at the office, make it for pennies only. We have some real card sharks that work for us." Alex made a mental note to warn his men.

"I know what you mean, Tori has cleaned me out more than once." She sipped her water and picked up a Jell-O cup. "Cards are a great way to break up the boredom while waiting for the orders to move out."

"Do you remember your missions?" Alex didn't want to ask specifics, but the more she remembered, the better.

"Sure. I'm just having problems remembering people." She lifted hopeful eyes to him. "When we get to Guardian, can we call my brother and ask him to come over? I want to fill in that blank."

"Absolutely, babe. Daniel has been very worried about you ever since you were taken to the hospital. He visited you several times, mostly late at night."

Her brows knit together once again. "I still can't picture him, as either a child or an adult."

"It's okay." Alex rubbed his thumb over the creases on

her forehead. "It'll be fine. Your brother loves you and he understands the situation."

"Will you call him for me?"

"How about I call him and I'll put it on speakerphone. Maybe his voice will bring back those memories."

"Okay." Katlin let out a deep breath. "Can we first call Barry and ask him to call Jack?"

"You bet, babe."

CHAPTER 15

JACK SAT SLUMPED IN HIS HIGH BACK EXECUTIVE CHAIR AND watched the gold dot pulse in Kosovo. He knew if he sent men to that location, Katlin wouldn't be there. The dot disappeared, reappearing in Johannesburg, South Africa. He'd put his best computer geek to trace the movements, but he hadn't been able to break the algorithm, nor pinpoint the origin which would lead them to Katlin's location.

His audio team had added Katlin's name as well as Lady Hawk to their search protocol. Not a single hit on either word in all the millions of communications they followed.

Where the fuck was his woman? Was there any chance that their babies had been saved?

Ever since he'd discovered that she was gone, he waited for the ransom note. He'd pay whatever it cost to get her, and their babies, back. Then he'd have his best men track down those fuckers and kill every last one of them using the most painful methods possible.

But no ransom had ever been demanded.

It had been as though she'd simply disappeared.

He'd assigned the head of his video department to go over

every frame recorded on each camera throughout the entire hospital. Again, she was there, and then she was gone. His technicians couldn't explain why that had happened.

His temper tantrum over the Katlin situation had gotten him another month of visits to the agency psychologist. At that point, Jack didn't care. Finding Katlin was the most important thing in his life.

The preceding beep of his intercom interrupted his sulking.

"Mr. Ashworth, I have a Barry Howell on the line demanding to speak with you. He's Katlin Callahan's attorney. He claims to have information about her." Jack bolted upright in his chair and adjusted his tie as though it were going to be a video call. "Put him through, Mrs. Ward."

As usual, he let the phone ring several times before he picked it up. People needed to know what a busy man he was. "Jack Ashworth," he announced.

"Mr. Ashworth, I'm Barry Howell, attorney for Katlin Callahan. She asked me to call you to let you know that she will not be back to work for a minimum of six weeks. Her neurologist has reserved the right to extend her medical leave for up to six months. At that time, she may be forced to go before a medical review board in order to stay in the military."

"Where the fuck is she?" Jack demanded, unable to wait any longer.

"Ms. Callahan is in a safe location."

"Where. Is. She?" Jack was losing his temper.

"Ms. Callahan is in a safe location." Mr. Howell repeated. "I am not at liberty to tell you her location. She has specifically asked that you stop spending valuable resources searching for her. She is in excellent hands and has already started her rehabilitation therapies."

"Mr. Howell, do you know who kidnapped Ms. Callahan? I intend to bring federal charges against the men who took her out of the hospital, thus kidnapping a federal agent." *Maybe that will scare him*, Jack thought smugly.

"First, Mr. Ashworth, I feel the need to point out that Katlin Callahan is not a federal agent. She is a lieutenant commander in the U.S. Navy. As such, she personally spoke with General Lyon at USSOCOM informing him of her condition. This is simply a courtesy call to you since she is temporarily assigned to Section Seven of Homeland Security."

"While assigned to my division, she was an acting agent of Homeland Security." Jack volleyed back.

Barry Howell chuckled. "You're going to have a tough time defending that to any judge, especially with General Lyon across the aisle. Moving on with your accusations, my second point is that Alex Wolf, her legal executor, had her removed from Walter Reed Medical Center in fear of her health and well-being. Your plan for implanting embryos you fertilized into Ms. Callahan's body was discovered just in time to have her removed from the premises. Thus, there was no kidnapping."

"I'm going to bring multiple murder charges against Alex Wolf. He killed my babies. There were viable embryos that have disappeared." Jack was breathing hard. Every time he thought about Katlin's belly round with his babies, raising them beside him, his anger boiled. Everything he'd planned so precisely had disappeared that morning with her.

Howell burst out laughing, which just made Jack more furious.

"Mr. Ashworth, I look forward to following that case, which I'm quite sure would end up in the Supreme Court. As I'm sure you're aware, those embryos have a forty-five-hour lifespan and cannot be refrozen. So, technically, you killed them when you insisted they be thawed, knowing that if Ms. Callahan were conscious, she would never agree to such a procedure."

No. He was not responsible. It was Alex Wolf's fault.

"But since you brought up the subject," Howell continued, "we would like to know exactly where and how you came into possession of eggs harvested from Ms. Callahan several years ago. According to the records at the fertility center where they were being held for her later use, those eggs disappeared along with several others from similar mothers. It was presumed they were stolen and sold on the black market. Exactly how did you come to be in possession of Ms. Callahan's eggs?"

"That's none of your Goddamn business. I haven't heard any charges, nor have I been Mirandized, and you're not a law enforcement officer so I don't have to answer any of your questions." Then he countered in a sassy voice, "Oh, but *I am* a law enforcement officer. I do have a federal badge. Perhaps I'll drag your ass in for questioning. Mr. Barry Howell, have you been associating with terrorists? Have you had contact with anyone who is a threat to the United States of America?"

"Nice diversion, Mr. Ashworth. Good luck with that. Now, returning to the reason for my call, Ms. Callahan will not be able to return to her duties until she is released by her neurologist and a psychologist. It is estimated that she will be out at least six weeks. If you try to contact her during her rehabilitation, I'm prepared to file a restraining order against you."

"What the fuck?" Jack was devastated that Katlin would take out a restraining order against him.

"Excuse me, Mr. Ashworth, but what part didn't you

understand?" Barry Howell was rubbing Jack's last nerve raw.

Jack would figure out a way to talk to her. He needed to hear her voice, reassure himself that she was okay. "What if I need to confer with Katlin about one of her previous missions?"

"Should you need to discuss anything business-related, you are to contact General Lyon at USSOCOM. If you need his number, I can give that to you."

"I have his fucking number." Not that Jack would ever use it for anything other than official business.

"Excellent." The attorney sounded gleeful. "I will consider you informed of Ms. Callahan's wishes and her doctor's orders. If anything changes in her condition, you are on the list to be notified. On a personal note, I find you to be the lowest of slime on this earth for what you attempted to do to my friend Katlin. I can assure you, we're going to address the issue when she's healthy." The line went dead.

Jack hung up the phone and rubbed his temples. He knew Guardian Security had retrieved the remaining eggs from the fertilization clinic he used for the IVF last week. But those weren't their only embryos. He had more stashed in a Pennsylvania fertility clinic. Three had already made it past genetic testing.

He grinned. His backup plans always had backup plans.

His intercom buzzed again. "Mr. Ashworth, Agent Chernakov is here per your request. Sir, Operations Control needs you right away."

Jack didn't bother answering his administrative assistant. He opened the door and strode past her desk. "I'll be in operations."

"Agent Chernakov, walk with me." Jack loved how the woman took orders, at work as well as in the bedroom. He mentally chuckled as he recalled all the places outside of his bedroom he'd fucked her, including the office he just left.

"How soon is Katlin coming back?" Nikkole asked as soon as they were out of hearing distance of Mrs. Ward.

"She won't be back for at least six weeks, possibly as long as six months." Jack's heart broke at the thought he'd have to go months without seeing his Katlin.

On the other hand, Nikkole could barely contain her excitement. "Does that mean you're putting me on the Black Swan team?"

"I have something much more important for you to do." The woman beside him had always been Plan B. If he couldn't have Katlin Callahan, at least he could have a part of her in his life. "We'll discuss it tonight at my house."

His covert Kat purred. "Good. I bought something special to wear just for you," she whispered just before she turned down a side hall.

He'd chosen Nikkole years ago because of her blood type…and willingness to do anything he asked. She and Katlin were both blood type AB, the same height, and similar build. Over the last several years, he had personally paid for Nikkole's new breasts, the blond hair that tickled his thighs as she sucked his cock, and several personal gifts. But the Agency had paid for her new nose due to an unfortunate training accident. With her specially made blue contacts, she looked as though she could be Katlin's sister.

He hoped she would agree to be Katlin's surrogate. Jack didn't think Nikkole would make a good mother, but women still died in childbirth and he could find good nannies.

CHAPTER 16

THE MOMENT KATLIN WALKED THROUGH THE DOOR OF Guardian Security D.C. Center, she was attacked by one hundred pounds of love and licks. Alex wasn't sure which was happier to see the other, dog or master.

Watching her eyes light up blue as a mountaintop summer sky when she greeted Damnit, her Mastiff Rottweiler mixed rescue dog, lifted Alex's heavy heart. She loved that dog, and seeing her smile for the first time since waking up, filled him with hope.

"How's she doing?" Tanner Hill, the dog's trainer and kennel owner, asked as Katlin fell to her knees and hugged her dog.

"The doctor believes she is recovering well. She'll sleep better when she's upstairs in our bed." A place he wanted Katlin to go, now. She was exhausted from the trip over. She had a long way to go before she was mission ready…if she ever made it there.

Alex would be okay if she didn't ever return to active duty. She owned half the stock in Guardian Security and the company made more than enough money for the two of them to live comfortably for the rest of their lives. She also had investments in real estate, stocks and bonds. Most certainly, they would never starve.

As Alex gingerly stepped past the reunion, Tanner asked, "Do you think Katlin would be up for a visit from Bailey? She's been so busy working and training that she hasn't seen hardly any of the women she served with."

"What a great idea. The rest of Katlin's team is away training. She's hoping for a call from them soon. Have Bailey call and set up a time. Is she still training for the Paralympics?"

Katlin's giggling was the only thing that kept Alex from pulling the large dog off her.

"Always. She now competes in both Summer and Winter Paralympics." Tanner chuckled. "She's in better shape than I am."

Katlin stood, leash in hand. "Thank you. I don't know what I'd do without you boarding him when I'm gone."

The trainer grinned. "Oh, you'd find somebody to take care of Damnit." He reached down and scratched the dog's ear. "He's just a big old gentle giant. Give me a call when you leave town again and I'll come get him. My kennels are his second home." Tanner waved on his way out the door.

As the three of them crowded into the elevator, Alex automatically moved away from the dog.

He'd never been comfortable around the big dogs. Growing up on the seedier side of D.C., he wasn't allowed to have a pet. That would've just been one more mouth to feed and his parents were stretched as thin as they could be feeding their family of five and half the neighborhood children whose parents couldn't bother.

He wasn't afraid of Damnit, he just didn't know what to do with the big dog. It was a good thing the mutt never left

Katlin's side, even as Alex tucked her into bed ten minutes later.

"What was his name?" Katlin asked just above a whisper.

"Whose name?" Alex glanced down at the big dog.

"His trainer. I should know his name, but I just can't think of it." Katlin seemed distressed so he took her in his arms.

"That's Tanner Hill. He married your friend, Bailey. Do you remember her?" Alex looked her in the eye so she wouldn't lie to him.

"Uhm. No." Her eyebrows drew together. "Maybe."

"Sleep for a couple hours if you can." Alex kissed her on the forehead. "I'm going down to my office for a while. I'll bring supper up with me."

When he turned to walk away, Katlin grabbed his hand and pulled him down for a kiss. With her arms around his neck, she held him in place.

"Have I thanked you for everything you've done for me?" Her eyes filled with tears. "Jack…if he'd—"

Alex put his index finger on her lips. "He didn't. And his fuck-up made it possible for us to have a family someday, hopefully. Silver linings, babe. I don't want you to worry about anything. I'm going to take care of you. We're going to get you better." He ran his fingers down the side of her beautiful face and wiped the tear off her cheek with his thumb.

All this crying was new. His Kat never cried. Never. She was hard as steel inside and out. Perhaps as she regained her muscle strength, her fortitude would return as well. He reminded himself once again, Dr. Tobias had warned him that she might not be the same woman she'd been before.

"Sleep, babe." He gave her a quick kiss on the lips. "I'll be back in a few hours."

Damnit followed him to the bedroom door then plopped

his large body down in the open jamb, positioned like a sentry guarding his queen. He carefully watched Alex as he strode out of the apartment.

In his D.C. office, Alex caught up on business phone calls before he tackled personal ones. He didn't recognize the telephone number, but the area code was definitely Los Angeles.

Hitting play he instantly recognized JJ's voice. "Hey there, hunk in my life. I got the part of the kick-ass detective. How soon can you get that tight ass of yours out here and teach me some moves? They want me to do as much of my own fight scenes as possible. They've got me taking some martial arts classes, and I've already had a few self-defense courses, but I'm sure there's so much more my personal bodyguard can teach me. Call me. Oh, by the way, this is my new cell phone number. I had to get a new one. Some motherfucker gave out my last one and I had all kinds of creepers calling me. Talk to you soon. Love you. Bye."

Alex shook his head and hit the icon to call her back. He was surprised when she answered. "Please tell me you're already here in town. I need your help." She dragged out the word *need*.

"I'm not sure when I'll get back out to Los Angeles." Although he needed to visit each site, he wasn't about to leave Katlin. "but I have a whole office of former special operators and I'm positive they can teach you anything you'll need to know for the movie. You'll like them." Grinning, Alex could imagine the men in his L.A. Center fighting over the chance to teach the starlet, up close and personal.

"But I want you, Alejandro," she whined in Spanish.

"As soon as I get to Los Angeles, I'll take over your training, but in the meantime, I'm going to call my office manager there and have him call you. Can he reach you at this number?"

"Yes," she pouted out the word. "But you'd better get here soon. You're the only one I truly trust."

"I know, Jae." Alex thought about his beautiful woman sleeping upstairs in their bed. "It might be weeks before I can get there."

"What could be more important than helping me?" JJ pleaded.

Typical Jae. The world revolved around her.

"My fiancée was in…" Alex almost said an accident then he remembered Katlin's words. The RPG was hardly accidental. "Was badly hurt. I'm taking care of her."

"Get her a nurse or something. I need you out here." She made an impetuous noise. "Let me talk to the producers and see if they'll pay for a nurse for her. They're paying well for your services."

Well, at least his men would be paid for working with her, a point she'd neglected to mention earlier. "Jae, I don't need them to pay for a nurse. Katlin is still under a doctor's care and we can't leave D.C. right now. You'll just have to do with my men from the LA office."

"Fine." She huffed. "But you'll get here as soon as you can?"

"Yes, Jae. Be sure to take the phone call from my office manager. He'll make all the arrangements. I'm quite sure you'll be satisfied with the men we send you." Before she could protest again, Alex said, "Goodbye, Jae."

"Alex," she quickly interjected before he could hang up. "Thank you for looking out for me, just like you did when we were kids. I'll always love you, you know."

"I know. I'm hanging up now, Jae." Alex ended the call. As he sat there with the cell phone in his hand, memories of his last day in that small clapboard house with the dirt yard came to him as clear as though it were yesterday.

He'd known he was in trouble the moment he stepped into the house. His mother stood in the middle of the living room with her hands balled into fists and planted on her hips. Jael Jimena Martinez stood beside her, arms crossed under her voluptuous breasts, making them practically pop out of her low-cut tank top.

You fucking little bitch. "You told her, didn't you?" Alex accused the most beautiful girl in the neighborhood. He only told her because she'd been targeted by the gang who was recruiting on their block.

Lifting that little pointed chin of hers into the air she admitted, "I did."

"So, it's true." His mother didn't ask the question, she'd made it a statement.

He knew better than to lie to her. His mother ruled the house, even before his father had been murdered.

"Yes, Mamá. I'm an initiate." Alejandro hadn't officially joined the gang. His loyalty was still being tested, but when the leader told him he had to lure Jael to the empty house two blocks away so all the initiates could gang-rape her, he couldn't do it. He had loved her since they were in kindergarten. He just wasn't *in* love with her.

Instead of doing as the gang had demanded, he'd gone to Jael hoping she'd tell her parents, not that he was sure they would do anything about it. Many adults in his neighborhood were as afraid of the gang as the kids were.

It was obvious—she'd told his mother about his gang involvement instead.

Within days, Alejandro had found himself in Little Havana, Miami living with his Nana Rosa where he'd finished high school...and met Katlin.

Jael had saved his life.

His mother had saved hers. Jae had moved into the Lobo house, sharing a bedroom with his younger sister until she graduated two years later.

Both Alex and JJ had repaid his mother back a hundred times over. As soon as Alex could, he moved his mother out of that neighborhood and into a nice townhome with her second husband. Recently, JJ had bought his mom another new car.

At the thought of his mother, Alex collapsed a little inside. He'd been back in town for weeks and hadn't been over to see her. Had she known Katlin was sick, she would've been at the safe house every day, cooking up a storm for everyone. Because he wasn't sure if Jack had put surveillance on his mother, he hadn't told her. Now that Katlin was safe inside Guardian, he'd better call her.

Grinning, he dialed her number. He'd kill two birds with one stone. She would come over immediately, and most likely bring supper.

CHAPTER 17

KATLIN WOKE UP FEELING REFRESHED FOR THE THIRD DAY IN a row. Automatically, she reached across the smooth sheets searching for Alex. He wasn't there. The sheets were cold but that wasn't a surprise, especially when she glanced at the clock on the nightstand. It was nearly nine in the morning. Most likely, he'd been up before six, taking his men for a run before breakfast, then working out in the gym for another hour.

Lately, she'd wake up when she heard Alex in the shower. Before the explosion, what she now secretly thought of as BTE, she would have joined him for the morning routine, especially enjoying the shower together. Now, he crawled into bed long after she'd fallen asleep and was gone before she awoke.

Last night, she had a nightmare and he'd held her until she fell back asleep. She wished he'd do that every night. Just hold her.

He didn't know she was scared to her soul. She was living by the creed; fake it till you make it.

Names. She hated it when there were more than three

people in the room that she didn't know. Sometimes, she forgot who they were a minute after being introduced. BTE she'd always been good with names, she was sure of it.

She'd felt like such an idiot when Bailey came to visit. They had trained together at the Joint All Female Special Operations School. She'd been on the mission when the IED had taken Bailey's leg. They'd been through so much together, but when her friend knocked on the penthouse door, Katlin couldn't remember her name. She knew they were friends, recognized her face, but couldn't for the life of her think of the name. Thank God her friend was a psychologist for the Veterans Administration and had worked with several TBI and PTSD veterans. She'd brought cards and they'd played gin rummy for almost two hours before Katlin was so tired she was practically falling asleep at the table.

It had taken her three more days before she remembered Marine Brigadier General Ava Standish's name. Even though she'd called the woman Aunt Ava all of her life, Katlin needed those days to put the pieces together. The amazing woman had been her father's friend since they'd been midshipmen at the Naval Academy. She'd been Katlin's babysitter, her Uncle Tom's on-and-off girlfriend, all while having an outstanding career as a Marine. Most recently, she'd been instrumental in creating JAFSOS and recommending Katlin for the program.

After a great deal of consideration and self-debate, Katlin decided that telling General Standish about all the things that Jack had done to her was the right thing to do. Although General Lyon was aware of the most recent events, Katlin thought a military woman's perspective might be better than a man's.

Although she wasn't sure of the current relationship status between Ava and her Uncle Tom, she needed him as well. In his position as deputy director of the CIA, he could give her insight as to what could be done with Jack from a governmental employee position.

When Katlin had started writing down things that Jack had done in the past, per General Lyon's instructions, she discovered an entire folder cleverly buried on her computer. Reading through it had been an education in sexual harassment. She'd clearly remembered most of the incidences, and the number of times she'd used Jack's indiscretions against him. Every day she could recall more memories.

She was thrilled when she called her Uncle Tom and Ava was with him.

Katlin smoothed down her pencil skirt in front of the cheval mirror in the bedroom. She thought it might be nice to dress up for her company…and Alex. For the past several weeks, all she'd worn was a hospital gown, yoga pants, and the towel on her way to the bed before she crawled in naked. Instead of her normal ponytail, Katlin had curled her long blond hair and swiped on a little makeup so she didn't look quite so pale.

The other oven buzzer went off at the same time she heard voices in the hall. Alex opened the front door, holding a bouquet of yellow roses already arranged in a crystal vase. The three of them were chatting like old friends do.

When Katlin opened the oven, the entire apartment filled with Italian spices.

"Oh my God. That smells delicious." Ava stepped next to her. "Can I help with something?"

"Thank you, no. I'm just going to let this sit and cool a minute."

Since neither woman was in uniform, they hugged.

Then her Uncle Tom hugged her. "I'm glad you

remembered how to cook. My freezer is almost empty of your meals." He held her tight in his arms. "I thought there for a while we'd lost you. That Jack-ass wouldn't tell me who'd been killed or that you'd been rescued."

When he released her, Katlin stood, processing his words. Her team still hadn't been able to call her, but each had texted letting her know they were looking forward to the day she'd return. They were working well with Black Swan Team Two, so that meant that no one on her team had been killed.

"Who died?"

Silence filled the kitchen.

Ava and Tom both looked at Alex, who immediately rushed to her side and threw his arm around her waist. "I'm sorry, Kat, I didn't even think about telling you. Jonathan didn't make it."

All eyes were pinned on her waiting for a reaction.

Although she could put a face to his name, she examined her feelings toward the man. She hadn't liked him. "I'm sorry he was killed but the world has one less arrogant and misogynistic asshole." She turned toward Alex. "Why don't you get our guests some drinks while I plate these appetizers?"

"You certainly tell it like it is." Her uncle dropped a kiss on top of her head before he meandered into the living room toward the wet bar.

Oh, fuck. Had she said something wrong?

She grabbed Alex's arm and asked quietly, "Should I have lied?"

"No, babe. Jonathan was everything you called him, and probably more." His lips brushed over hers. "You look beautiful."

"Thank you. I tried." She wasn't sure why she was

nervous. Everyone here was family. Better yet, she'd remembered their names.

Minutes later, Katlin sat down on the couch beside Alex. Everyone had a small plate of hors d'oeuvres in their lap. While she drank water, the two men sipped scotch and Ava seemed to enjoy the white wine.

"These are absolutely delicious, dear." Ava sat her plate on the glass and chrome coffee table. "You didn't call us here to sample your latest Italian finger food. What can we do to help you?"

Katlin let out a deep breath. That's exactly what she needed the woman to say. Opening her laptop, she started down her list of Jack's harassments. She glanced up a few times to be sure that Ava and her Uncle Tom were still following. The average person wouldn't have caught their anger, but since she'd known them all of her life, she could read them. Their professions had taught them to hide their emotions, but each had small physical indicators.

She didn't need a list for the last one.

"As you both know, I was considered AWOL for nearly a week. Thankfully, General Lyon changed my status after I was able to call him. I was not kidnapped." She emphasized the word not. She reached for Alex's hand at the same time he extended it. "The Ladies of Black Swan sneaked in to see me before they left for training. Jack had forbidden them to do so, but they did it anyway…and I thank the good Lord every day now that Nita looked at my file."

Katlin tried to swallow over the large lump in her throat but couldn't seem to moisten it enough so she picked up her water and took a large drink.

"It's okay, Kat." Alex bounced their joined hands on his thigh. "I'm right here beside you. You're safe."

She sucked in a ragged breath. "Nita discovered that they

had been pumping pre-pregnancy steroids into my body so they..." Her voice cracked. "Jack had fertilized my missing eggs and they were going to implant the embryos into my uterus the next morning." Katlin was so proud of herself that she'd made it through the explanation without crying. She didn't need any more useless tears. Finally, her soul-wrenching pain for the children she couldn't have because he'd ruined those eggs, had transformed into unadulterated anger.

"What the fuck!" Her Uncle Tom flew out of his chair and started pacing in front of them.

"Jack…your eggs…the ones that went missing years ago?" Ava shuddered. "You got her the hell out of there, right?"

"It wasn't me. I was on the West Coast. But it was my men." Alex said with pride. "And Daniel."

Uncle Tom stopped in his tracks. "They didn't kidnap you, they rescued you."

Katlin smiled. "They most certainly did."

"You need to have him arrested." Ava leaned forward.

"That's why I told the two of you. What legal recourse do I have?" Katlin took another long drink of her water. "General Lyon knows what happened, but as he pointed out, Jack isn't military so he isn't subject to the Uniform Code of Military Justice. Even though I'm active duty and TDY to Homeland, the UCMJ doesn't protect me from him."

"Goddamnit, he's right." Ava pulled out her phone. "But there's definitely a history of sexual harassment and the attempted rape three years ago."

"The attempted rape charge would just be your word against his. He'd get a slap on the wrist at most." Her uncle started pacing again. "The IVF, I'm not sure he can be touched on that, either. I should just go kill the fucker myself."

"You'll have to get behind me. The line to kill Jack Ashworth is longer than you might think." Alex was right. So many men wanted to kill Jack on Katlin's behalf.

Little did they know, if she ever got the chance, she'd take him out, and as far as the world would know, the man would just disappear. She had planned Jack's death countless times in numerous ways. All of them involved hours of torture, most to his genitals. But then she considered the ick factor of seeing, or worse, touching, his junk and decided against any of those methods.

Lady Hawk was the most lethal woman in the world. She had eliminated dozens of men and Jack Ashworth would be just one more dirtbag that needed disposing of. She was making her way back to her BTE strength. Her hatred for Jack was enough to push her physically and mentally. She would be Lady Hawk once again.

At that moment, Ava acted more like an aunt than a general, moving to Katlin's side and hugging her. The men were incensed that Jack would try to do something so vile to *their* Katlin, but Ava understood the violation on a feminine level. Very few people knew that the highest-ranking woman in the United States Marine Corps had been raped as a new lieutenant. The captain had been killed in action before he could be brought to justice.

"Certainly, he could be charged for stealing the eggs." Ava put her arm around Katlin.

Her Uncle Tom shook his head. "It would have to be proven that Jack stole the eggs. Or, if someone else stole them and Jack purchased them, that would also have to be proven. It would be federal if it crossed state lines, but again, that requires proof. I'm not sure what laws he broke when he attempted the IVF."

"I hate it when you're right." Ava gave her uncle a small smile. She gestured toward the computer. "All we have here are allegations."

"The whole frozen egg and sperm situation is so new I couldn't even find where it had been tested in a court." Alex squeezed her hand as he looked at Katlin. She had no idea he'd already looked into the legalities of what Jack had done to her.

She mouthed the words *thank you.* Alex's eyes said everything a second before he leaned in and brushed his lips over hers.

Her uncle's phone beeped three times. He instantly pulled it out of his pocket and checked the message. "Fuck. I'm sorry, little one, but I have to leave immediately." He glanced at Ava. "Sweetheart, it's going to be a late night." Turning to Alex, he asked, "One of your men take Ava back to Quantico for me?"

"Of course." Alex immediately reached for the house phone on the end table. "I need a car to take General Standish to Quantico."

"Please email me that list." Her Uncle Tom moved her way, so Katlin stood to hug him goodbye. "I have a few attorney friends, that with your permission, I'd like to get their opinion."

"Of course. Anything that will help me see Jack Ashworth get what's coming to him."

Standing, Ava asked, "Would you mind sending me a copy as well? I'm not sure how I can help, but maybe I can get you transferred away from Homeland Security."

When the four of them headed toward the door, Damnit appeared at her side and followed them into the elevator down to the garage level where they were met by a Guardian driver for Ava. With only a nod from Alex, he got into a company SUV.

Their goodbyes were quick because everyone understood her Uncle Tom was needed elsewhere.

Alex threw his arm around Katlin as they headed back to the elevator. "You look tired."

"I am. Probably more emotionally exhausted than physically," she admitted. "I'll clean up then head to bed." She leaned over and kissed him as the elevator opened on the top floor. "It's early. If you need to go back to work, don't let me stop you."

He pulled her tighter into him as they stepped out of the elevator. "I'll help you clean up then I'll tuck you into bed."

CHAPTER 18

DAMNIT NUDGED KATLIN'S HAND.

When she sat up in bed, she realized how fast she was breathing. She had a nightmare about Jack raping her. In her nightmare, he'd tied her to a bed and was about to slide into her open sex when Damnit had awakened her. She looked down and realized she'd been rubbing her wrists as though they had been bound.

Her heart was pounding. She was supposed to remain as calm as possible so she used the breathing techniques they'd been taught to help control adrenaline. When she sat up on the edge of the bed and flipped back the sheets, a note from the night table fluttered to the floor.

Damnit has already been out. Breakfast is in the fridge. The coffeepot is waiting for you. Alex

As Katlin read the note for the second time, it dawned on her that Alex had never said he loved her since she'd awakened from the coma. Was it possible he didn't love her anymore? Was he taking care of her out of guilt or some sense of responsibility? They weren't married so the *through sickness and health* clause didn't apply. She started to wonder how often he'd said I love you BTE. She couldn't remember.

The yellow roses he'd brought her the other night when Aunt Ava and Uncle Tom were there tickled in the back of her mind. The color…they were special.

She got out of bed and padded to the foyer where she'd set them on the side table next to the silver tray that contained her keys. Placing her keys there had been automatic. She'd reached for her weapons as well before she realized she wasn't carrying any on her body. They belonged on the same table.

Leaning in, she inhaled the sweet smell of the roses which were now opening wide. She closed her eyes to savor the scent. The rush of memories that overtook her almost knocked her backward.

Popping her eyes open to stabilize herself at the same time she reached out for the narrow table, her body seemed to fill with love. Then, and now. Katlin could picture the yellow roses that had been delivered by mistake for her sixteenth birthday. Alex had ordered red ones but they'd all been sold out for Mother's Day the weekend before. Since that moment, she'd always preferred yellow roses.

She needed to thank Alex.

As she reached for the doorknob, Damnit's cold nose poked her butt cheek. Looking down at her naked body, she rolled her eyes. She'd always slept naked and felt as comfortable nude as she did wearing clothes. "You're right, big boy." She scratched the dog's ears. "Clothes would be a good idea. So would a shower." But when her stomach growled she diverted to the kitchen, grabbing a cup of coffee and the plate of fruit and cheese she found prepared for her in the fridge. Taking everything with her, she headed to the bathroom. She could thank Alex after she was dressed.

Wrapped in nothing but a towel, Katlin stared at the uniforms, coordinated suits, clubbing dresses, and formal attire on her side of the huge walk-in closet. She glanced toward the dresser in the bedroom. Although a morning nap sounded nice, at her checkup yesterday with Dr. Tobias, he told her that she could start working out. She was not to push herself and to keep her heart rate under one hundred. For her, a light workout was one hundred and sixty beats per minute. When in training, she always maintained two hundred for at least thirty minutes.

Changing into workout clothes, she took the stairs down to the company gym. She'd start with stretches, a slow jog on the treadmill, then lift a few weights. That would be a light workout.

Winded by the time she got to the gym level, Katlin was embarrassed walking in already sweaty. Unrolling one of the yoga mats, she got her breathing back under control while stretching. She cut her usual routine short, wanting to curl up like a kindergartner for a short nap on the padded mat. She might've done it if there hadn't been several men pumping iron and sparring in the room.

She checked her smart fitness watch. Her heart rate was already at one-twenty. She also had several emails and considered reading them on her phone as an excuse to stay seated.

She had to get better.

The only way to improve was to get moving.

She stood, wiped down her mat, and put it away. With all the determination she could muster, she programmed the treadmill. Damnit followed, sitting down next to the machine. It took her almost ten minutes to find her pace and adjust her breathing. She wasn't sure how long she'd been fast walking, but Damnit started to whine.

Damn. She hadn't taken him outside. He probably had to go.

Punching a few buttons, she slowed the machine, but before it came to a complete stop, one of the men was by her side. Fuck. She couldn't remember his name. Panic ripped through her. She should know who he was. He was an assistant manager for Christ's sake. There were only three of them at each center. What the hell was his name?

The man with hazel eyes, about her age, grabbed Damnit's leash. "I'm done. I'll take him out for a walk."

Katlin gave him what she hoped was a thankful smile, but she was breathing too hard to be sure. "I appreciate that," she said between huffs.

"Come on, Damnit. Walk with me."

The dog didn't move.

He poked his muzzle at Katlin.

The machine came to a complete stop. Between gasps of air, Katlin told her puppy, "Go on. He's going to take you out."

The dog didn't move.

Katlin gave a heavy sigh and she stepped off the treadmill. "Okay, big boy. I've got you."

Damnit instantly came to his feet and walked right beside Katlin. "I'm sorry. I don't know what's gotten into him today."

"I do," Top called from the door, his feet spread wide, powerful arms crossed over his broad chest. "Damnit is smarter than you are. What the fuck do you think you're doing?"

At the moment? Trying to walk on legs that felt like cooked noodles. Her lungs burned. She seemed to have to think about every step to make her legs move. She wasn't sure she'd felt this bad after running the Marine Corps

Marathon two years ago. She couldn't answer Top's question. She didn't have the breath.

When she was within reaching distance, he grabbed her wrist, flipping it around so he could see the numbers. "One hundred seventy," he growled. That's almost twice as much as the doctor allowed. From now on, I'm in charge of your workouts."

Top reached down and scratched Damnit's ears. "Good boy."

Katlin swayed but managed to lift her hand and caught herself on the doorjamb.

Good.

She was still upright.

"Whoa."

Katlin whipped her head around to see who had spoken. They felt too close.

Her brain swam within her skull. She felt like she was stepping out of the Tilt-A-Whirl at a traveling carnival.

Suddenly, she was in the air. "I've got her, Top. You deal with the dog." She recognized the man's voice but still couldn't think of his name. He'd picked her up bride-style.

Damnit was licking her hand that swung loosely to the side, then he was gone.

She heard nails scampering down the hallway.

"Somebody grab Damnit," Top called. "Take Kat to the penthouse."

Katlin inhaled deeply several times. Her head quickly cleared. "Put me down, please. I can walk."

"Not until we get her upstairs," Top ordered.

Katlin heard boots running down the hallway. Fuck. She knew who that would be, and he wouldn't be happy.

"What the fuck happened?" Alex's distinct voice cut through the noise.

"I'm all right," Katlin yelled as loud as she could. She turned to the man carrying her. "I'd truly appreciate it if you'd set me down. I really can walk."

Alex was on the other side of her, lifting her out of the man's arms. "I've got you, now. You're safe."

She rolled her eyes at him. "I'm fine. Please, put me down. I can walk." She swallowed her pride. "I may have pushed myself…a little. I got a little dizzy." She quickly added, "But I feel fine now." And she did. Embarrassed, but physically well enough to walk on her own.

As soon as someone punched the button for the elevator, the doors opened. Damnit followed them in, dragging his short leash.

"Damnit came sliding into my office." Alex's voice shook. "All I could think was—"

Katlin put her index finger over his lips. "I'm fine." She leaned up and gave him a quick kiss. "You don't have to carry me."

When the doors opened, she already had her key fob out and unlocked the apartment door.

She giggled. "You're not supposed to carry me across the threshold until I'm in a bridal gown and you're bringing me home for the first time as your wife."

The look he gave her was completely unreadable.

Had he changed his mind? Was he going to call off their engagement? More than once Dr. Tobias had told them that it could take years before she was back to being the same woman she'd been BTE. She'd also heard the doctor say that she may be a totally different woman when she regained consciousness. Had Alex decided he didn't like this woman she was now? Maybe he didn't want a damaged wife.

He hadn't once told her that he loved her since she'd awakened.

Katlin thought she'd been making amazing progress. Sure, she was hiding a lot from them, but it wasn't that big a deal. So what if she couldn't remember everybody's name? She didn't think her personality had changed… much. She seemed to cry a lot which was new. Her body wasn't as strong as it was before, but it hadn't changed that much.

"My memories are coming back!" She announced as they passed the bouquet on the foyer table. She squeezed his neck and gave him a kiss on the cheek. "Thank you for the yellow roses. I remembered all about them this morning."

He laid her down on the bed, then sat on the edge. With his elbows on his knees, he dropped his head into his hands. "Christ, Kat. You scared the shit out of me."

She sat up next to him and rubbed her hand up and down his back. "I'm sorry. I didn't mean to. I just got a little lightheaded while working out in the gym."

"Dizzy enough that Sam had to carry you." Alex's worry was evident in his tone.

Sam. That was his name. Samuel Baden. See? She was getting better.

"They were all overreacting." She bumped his shoulder with hers. "You only hire macho men. Of course, they would swoop in and scoop up a woman if they thought she was going to faint."

He rolled his head to look at her. "You were fainting?"

Well, hell. That was the wrong choice of words. "No. I just felt a little wobbly."

"Why don't you lie down and take a nap?" Alex suggested.

"I stink. I'll see how I feel about a nap after I take a shower." Standing, she held out her hand to him. "Join me?"

"No. But I'll wait in the bathroom while you shower, just

in case you get lightheaded again." The smile he gave her didn't reach his eyes.

She stripped on the way to the bathroom, giving him a little extra swing in her naked hips, tossing the stinky clothes in the hamper. She'd show him exactly what he was missing. But when he followed her in and leaned against the counter, crossing his arms over his chest, his body language screamed his unhappiness at being there. She didn't want to stand naked in front of him while the water warmed, so she stepped into the tepid shower. Closing the door she turned on all eight showerheads.

Maybe with water pelting her body, she wouldn't think about how many times they'd made love up against those marble walls. How many times Alex had soaped her body, washing their lovemaking off her and she'd reciprocated. She loved rubbing her hands all over his body, whether with soap, or oil, or sweat.

She'd been awake for nearly a week and Alex hadn't even kissed her. Little pecks didn't count. When she and Alex kissed, BTE, it had been all-consuming. These days, when she awoke in the middle of the night, he was spooning her from several inches back or had a hand on her hip. BTE, he'd be right up against her, one hand cupping a breast. She didn't even know if he went to bed or awakened with a hard-on.

Katlin would gladly take care of it for him. They had always been a very sexual couple. When together, they seemed to need to make up for the lost time, often having sex several times a day. Location didn't matter. They had christened almost every surface in the apartment.

Her shower poof scraped over her hardened nipples as she spread the suds over her body. Aroused, Katlin decided to ask Alex one more time to join her. Sliding open the door she asked, "Can I change your mind about joining me?"

"You done?" He asked at the same time, leaning forward to grab a towel.

"No." They said in unison.

With tears in her eyes, Katlin stepped back into the shower and quickly rinsed. When she moved out onto the rug, she snatched the towel from his grasp. "I told you I was fine," she snapped, wrapping the towel around her.

"Babe." That was the only word he said.

Without looking at him, she strode to the bed. "I think I will take that nap." She dropped the wet towel onto the wood floor and crawled under the covers…naked. "Hang that up for me, would you, please?" She couldn't watch him walk out of the room, so she rolled toward the other wall. She heard him pick up the towel and hang it in the bathroom before he walked out of the bedroom.

When the tears started to flow, she didn't bother wiping them away.

Damnit jumped up on the bed, leaped over her body, and got in her face. He wasn't allowed on the bed and knew it. But when her puppy licked away her tears, they just flowed until she cried herself to sleep.

CHAPTER 19

"Babe, wake up." Alex kneeled next to their bed and spoke quietly to her. With his fingertips, he brushed stray hairs off her face and tucked them behind her ear. He needed her to wake up. "Katlin, wake up and look at me. You have company."

She whimpered and pulled the blankets over her shoulders.

"Do you want me to ask them to leave? I will if you're too tired." He really hated to do that to Daniel, but he would for Katlin.

Exhaling a deep breath, Katlin rolled over. "Who's here?"

"Your brother, Daniel. He brought the kids." Alex ran his fingers through her hair from her temples to the back of her skull. "But if you're too tired, I'll ask them to come back another time."

"Aunt Katlin," Simon practically sang. "Can you come out and play?"

"I'll be right there," she called loud enough so her nephew could hear her through the closed door.

"Do you know how beautiful you are when you first wake

up?" Alex bent and laid a gentle kiss on her lips. "For nearly a week I was afraid you weren't going to wake up. Then I was afraid you would and that you'd be some other person. Somebody who didn't know me. Somebody who didn't love me the way I love you."

He kissed her again. "I'm sorry I was such a dick earlier today."

The kiss he gave her was slow and sensual. "I know you wanted me to rip my clothes off and join you in that shower...but I couldn't. I knew if I did, I'd want to bury myself deep inside you up against the wall like we have so many times before. I had to hold my hands down under my arms so I didn't touch you. The doctor doesn't want you working out hard, so I know he doesn't want us having mind-blowing sex."

He tried to pack everything he felt into his next kiss. "Don't think for one millisecond that I don't want you." He looked down at his obvious erection trying to poke through his basketball shorts. "Now, quickly get dressed and go out there and play with your niece and nephew. Tell them Uncle Alex will be out as soon as he showers."

It was a good thing Alex was used to showering and getting dressed in a hurry. Daniel had stopped by to visit the first day she was at Guardian and things had been a bit rough for the first few minutes. Fortunately, Katlin recognized him, but she couldn't remember his name. When she asked about their childhood together, admitting she couldn't remember what he'd look like at different ages, Daniel finally explained that they had grown up mostly apart. He'd been left to attend school in the United States while she lived in embassies with their parents, only visiting her much older brother during holidays. Those memories of her entire family together still hadn't returned.

Fortunately, Katlin did remember the children who he'd brought with him this time.

When Alex stepped into the living room, Katlin had the adorable dark-haired four-year-old, with eyes that matched her own, in her arms. "When did you get so big?" She asked dramatically.

The child put his small hands on each side of her head. "Daddy said your head got hurt. Where? I kiss it, make it better."

Alex's heart melted. Katlin loved that little boy so much. He wondered if they could have a boy. There were very few eggs left and their success chances were slim, but better than none. He would do whatever it took to give her a baby. He corrected himself. Give *them* a baby.

Katlin forced a smile. "My brain was hurt inside my head so you can give me a kiss right here." She tapped her lips with her index finger.

Simon leaned forward and gave her a smacking kiss like only small children can do. "All better?"

"I'm gonna need lots more medicine like that before it's completely healed." She scrunched up her face overdramatically. "Do you have more where that one came from?"

Simon's blue-on-blue eyes lit up. "I've got lots of kisses." He leaned in and gave her another. "Let me know when you need more." He pointed to the superhero rolling bag. "Do you want to play with my trucks?" His face fell. "Daddy made me bring puzzles, too, in case I needed to play quietly while adults talk."

Katlin carried him over to his bag. "How about you get your trucks out while I say hello to your dad and snuggle Isabella for a few minutes?"

"Will you hang on to her while I do my job? She walks,

you know. And she likes to put my toys in her mouth and gets them all slobbery." Simon turned his back on everyone as he unzipped his bag and began unloading.

"Let me have that little girl." Katlin lifted baby Bella out of her brother's arms and sat down on the couch next to him. "Thank you for bringing them over."

She was so damn good with kids. And he promised himself that he would be better with his next children than he'd been with Jenny. Although he had to admit that Katlin had helped him learn to enjoy his daughter. He'd been so afraid of doing something wrong with her as an infant, then she and her mother had completely left his life for years. He'd only been able to see her for a few hours every six to eight weeks, sometimes less when he'd been on deployments.

"How are you doing?" Daniel asked. "And don't sugarcoat it."

"I might've done too much today in the gym. I got a little dizzy." Katlin drilled her nose into the baby's rounded belly. "But I'm much better now, aren't I Bella?" She looked so happy to be with the children.

"Christ, sis. You need to be more careful," Daniel scolded.

"It was my first day in the gym. I had to figure out my limits." She smiled at her brother. "And now I know I can't maintain a heart rate of one hundred seventy beats per minute."

"Top told me on the way up here that he's going to take over as your personal trainer." The edges of Daniel's mouth twitched. "I'm not sure if that's a good thing. He's used to conditioning Marines for Embassy duty."

"And sometimes he treats me as though I'm still four years old." Katlin loved the hard as nails retired Marine and would do anything for the man. Alex was glad for his protectiveness.

"Have you been keeping up with the news?" Daniel's question was tentative, and Alex completely understood.

"If you're asking me if I heard about Jack's parents being murdered, the answer is yes." She grinned and rattled keys for baby Bella. "It would be pretty hard to live in D.C. and avoid the barrage of media. They're feasting with speculation."

"Do you think Jack killed them?" Daniel asked with all seriousness.

"Fuck, no." Katlin slapped her hand over her mouth, her eyes apologetic toward her brother. "Sorry. I don't think he has anything to gain by their deaths. His father was a known hound dog. If the rumors are true, he kept several women on the side. I think his mother was just as bad."

"With women?" Alex couldn't help himself.

Katlin shrugged. "More than once I'd heard that she thoroughly enjoyed her workouts with her trainer."

"I'm quite sure I don't want to know why she was in training." Alex looked to Daniel. "Have you ever met her? The woman has domme written all over her."

"The newspaper said the wife was killed first." Daniel handed Katlin a burp cloth. "You keep bouncing Bella around like that she's gonna throw up on you. Peas, the second time around, aren't pretty."

"Do you want to stay for supper?" Alex asked as he kneeled next to Simon and helped him unload trucks.

"Thanks, but no." Daniel glanced at his son. "The kids have already eaten. They'll probably fall asleep in their car seats on the way back home. Their bedtime is seven-thirty and you guys are still eating appetizers then. Sometimes I miss late-night dinners." Daniel's lips pulled tight. "When

Nita is home, we'll feed the kids and get them in bed so we can have our own quiet supper. But she's still off training." He made air quotes around the last word. "Have you heard from your team? I haven't heard a word from Nita."

"If it's any consolation, I believe they truly are training. I've been told they're working with Team Two. I did get a text from everyone a few days ago wishing me a fast recovery." Katlin put her niece down on the floor. The baby immediately pulled herself to a standing position and she toddled straight toward her older brother.

"I've got her," Alex said as he intersected the wobbling child. Scooping her up, he held her high above his head. "And where do you think you were going?"

He loved Katlin's niece and nephew. Bella reminded him so much of Jenny at that age, so curious. He hoped that perhaps as soon as Katlin was given permission to travel, they could make Miami their first stop so they could visit his daughter.

Isabella soon slowed and crawled into her father's lap. Simon was secretly rubbing his eyes as well.

"I need to get these creatures home." Daniel stood and wrapped his arms around Katlin. "It's good to see you up and about." He squeezed her tighter. "I couldn't stand seeing you in the hospital bed hooked up to all those machines. When we rescued you, Top and I agreed that I shouldn't come over to the safe house and visit you in case Jack had agents following me. I had a tail coming home from work almost every night. I couldn't tell which agency had somebody on me."

"Take it slow, give yourself time to heal." He kissed her on the temple then stepped back, deftly grabbing his daughter as she toddled past with a last-minute burst of energy.

Alex got down on the floor and made a game out of collecting all of Simon's trucks, farm animals, and puzzle pieces. Hope filled his heart as he thought about doing the same thing with his own son. Someday, by the grace of God.

Katlin had to get better, first. He wanted to be married before she got pregnant, so they needed to plan a wedding. Then, they'd want some time to themselves as husband and wife before throwing pregnancy into the mix. Could she even get pregnant? Carry a child to term? He hoped so, but if not, they could adopt.

"Bye, Aunt Katlin." Simon held his arms in the air so she picked the boy up. "More medicine kisses before I go?"

"You bet." They puckered lips and kissed several times. "I'll carry him down for you." She slid the small child to her hip and headed for the door.

"That means I get you." Alex held the tired toddler in his arms. Schlepping the diaper bag and rollie, Daniel held open the door and pressed the button for the elevator.

"Thank you for bringing them by." Katlin held her brother's gaze.

"Anytime." He grinned. "And I mean it, anytime. You're welcome to tire them out for me."

As they all headed to Daniel's SUV, he stopped in his tracks. Smiling, he extracted a long chain with the ring dangling at the end. "I thought you might want this back, sis. Nita grabbed it before you were taken by ambulance to Walter Reed Medical Center. She was afraid it might disappear there."

Alex had never been so relieved to see such a small piece of jewelry. Kat always wore her engagement ring on a titanium necklace while on a mission. Alex inquired of its whereabouts at the hospital but no one seemed to have seen it. For a while, he wondered if Jack had stolen it, knowing how much it meant to Katlin and Alex.

"Thank you." Katlin threw her arms around her brother. "I

thought it was gone forever." Apology was in her eyes when she looked at Alex.

He'd been afraid she'd forgotten they were engaged.

She took it off the chain and slid it onto her ring finger. "There, back where it belongs. I'm going to text Nita and thank her for saving my ring."

Yes. Katlin's engagement ring was exactly where it was supposed to be.

Once they had the children situated in the car, Alex gave Daniel a back-thumping bro-hug. He liked his future brother-in-law. Daniel was a good man.

Katlin hugged Daniel tightly. "In case I didn't say it before, thank you for your part in my rescue."

When they parted, Daniel said through clenched teeth, "What you really need to thank me for is not killing Jack Ashworth, yet."

"I get that privilege," Alex announced as he threw his arm around Katlin.

She giggled. "Oh, no. He's mine."

CHAPTER 20

"So, how is our patient doing this morning?" Dr. Tobias asked Alex and Katlin when he came into the exam room.

"I think she's doing quite well, especially since it's only been two weeks since she was brought out of the medically-induced coma." Alex reached over and grabbed Katlin's hand, weaving his fingers between hers. He wanted her to know just how proud he was of her progress.

"Any more fainting? Dizziness?" The doctor began his examination, starting with shining the light in her eyes.

"None." She smiled. "Top Cooper has me on a strict workout regimen. I'm now up to one-hundred thirty beats per minute sustained for twenty minutes. No side effects whatsoever."

"Good. Prove it." The doctor challenged.

Shock, then questions, crossed Katlin's pretty face. "How?"

"Follow me," the doctor instructed. "I'm going to hook you up and put you on a treadmill."

Forty-five minutes later, Katlin stepped off the belt and a

nurse handed her a small towel. Dr. Tobias continued reading strips spit out by one of many machines while the nurse unhooked the two-dozen wires.

Finally, the doctor looked up. "Let's talk about this back in the examination room."

Alex once again took the chair in the corner as Katlin sat on the raised bed. She shifted nervously, making the white paper crinkle, but they said nothing to each other. He wanted to pull her into his lap and tell her everything was fine. He was impressed with how well she was doing. Top wouldn't let her push herself too much, but he also knew how to develop muscle groups with different exercises each day.

"I'm sorry. That took a few minutes longer than I had expected." Dr. Tobias flew into the room with paper strips flowing from his hands. "I wanted to talk with a colleague of mine. He's my counterpart in the Navy, another neurologist. I specialize in traumatic brain injury, so I primarily deal with cranial nerves, reflexes, coordination, and cognitive function. You might think of me as step one." He reached out and patted Katlin's hand then gave her one of those smiles that looked more like a sneer. "You have recovered so much faster than I expected. I attribute that to the immediate care you got on-site."

He glanced at Alex. "What did you say the medic's name was?"

"Dr. Nita Callahan." Katlin offered before Alex could utter a word.

"Yes, her. She did a wonderful job of stabilizing you immediately. I believe that made all the difference in the world as to the speed of your recovery." Dr. Tobias looked genuinely pleased. "I'm rewriting the procedures as to how we treat brain injuries in the field. We could improve the quality of life of so many soldiers with just a few minor procedural adjustments and modifications in the equipment they carry."

"Nita will be very happy to hear that." Katlin smiled impatiently. "So, what did you learn from my twenty-minute workout?"

"Captain Abrams agrees with me, your results are at the six-month benchmark for a mild TBI. For a moderate TBI, you're at about a two-year benchmark. Muscle strength is the only thing that is keeping us from declaring you at that point. Less than ten percent of severe TBI patients ever make it to where you are right now, even after years of therapy. The good news is that you'll continue to improve."

"That's wonderful." Alex went to stand by Katlin. He reached for her hand and she automatically slid her palm next to his. "So, what does this mean? Is she ready for duty?"

The doctor scoffed and shook his head. "No, not yet." He turned his attention to Kat. "We have to make sure your strength and coordination returns. I'm very pleased we haven't seen any seizures, but we need to be on the lookout for them as I slowly wean you off the blood thinners. As you continue to improve, we have to be alert and aware of any changes in the nerves. If you lose feeling in any extremity, even a slight tingling in your toes or fingers, call me immediately and head to the hospital."

The doctor shifted his gaze to Alex. "She might not realize any difference, but if her gait changes, the way she holds her body, how she runs, I want to see her immediately."

Alex thought everything sounded wonderful. He'd be sure to watch her more carefully and share this information with Top.

"I'm releasing you to increase your physical workouts. You may now maximize your heart rate at one-hundred eighty beats per minute." His gaze bounced between the two of them then down to where their hands were joined. "You may also resume sexual relations. Keep in mind that one-hundred eighty beats per minute rule."

He wrote a few numbers down on the strips of paper then transferred them into her electronic chart. "I'm going to have my assistant send you a list of suggested video games. I'd like to see you playing first-person shooter games, especially those in 3D. I'd like to see you back on the range, too, but I want you to wear double hearing protection. By that, I mean the kind that fits into your ear as well as the kind that covers the entire exterior ear."

Stepping back, the doctor made a few more notations in her computerized records. "I don't need to see you for two weeks."

"Can she fly?" Alex asked.

Dr. Tobias lifted his eyes to Alex as though saying he was crazy. "I still don't want her driving so I certainly can't condone her piloting a plane."

Alex chuckled. "No, sir. I need to visit some of our other locations, and I was hoping Katlin could go with me."

"Cabins are pressurized at ten thousand feet. You shouldn't have a problem with that, but call me immediately after you land the first time." The doctor continued to write. "I want to be sure that Lieutenant Commander Callahan doesn't experience a headache during or after landing. Do you have an office in Denver?"

"Yes, we do." Alex and Kat exchanged a glance.

"I think I'd rather she not go there right now. The elevation is too high and often stresses a normal body. Let's give Katlin a bit more time." Standing, the doctor gathered the test results and her file. "I'll see you in two weeks, then. I may call in Dr. Abrams and have him conduct his testing. Who knows? He might release you to drive a car."

As soon as the door closed behind Dr. Tobias, Alex cupped Kat's face in both his hands and kissed her the way he had wanted to for weeks. "What do you say we go home and spend the next few hours in bed?" He laid his lips on hers again. "I promise to keep your heart under one-hundred and eighty beats per minute." He grinned. "But I'll have you riding that edge until you beg me to make love to you."

Katlin pushed him back and jumped off the exam table. "Hey, Wolf, you big stud, take me to bed or lose me forever." Quoting the line from the famous movie they'd watched a few days ago reassured him that her mid-term memory was there.

"I know the way home." Alex didn't give the response line as it was said in the film, but his intent was there. He could finally touch her, sink inside her hot wet heat, show her how much he loved her with his body.

When they reached the apartment, Alex couldn't hold in the silence any longer. Katlin hadn't said a word the entire way home. He used his fob to unlock the door, following her in.

Grabbing her hand before she could leave the foyer, he pulled her back to him. Her hand in his, she stood nearly a foot away. "Look, Kat, just because you're allowed to have sex, doesn't mean we have to."

She stared at the floor, not meeting his eyes. After a deep reinforcing breath, she raised her head to look at him. "Are you telling me you don't want to make love with me?" Her voice cracked.

Alex pulled her to him and wrapped his arms around her. "Christ, no. Kat, there's nothing I want more than to strip you out of those clothes and sink into you." He lifted her chin until their eyes met. "I just want to be sure it's what you want. I don't want to rush you."

"Why are you treating me like a teenage virgin?" Anger flashed in her eyes and then it was quickly gone. "I'm not fragile, and never have been. You heard Dr. Tobias, I'm years ahead of expectation." She dropped his hand. "Have I changed that much you don't want me anymore?"

Fuck. He'd been warned that she could get very paranoid. It was actually part of the healing process.

"No, babe." He stepped to her, wrapping his arms around her again. "You really haven't changed at all." It was a lie. She had changed, in small ways. She wasn't as confident as she'd been before.

Katlin Callahan had been decisive. She would quickly assess the situation and make a decision. Alex had watched her start toward the stair stepper, then turn to the free weights and work on her biceps. Top had cleverly redirected her more than once while overseeing her workouts, noticing the same problem.

He brushed her soft blond hair away from her alabaster face. She'd lost any tan she had before the explosion since she almost never went outside. "You're still the most beautiful woman I've ever known, inside and out. You're the only woman I want in my life." He slowly lowered his head, giving her plenty of time to turn away.

When she tilted her face to meet his, he considered it a major hurdle overcome. Their kiss was tender, sharing, and slow. She wasn't tentative, but she wasn't aggressive by any means. Before, when Kat wanted him, she didn't hold back.

Alex decided he needed to take it slow. He kissed his way down her jaw and traced her racing heartbeat with his tongue. At least he was turning her on.

He unbuttoned the shirt she wore over a tank top, kissing every inch of skin as it was exposed. Curling his fingertips under the stretchy top, he pulled it over her head, taking the blouse with it.

"You're perfect, and that hasn't changed one bit." Alex traced the lace edge of her bra with his tongue while he reached behind and unhooked it. She pulled it off and tossed it on the floor with her other clothes.

He held up one breast, taking the dusky pink nipple into his mouth. With the other hand, he ran his finger on the underside of her breast before he took her nipple between his thumb and forefinger and rolled the hardened bud. He nipped the tip before moving to the other side, paying it equal attention.

"You're wearing way too many clothes," Kat informed him as she tugged on his polo shirt, pulling it from his khakis. Reaching his hand behind his neck, he yanked it off in one quick motion.

Her hands instantly went to his chest, running her fingers through the smattering of hair. She circled his flat nipples before she pinched them. Alex loved it when she touched him that way. This seemed normal. This seemed like them.

While she was entertaining herself with his chest, he unbuckled and unzipped her pants. Kneeling as he pulled them down her long shapely legs, he held her pants around her ankles as he leaned in, inhaling. Her unique scent went straight to his cock. It was as though it knew where it belonged and stiffened, straining at his zipper.

He rubbed his thumb over her panties directly across her clit. The already moist lace suddenly became soaked.

Thank Christ she still wanted him.

He pulled down her panties. "Step out," he instructed.

She obeyed wordlessly and he tossed the last of her clothes to the side but didn't stand. Instead, he spread her folds. She automatically widened her stance. When he sucked her clit into his mouth, her fingers dug into the back of his head.

Yes. That was his Kat. She would hold him there until she couldn't stand it any longer before pulling his face away and up to hers. That afternoon was no different. Within a few minutes, her legs were shaking.

"Take me to bed," she insisted.

Alex stood, scooping her up in his arms and carrying her to their bed. He quickly dropped his cargo pants and boxer briefs before joining her on the silky sheets. He continued to kiss every inch of her body until she had enough.

She gently shoved him onto his back and straddled him, lowering herself onto his erection. This had become their favorite position. His hands were free to play with her luscious breasts, rolling her nipples between his thumbs and forefingers, exciting her even more. When she was close, he'd often pinched the nipples, or he'd sit up and suck them deep into his mouth. Kat had the most sensitive breasts he'd ever known.

As she rode him hard, he covertly looked at her heart rate on her watch. She was reaching her max. He had to take her over the edge. He moved his hand between them and stroked her clit with his thumb as he thrust up into her. Her inner walls quivered, grabbing and releasing his shaft. Alex couldn't hold on any longer. He'd been too long without her.

Pressing down on her clit, Katlin exploded, and Alex followed her into oblivion. More out of muscle memory than actual thought, he rolled them to the side as they fell asleep, connected in the most intimate way possible.

The next morning, they boarded the executive jet service for Miami, Damnit at Kat's side. Jenny joined them for a few days, staying at Kat's condo on the beach, and taking in a musical matinee. Strangely, though, it was Alex and his daughter who stayed up late talking and playing board games because Katlin fell asleep most nights shortly after nine. His daughter was turning into quite a delightful young lady.

They hit the Houston and Dallas offices next but their routine was the same.

Alex and Katlin would work out side-by-side in the gym for over an hour before showering together. Often too exhausted to do anything else after breakfast, Katlin would take her morning nap. She would join Alex for lunch then spend a few hours at the indoor range available to employees at every Guardian office. He would sometimes find Katlin playing cards with several of his men in the game room or challenging one of them on a videogame.

She would often catch an afternoon nap before they had supper with all the men. At least one night at each center, Alex and Katlin would take out the manager and assistant managers for a special supper. By the end of the evening, Kat was exhausted. Although she'd go to bed early, most often she'd awaken when he crawled in and they'd make love one more time that day.

At the end of the two weeks, they returned to the Guardian Security D.C. Center.

"Are you nervous about tomorrow?" Alex asked as Kat slid naked between the sheets.

"No, why? Should I be?" She sounded slightly worried.

"Not at all." He pulled the covers up around her and dropped a kiss on her lips. Although her body was getting stronger, Kat still wasn't making quick decisions. She would change her mind about doing something two or three times before she proceeded. Names still caused her difficulty and she was still missing so many memories. Alex was also concerned about the amount of sleep she seemed to need. The more sleep she got, the more nightmares she had. He wanted to be sure it was normal for a TBI patient.

Alex hoped he'd be able to discuss his concerns privately with Dr. Tobias, but he had the man's phone number in case he didn't have the opportunity at Katlin's appointment.

CHAPTER 21

KATLIN FELT A LITTLE QUEASY AS ALEX DROVE HER TO Walter Reed Hospital. Her usual toast and fruit washed down with two cups of coffee sloshed around in her stomach. It was nerves. Had to be. She hadn't made the progress in the past two weeks she should have. She was failing everyone. Alex. Top Cooper. Dr. Tobias. And herself. But all she wanted to do was curl up and go to sleep.

Maybe she'd done too much. Maybe she hadn't pushed herself enough. Either way, she'd failed.

The nightmares wore her out. Thankfully, Alex was there by her side each and every night. It didn't matter whether she had one horrible dream or three. He'd move in close, perfectly aligning his body with hers as he gently woke her. All too often, she was soaked in sweat so they would take a hot shower together before returning to their bed where he changed the damp sheets.

He wasn't bothered by her nightmares, but she was becoming afraid to fall asleep. The more she fought sleep, the more tired she became. Sometimes she was so exhausted that she'd fall into a deep sleep during an afternoon nap and wake up screaming, her heart beating so fast it made her head hurt. The worst part of those nightmares—or were they really "day" mares?—was that Alex wasn't around. She had to handle them by herself. She never told Alex about them.

She wouldn't allow herself to take up any more of his time nursing her back to health. She could take care of herself. She knew when she'd had enough and politely excused herself for a nap or bedtime. He had ten security centers to run, hundreds of employees, and thousands of clients. He'd already dedicated far too much time to her.

Her lack of sleep left her without enough energy to complete her morning workouts. She could see the worry in Alex's eyes that she was backsliding.

"I'll drop you off here and you can check in while I find a parking space." Alex pulled up to the physician offices wing.

"I hate to make you wait around while I see the doctor," Katlin said as she got out of the Guardian SUV. "You know this sometimes takes hours. I can call Guardian's operations center and have them send over a car when I'm done. That way you can go back to work."

He gave her that killer smile that said she was the most important thing in the world to him. "You trying to get rid of me? Not happening, babe. I'll be there in just a few minutes, probably before you're finished with the paperwork."

She wouldn't mind having him next to her when she received the bad news she was sure to get. Forcing a smile, she stepped back. "I'll see you inside."

Sure enough, it took more than thirty minutes before she was moved from the waiting area into an examination room.

"So, how were your travels?" Dr. Tobias began his examination as soon as he stepped into the room.

"Traveling was fine, but I seem to be tired all the time." She glanced at Alex then decided to push forward. "I'm having nightmares every night, sometimes two. Then I don't want to go to sleep because occasionally I fall right back into the bad dream picking up where it left off."

"Uh-ha." His grunt of acknowledgment was all he said as he continued testing her reflexes.

When he was finally finished, he sat down on the short round stool on rollers. "I expected this." He patted Katlin's hand. "Nightmares at this stage are very common. Sometimes they'll make sense, other times they will be bits and pieces of things that have happened in your past that are all jumbled together. On occasion, they'll be nonsensical, and your brain will spend several unconscious hours trying to unweave the elements. You wake up feeling more tired than you did when you went to bed."

That's exactly what was happening. Normal. Thank God.

Dr. Tobias looked at Alex. "I'll also bet that her workouts aren't anywhere near the level they were before you saw me last time."

Alex lit up. "Exactly."

The doctor redirected his questions to Katlin. "Have you been indecisive? Maybe even a little depressed with your progress?"

Katlin wanted to cry. "Yes," she croaked, trying to hold back the tears.

"This is a vicious, downward spiraling cycle we often see in TBI patients." The doctor held Katlin's gaze. "I don't want you to worry about this. It's perfectly normal. I'm sure you'll feel better once you start sleeping."

He turned to his computer, clicking, and typing. "I'm ordering you some mild sedatives. They may help with the nightmares." He paused for a long moment staring at his screen before he bounced his gaze between Katlin and Alex. "Are you two going back on the road?"

Alex glanced at her before answering. "I'd like to take her with me." His smile was loving and gentle. "I like having her at my side. We've established a daily routine."

And a nightly one.

When Alex's gaze met hers, they were both thinking the same thing.

Dr. Tobias spun around on his stool to face Katlin. "I don't know how you feel about psychiatrists, but with TBI's, they're automatically part of the healing process. I'm going to put in an order for you to speak with Dr. Eloise Bowden. I'd like you to meet with her in person before you fly off to the next city. After your initial session, I'm going to suggest you do videoconferencing with her every few days. And, before you ask, her clearance is higher than yours. Normally, she only sees special operators, and we all know that the U.S. military doesn't have any females in SpecOps."

When the man winked at her and then slid a glance to Alex as though he didn't know, Katlin thought she was going to burst out laughing.

"Thank you, sir. Actually, Dr. Bowden and I have known each other for years." Katlin gave a brief thought as to tell him exactly how many years, then mentally shrugged. "When I was kidnapped in a South American country at the age of four, Dr. Bowden was just starting in psychiatry as a new Lieutenant Junior Grade. They sent her down to work with my mom and me. I've seen her professionally from time to time over the years."

Katlin wasn't going to mention that the familiar psychiatrist tested every woman before she could graduate from JAFSOS. The doctor had also made a personal phone call to Kat when each of her parents passed away, as well as shortly after Ty had been buried.

"I look forward to talking with Captain Bowden." And she truly did.

"Very well, then." The doctor spun back to his computer. "I'd like to see you again in three weeks. Stop by the pharmacy and pick up your prescription."

On the way back to Guardian's office, Katlin texted Dr. Bowden. She was shocked when the older woman called minutes later.

"Katlin, I just read your file. I'm so sorry but I'm in San Diego debriefing a SEAL team. I'm fine with videoconferencing if you are." The psychiatrist sounded genuinely apologetic.

Katlin glanced over to Alex. "Do you mind going out to the Los Angeles office first? I might be able to get in and see Dr. Bowden there more quickly."

"That will actually work out well." Alex seemed a little hesitant, as though he had more to say but decided against it.

"I have wonderful news," Katlin told the woman who knew more about her than anyone else on the earth. "I'm headed to Los Angeles, but I can take the car down to San Diego. I'll let you know my schedule within the next few hours." She was actually excited to see the psychiatrist. Katlin had always found the older woman easy to talk with. After her mother had been suddenly killed in a car accident, Katlin would occasionally call Dr. Bowden for motherly advice.

"That sounds perfect. I'll see you in a few days. I've got to run, my next appointment is here." When the doctor hung up, Katlin already felt better.

"Are you sure you don't mind going to Los Angeles?" Katlin laid her hand on Alex's bicep that stretched the company polo shirt he wore.

"Not at all. I need to go back there. I was headed to the

L.A. Center when I heard you were hurt." His eyebrows drew together as though he was worried, or perhaps thinking hard. He reached out his hand and she slid hers down his arm and interwove their fingers. "I got a call a few weeks ago from Jae…the world knows her as JJ, the actress, but we grew up together so she's Jae to me. Our history goes back to kindergarten. She's a special friend. We dated a few times when I bought the Los Angeles office two years ago, before you came back into my life."

He slid her a glance, watching her as though she might go apeshit-girlfriend crazy.

"I know you weren't celibate after your divorce," she squeezed his hand. "But you'd better be monogamous now."

He picked up her hand and kissed the engagement ring he'd given her nearly a year ago. The large blue diamond, a family heirloom, with a clear diamond on each side, was perfect. She loved the ring as much as she loved Alex. "Kat, I don't want any other woman in my life except you."

"Good. And you'd better keep it that way." Katlin wondered why he was telling her about his childhood friend, Jae.

He squeezed her hand. "While you were on that last mission, she had a stalker, but we caught him just before I got the news that you were hospitalized."

"That's good, right? You caught him." Katlin felt like she was missing something.

"Yes. We did. But there were a lot of pictures, and speculation, about the two of us in the trade rags and celebrity blogs." They stopped at a red light and he turned to face her. "I swear to you, nothing happened between us."

"Good to know." There was more to this that Katlin just didn't seem to be able to read between the lines. "What aren't you telling me?"

"Jae asked me to help her train for the movie she's filming. She's supposed to be some kind of kick-ass-and-take-names detective. I've had her working with several of the men at the L.A. office, but I really should go help her for a few days while I'm there."

"That might work out well since I'll need to go to San Diego to meet with Dr. Bowden. I'm sure we can get one of the men to drive me there." She'd already held him back from so much of his work, she wasn't going to pull the fiancée card and insist that he go with her. Hell, had she been released to drive, she'd just take one of the cars and drive herself. But she wasn't quite there, yet.

"You're the best fiancée a man could ask for." He bounced their joined hands on his thigh.

"You'd just better remember that." Katlin didn't need to warn him. Alex was not like her first husband at all. She trusted Alex completely. Paranoia crept in every now and again, but then she remembered who he was…and wasn't.

"See how soon we can catch a flight to L.A.," Alex asked as he released her hand. "I'm thinking maybe five days there, then we'll go up to San Francisco. We can catch Denver then Chicago on our way back to D.C.." Alex frowned. "Fuck. I forgot to ask Dr. Tobias if you can now go to Denver."

"I'll send him an email and confirm one way or the other before we schedule that leg." Katlin quickly checked the executive jet service they used and scheduled their flights.

Three days later, Tim was behind the wheel of the Guardian SUV taking Katlin to the Naval Base in San Diego, a two-and-a-half-hour drive in good traffic. But it was Southern California. Traffic was always insane.

She turned to pet Damnit, who'd decided to take up the whole backseat, when she asked, "Were you assigned to helping train JJ?" She already knew the answer.

"Yes, ma'am."

"Do they always work such long hours?" Since arriving in L.A., she hadn't seen much of Alex. He left for the studio early in the morning and often didn't return until long after supper.

Tim chuckled. "They did the days I was assigned to her. The movie director is a real taskmaster. He wants JJ to perform all the fight scenes, so we ended up working with her for hours. Then they wanted to be sure they got the right camera angles. More than once, I felt like the stunt coordinator. The guy getting paid for that job sat on his ass, talking on his phone, while I re-scripted the movements to more realistic ones."

That made Katlin feel a little better. She probably wouldn't see Alex at all that night. When arranging the appointment with Dr. Bowden, the psychiatrist thought she might want a sleep study, so Katlin was scheduled late in the afternoon. Just in case, they'd made reservations for Tim at a nearby hotel.

"Thanks again for being willing to take care of Damnit if they do the sleep study." She loved having the dog by her side. Lately, he'd been as diligent about her workout routine as Top Cooper. If she pushed it too hard, the dog would push her. More than once, he shoved his nose at her when her heart rate was too high. Even the damn dog wanted to take care of her. She was surrounded by protective Y chromosomes.

"No problem, ma'am." He reached back and petted the oversized puppy. "I love dogs. I miss mine."

"Oh, no. Did he take that trip over the rainbow?" Losing a dog was so heartbreaking. It was like losing a family member.

"No, ma'am. I couldn't take him when I left the military."

He gave her a big smile. "When they decide to retire him, I'm on the list. Maybe I'll see him again, someday."

Katlin stroked Damnit's smooth coat. "I hope you do." She loved her dog. She was surprised and thankful that Dr. Bowden allowed her to bring Damnit to the session.

They greeted each other with warm professionalism. Katlin knew the routine. She also knew how useless it was to lie. She wanted to get better. She wanted to return to her team. Although no one had said so, most likely Dr. Bowden would be the one to give the final okay, allowing her to return to full duty.

At the end of an hour-and-a-half of intense questions, Katlin was drained. "Well, am I insane?" It was an old joke started by a sassy four-year-old.

Dr. Bowden smiled and gave her routine answer. "Nope. Not yet." She sat back in her chair and glanced at the notes she'd taken on her computer. "Okay. First, we don't need the sleep study."

Yay. They could go home, and she could sleep in the Guardian apartment with Alex. She hoped Tim wouldn't mind if she slept most of the way back, but she was exhausted.

"Second, you're not experiencing typical nightmares. Your subconscious is trying to remember the explosion. They are two very different occurrences." She went on to explain, "Most nightmares consist of bits and pieces of memories, but they are rarely the same. They are like a jigsaw puzzle and your mind tries to rearrange the pieces each time. The theme may be similar, and the result is always that the person wakes up before the fear reaches a certain level."

The doctor leaned forward in her chair. "Your dreams are exactly the same, beginning to end, element to element. Each dream adds just a little more to it."

She typed into her computer and put a workbook away that had been lying on her desk the entire meeting. "I was all set to start you on Imagery Rehearsal Therapy."

"What's that?" It sounded interesting to Katlin.

"It's a method by which you reimagine your nightmares with a different, less frightening outcome. Basically, you reprogram your nightmare. We've had great success using it with PTSD patients. But you are actually re-experiencing your trauma."

"Okay, so what do I do about it?"

Dr. Bowden smiled. "You remember."

"Yeah, right. If I could remember what happened, I wouldn't have the nightmares."

"You're absolutely right." She took out a small book that looked almost like the old-fashioned logs the military used. The small green book was filled with lined pages and had an attached pen.

For the next ten minutes, Dr. Bowden explained how to awaken and remember the dream. "It takes practice. And don't worry if you can only remember a snippet the first few times. It'll come. And as it does, I want you to write down everything you remember in the book. I could go into the whole psychological reason why you write it down, but you don't care."

Katlin giggled. "You're right about that. Just knowing that these are memories trying to fight their way through makes me feel better already."

"These memories are real, and what your nightmare is telling me is that you felt a great deal of anxiety while trapped in the vehicle." The doctor's tone softened. "You carry a great deal of emotional responsibility for your team. The inability to act is what I see as the key component of your fear. You feel the need to be in control of every element of a situation, but when the SUV was on its side and you couldn't get out on your own power, it was the most frightening thing your mind could concoct. Your mind shut down."

Dr. Bowden let out a short breath. "The fact that your brain was physically swelling was another factor. The mind doesn't like pain. In your case, internal and external forces made it shut down. Thankfully, your mind is smart enough to know that certain parts of the brain need to keep functioning. You are very fortunate that they didn't have to put you on a ventilator. I can tell from your records that your subconscious was very active during your coma. From a physical standpoint, that's excellent."

The doctor smiled. "Now, we just have to get your mind to open those doors so we can deal with the locked-up emotions and memories."

The doctor handed her a bottle of peppermint essential oil. "It may seem weird, but it works. I want you to put a drop of this oil on a washcloth that you keep under your pillow." She giggled. "Yes, you might have to move your weapon. Many of my SEALs slide theirs between the mattress and box springs."

Pointing to the small bottle in Katlin's hand, Dr. Bowden continued, "As you're fighting your way out of the nightmare, I want you to grab the washcloth and bring it to your face. When you inhale, the mint will ground you. Part of your brain will realize that the peppermint is real, and the dream is not. You wake up much quicker. Give it a try."

When the doctor stood, so did Katlin. Damnit rose, too.

"I like that you have a service dog." Dr. Bowden said on the way to the door.

"Oh, Damnit isn't a service dog. He's a rescue mutt." She petted the furry creature and scratched his ears.

"Didn't you tell me that Tanner Hill trained him?" The doctor opened the door.

"Yes. To all the basic commands." Katlin turned and made a fist. "Sit." Damnit's butt hit the floor. They went through a few others showing off. "See? Just a mutt."

Dr. Bowden gave her a knowing smile. "He's good for you. I want you to conference me in five days after you practice the techniques we discussed."

"Thank you, Dr. Bowden." Katlin turned her attention to Tim who was waiting beside the car. "Guess what, we're going to sleep in our own beds tonight. Let's go home."

CHAPTER 22

"AND, CUT." THE DIRECTOR STOOD AND CLAPPED HIS HANDS. "That's a wrap. I'll see everybody in three days in Vancouver where we'll shoot the outdoor scenes of *Finding Justice*." The extremely thin man dashed to Alex. "Mr. Wolf, I'd like to thank you and your men for working with our talented JJ making her scenes completely realistic." He threw an arm around his female star and stared down at her. "Those scenes alone are going to get you an Oscar nomination."

"Don't tease me like that," JJ chided. "I wasn't that good."

Alex's friend was still acting. Currently, she was acting humble. Last night, as he'd taken her home, she'd been bouncing in her seat, squealing at how well she'd performed the big fight scenes that day. They were child's play compared to the real hand-to-hand combat he'd seen from Katlin and her team as they'd taken on terrorists with their bare hands.

He truly hated most things about Hollywood, starting with the fact that nobody was real, and anything could be faked. As he turned to leave for the last time, he watched JJ's bodyguard wander off the set. Concerned, he turned to his friend. "Do you need a ride home? I see your bodyguard is gone."

Jae threw her arms around Alex's neck. "We're done with this segment and we get two days off. Come on, we're all going out to celebrate."

Alex didn't think it was a good idea for Jae to go out drinking without a bodyguard. She received dozens of threats a day. He pointed to the man's retreating back. "Are they sending a replacement for you for tonight?"

She playfully slapped him on the bicep. "No. I'm free of my watchdog, too. At least until I get to Vancouver." She hooked her hand into his elbow. "Come on. You deserve a drink as much as the rest of us."

"Come with us, Alex." Noah, the male lead slapped his shoulder. "You're part of this crew, so you need to come out and party with us."

Alex didn't have to get back to Guardian early since Katlin was staying in San Diego. He could go and have a drink with the men and women he'd gotten to know quite well over the past few days. "All right, just one though."

"And one dance with me." Jae moved in front of him and slithered her body against his. "I know you're a good dancer." She threw a sassy glance at Bexx, the supporting actress. "That's not all he's good at."

"I'll just bet," the other woman said in a husky voice. "Alex, promise me at least one dance, too?"

"And what am I? Dog food?" Noah moved in behind Bexx as they danced to the beat in their heads.

Thirty minutes later, they were in the VIP section of a trendy Los Angeles nightclub. When the waitress came by, Alex asked for his standard beer while everyone else ordered exotic concoctions. The one-upmanship never seemed to end with these people. Jae was just as bad as the rest when she was around them. When they were alone, she was Jael Martinez. He much preferred that woman.

"Come dance with me, Alex." Jae stood and grabbed his hand just as the drinks arrived. "Somebody stay here and watch our drinks."

Noah sat back in the club chair with his classic Blood and Sand. "I'm too comfortable to move right now. Go have fun."

Alex took a swig of his beer before setting it down on the coffee table. A number of the crew slid onto the two couches while others filled the chairs, excited to get the night started.

Jae loved to dance but wasn't comfortable with other men trying to wiggle their way in, so most of the time, she had a hand on Alex. He was good at emitting a keep away vibe, but since they'd arrived at the club close to midnight, many of the men who tried to barge in were too inebriated to get the message. Alex certainly didn't want to hurt anybody, but he wasn't going to let someone maul his friend.

"Let's go sit down for a while," Alex finally suggested after elbowing the last asshole who tried to dance with Jae by stepping in front of him. When they sat back down, she got sucked into a conversation with the people next to her. Alex decided this was a great time to check his messages as he finished his beer. Given the number of empty glasses that littered the table, he was quite sure everyone was making up for lost time. There had to be two-dozen empty shot glasses.

He'd just started scrolling through his voicemails when JJ playfully plucked the phone from his hands. "All work and no play makes Alex…no fun at all." She slid his phone into her bra then raised one eyebrow in challenge.

Alex was not going to go there. No way in hell.

"JJ, may I have my phone back?" He tried to sound stern, but the pounding music was so loud he had to yell.

"Dance with me one more time, and I'll give it back." She teased.

He could dance with her.

"But, Alex, it's my turn." Bexx stood and grabbed his hand, pulling him off the couch.

"I expect to get my phone back as soon as we're done," he warned Jae as he finished the new beer someone had ordered for him.

JJ crossed her long shapely legs as she flagged down a waitress and signaled for another round. Two was Alex's limit. He didn't like the out-of-control feeling he got when drunk.

Bexx was a nice person, probably the reason she'd never make it any further in Hollywood. Her dancing was sexy, but not sultry like JJ. He and the supporting actress moved like the acquaintances they were, but he became protective of her as well when a couple of drunk college boys tried to grab her, insisting she dance with them. As a trained bodyguard, Alex made quick work of the young men in their early twenties. Idiots.

When they returned to the exclusive area, Noah pointed to his fresh beer. "Yours was getting a little stale so we bought you another one."

He was quite thirsty by then and downed half of it.

JJ grinned at him. "Finish your beer and then I demand another dance." She stood and ran her fingers up and down his chest. "And if you're good, and I mean *very* good, then I'll give you back your phone."

She pressed her breasts up against him. He looked at his phone tightly nestled between her large natural breasts. She looked up at him with those big Bambi eyes that popped on camera, making her a favorite for close-ups.

"Go ahead, take it from me," she taunted.

He stepped back and drained his glass of draft beer. "I'll dance with you one more time, but I really do need to get home. Unlike you, I can't sleep in tomorrow morning. And I really should check my messages."

"After we dance." When they walked down to the dance floor, JJ wove, wobbling on her extremely high stilettos. She giggled. "I'm glad you're here to hold me up."

"How many drinks did you have while I was dancing with Bexx?" He swung her out then pulled her back to his body.

"A few." She danced away from him.

"How few?" He insisted.

"I was doing shots with Noah." She plastered herself to him, kissing her way up his neck. "You could come and stay with me tonight. Then you wouldn't have to get up so early in the morning." She snickered. "And you could make me come…and I'd make you come…" She giggled again. "But you'd have to come to my place."

Her movements weren't very coordinated, and she was slurring her speech. Alex was afraid she was drunk.

"How about I take you home now so you can go to bed? I think you've had plenty to drink." His suggestion was met with a dramatic frown. Then suddenly she smiled.

"Are you going to tuck me in?" JJ ran her arms around his neck and wove her fingers into his long hair as she kissed and nipped at his neck. When he lowered his face to talk to her, she went on tiptoes and kissed him.

Alex instantly pulled back, but he lost his footing for a second. "JJ, I drunk you think too much." The words didn't come out quite right.

She giggled up at him. "I think you're drunk, too."

What the fuck? Had somebody drugged his beer?

"Let's get you out of here." Alex took her hand and they started back toward the VIP area so she could pick up her purse. When they reached the exclusive area, the entire cast and crew were rolling around, laughing.

"One more time." When Noah lifted the shot glass, everyone in the area followed suit. "To an Oscar nomination. *Finding Justice* for Best Picture award." The drinks were downed, then someone poured a shot into his beer and JJ's Sex on the Beach drink.

Swaying, she picked up her glass and swallowed most of it.

Bexx handed him his beer. "Drink it down so then you'll be caught up to us, again."

"You put shots in my beer?" he accused.

Everyone in the area cracked up laughing.

"Of course, we did," JJ announced in a loud voice. "We're all doing shots and we know you wouldn't want to miss out."

Fuck. It'd been years since Alex had been drunk. Now, he really needed his phone. There was no way he was going to drive back to Guardian. He'd just call the operations center and have them send a limousine to take home all the drunks from her movie. He'd have one of his men drive him to JJ's place and he'd see to it that she got in safely. After that, she could be on her own. Then Alex could go up to his apartment and collapse. Thank God Katlin wasn't around.

"I need my phone." Alex almost stumbled on his way over to the couch. He plopped down beside JJ and rolled to face her. "If you don't give me my phone right now, I'm going to start telling people your real name."

"No!" She screamed at the top of her lungs. "Please, Alex, don't do that."

Alex went flying backward through the air and landed on his feet thanks to the strong hands that held him up. "We don't allow anyone to harass our guests, especially the ladies. I think you've had enough to drink. It's time for you to go home." A second bouncer showed up and grabbed Alex's other bicep.

"No." JJ held out her hands in front of the two men who were bigger than Alex. "It's all a misunderstanding." When she pulled his phone from between her breasts, they almost popped out of the dress. "I had his phone and I didn't want to give it back to him because he was going to call for the limousine and make us all go home."

Everybody from the movie started speaking at once.

It took nearly fifteen minutes, the manager, the waitress, and a call to Guardian's operations center, to sort out the situation. As the bouncer helped Alex load the last of the crew into a Guardian limousine, the big man guided JJ to the waiting SUV. Once she was securely inside, the bouncer turned to Alex.

"Your friends are assholes. Dumping vodka shots into your beer is uncool." He shook his head.

"They're not my friends. Nor are they clients." Alex shook the man's hand. "I appreciate you taking the time to get to the truth."

"Fucking actresses," the bouncer said on his way back inside. "You'd better get your girlfriend home before she passes out or pukes in your ride."

"She's not my girlfriend, either. My fiancée is down in San Diego tonight." He felt the need to explain, "JJ is an old friend. Just a friend."

The bouncer looked back over his shoulder. "You are so fucked. Everybody in the house tonight was taking pictures of the two of you. I hope your fiancée is the understanding kind."

At that moment, Alex hoped so, too.

It was almost 3 o'clock in the morning when he trudged into his penthouse apartment.

"Help me," Kat screamed from the bedroom.

Alex had his weapon in his hand as he crept toward the bedroom door.

"Don't let them take me," she pleaded.

Recognizing the words from almost every nightmare Kat had, Alex holstered his weapon. Feeling like an absolute shit for not being there sooner to help her wake up, he crawled into bed beside her, boots and all.

"I've got you, babe." He held her tight to him.

Kissing her damp forehead, he told her over and over, "You're safe. It's me, Alex."

Kat's eyes popped open. She crawled over him as though she was trying to get out of the bed. He held on tight to her.

"Babe, it's me, Alex. You're safe, now."

She twisted and turned, eventually squirming from his grasp. When she reached the nightstand, she grabbed a book and pen.

"What you doing?" He watched as she frantically scribbled words and phrases.

"I have to write this down."

Once she finished, Alex pulled her back down onto the bed. "Are you all right?"

Katlin smiled. "Yes." She tapped the book. "Dr. Bowden explained that what I have are not nightmares but my brain trying to remember. She'll be so pleased that I was able to recall part of the dream."

Alex could accept that. "Okay," he said nonchalantly. "I need to take a shower."

Katlin sniffed him playfully. Then her eyes went wide. "It wasn't the peppermint that made me wake up. It was the smell of you. You ground me." She sniffed him again and her eyebrows slammed together.

He dropped his head and inhaled deeply through his nose. He smelled sweaty. "I know, I need that shower." He stood and gave himself a second for his head to stop spinning.

"You smell like a woman's perfume," Kat said through clenched teeth.

Alex almost fell over on his next step.

"They were done shooting here in L.A., so everyone went out for drinks and dancing." He sat back down next to her. "While I was out dancing, the fuckers poured shots of vodka into my beer."

"So, you're drunk. That explains the smell of alcohol." She ran her finger over his neck then held it in front of his face. "I can't wait to hear how you're going to explain this lipstick."

Fuck. JJ had been all over him most of the night. He practically had to fight her off when he'd taken her unconscious body into her condo and put her to bed.

"Is that why you're in such a hurry to take a shower? Maybe hoping to wash the lipstick and perfume off before I discovered it?" Kat stood, completely naked as usual. "I'm going to take a shower. You know these nightmares wring me out."

"I'm right behind you." He started to follow her.

Katlin whipped around and punched her fists on her bare hips. "No, you won't be taking a shower with me. I'm still waiting for the explanation."

"I'm sorry, Kat." He was so drunk he'd forgotten she even asked the question. "JJ passed out in the car so when we got to her place, I had to take her inside and put her into her bed. She was kissing me, trying to get me to stay."

He slowly approached her, using every ounce of his

ability to stay upright. He cupped her face in his hands. "You have to know I would never have stayed." He laid his lips on hers, giving her a gentle kiss. "I'm sorry I wasn't here when the nightmare first started." He kissed her again. "You are everything to me."

As he kissed her that time, she responded but cut the kiss short. "You smell like her perfume. Go shower. I don't even want to kiss you because all I smell is her."

"Babe, I'm sorry." He started stripping out of his clothes on the way to the bathroom. At the door to the shower, he looked back at Kat. "Are you going to join me?"

"I haven't decided, yet, but definitely not until you've removed every remnant of her from your skin."

Alex scrubbed from the top of his head to his toes, rinsed, and scrubbed again. The hot water felt wonderful, but he knew if she caught even a whiff of Jae's perfume, he might never get laid again.

When the door opened and Kat stepped in, his world had righted itself.

"You can change the sheets while I shower." She reached for her shower poof and squirted her body wash on it, her back to him.

Alex took it from her hand and worked it into suds. He started with her shoulders then worked his way down her left arm. Stepping in close behind her, he raised her fingers. "When I gave you this ring, it was more than a promise to marry you. It was a promise that you would be the only woman in my heart and my bed. I've never broken that promise, and I never will. I did nothing wrong tonight. I put a passed-out drunk friend in her bed."

She turned in his arms and kissed him. Taking the poof from his hand, she asked, "Will you please change the sheets on our bed while I finish my shower?"

"Are you going to take advantage of my condition?" He said with a grin.

She shook her head. "I can't take advantage of a drunk man any more than you could take advantage of that drunk woman." She kissed him and pushed him toward the shower door. On his way out, she smacked his ass. "Besides, I know how much you like morning sex."

Oh, yes. He loved morning sex.

CHAPTER 23

SURROUNDED BY FOUR THOUSAND PEOPLE, JACK SAT ALONE IN the front row of the National Cathedral, sorrowful music saturating the air. The seat beside him was vacant, the aisle on his right. To his left was the vice president of the United States and his wife. The President's Secret Service thought it was too risky for him to attend, but he and his wife had sent their condolences.

It was only right that POTUS be concerned because the man was up for reelection and Jack's parents had seen to it that he'd been elected the first time. John Edward Ashworth had been a gray eminence in world politics for four decades. No one got nominated for the highest offices in government without the seal of approval of the Ashworth family. That stamp included the wife passing Suzanne Koch Ashworth's etiquette and grace standard.

The priest and his entourage moved onto the dais.

Most likely, everyone who filled the sanctuary owed his parents in one way or another. Many had approached him privately over the past five days, since the murder of his parents. So many people wanted to know if he was going to assume the void they'd left.

Fuck. No.

But that was Jack's secret.

He hated politics. He detested the way his parents had used people, often against each other, playing a real-life game of chess. They had wielded their old wealth, old power, and old attitudes as though they were Emperor and Empress of the world. As the only son of an only son, Jack would end the Ashworth reign.

He was a man of action. That's what he loved about his job. He gave the word and people died leaving the world a better place.

For nearly fifty years, his parents had used their money and influence to nudge the world in a particular direction. Jack could change the world with a well-placed bullet, his influence immediate.

"All rise." The priest lifted his arms as everyone stood and turned toward the back of the Cathedral.

His mother's white pearlized casket preceded his father's made from dalbergia. Each represented them so well, and should, because they had selected their caskets and had them custom-made years ago when his mother had a breast cancer scare.

The lump she was sure was cancerous turned out to be nothing more than a swollen lymph node caused by a cold. His hypochondriac mother had taken to her bed for weeks, sure she was dying. During her time sequestered in her rooms on the east side of their mansion, she insisted that her husband also prepare for death.

As he watched the two caskets move down the long aisle, he was thankful for their preparation. He had been left with very few decisions. His mother had even prepared the agenda for her funeral. Jack had just included his father with her mandates since his father hadn't bothered with such trivialities.

His mother would have been disappointed in him, though, because he'd refused to have an open-casket viewing. She wanted her silver hair to glisten—using a specified high-gloss hairspray—on the light blue satin casket lining. Although the gunshot wounds went straight through their hearts, the autopsies weren't nearly as kind to their bodies.

Jack had insisted on closed caskets.

Over the next hour, he was subjected to endless accolades, which included a personal letter written by the President, read by the Vice President. Several Middle Eastern princes spoke about his parents' generosity to their countries and his mother's art donations. What they didn't mention was the billions of barrels of oil his mother's family bought and refined before selling it to the Africans in Third World countries who couldn't afford the price.

After the fourth eulogy, Jack blocked out the blubbering behind the pulpit. He was furious that he'd missed Katlin's first week back at work while dealing with his parents' murder. Sure, she was on light-duty, but she was in the building. He'd been personally warned by the Secretary to stay away from Katlin. He was not to have any contact whatsoever with her.

Jack inwardly grinned. If she was in the building, he could see her. He'd be able to watch her. He'd been tapping into the security feed, which covered almost every inch of the building, for years. He knew secrets about the people all over that building. His parents had taught him human manipulation very well. Several of those people were included in the large contingent of Homeland Security employees that sat in the row right behind him.

Katlin wasn't there, though.

Neither was Nikkole. Earlier in the week, he'd needed stress release, and fucking his Katlin look-alike was the answer. He'd warned the near-perfect stand-in not to attend the funerals. The last thing he needed was her distraction.

Had Katlin shown up on her own, though, it would've proven to him that she truly cared about him as a man, not just her boss. But she hadn't shown.

Six hours later, Jack stepped into his Georgetown home and loosened his tie. He took off his suit jacket, folded it neatly, and placed it over the back of the antique couch. As he headed toward the wet bar in desperate need of his favorite scotch, the doorbell rang.

He closed his eyes hoping that it wasn't Nikkole. Although it had been an extremely stressful day, he didn't want her company. He poured himself a drink. Maybe if he ignored the bell, whoever was on the other side would simply go away.

At the third ring, Jack gave up and checked the peephole.

Fuck. The homicide detectives were back.

"Detective Schultz, Detective Weber, it's been a long and stressful day. What do you need from me?"

"We were hoping you might be able to help us identify some of the people at the funeral." Schultz waved a stack of pictures.

"Jesus Christ. There were four thousand people there. Those were my parents' friends, not mine."

"Could you just take a few minutes and look through these faces?" Detective Weber seemed to be the nicer of the two. "Something might click that could give us a new lead in the case."

With a heavy sigh, Jack opened the door wide and gestured for them to come in. He indicated the uncomfortable

16th-century furniture. He shuffled through the stack, sneering at several of his father's former fuck babes.

"You recognized someone." Weber held out his hand for the picture.

Jack pulled three from the stack he'd just perused. "I'm quite sure my father had affairs with all three of these women, but they're old news. I hadn't had drinks with him in nearly a month, so I hadn't been subjected to his bragging lately."

Weber's eyes widened at the young beauties. "All three? When?"

"Two, maybe three months ago." Jack glanced up at the detectives. "He was easily bored. I don't believe he's kept a steady mistress for years. When I was young, he often had one or two women he'd visit regularly. They were well-kept. He provided them with an apartment, a driver, and credit cards. He also had other women for a night here and there."

"Did your mother know about these affairs?" Schultz asked.

Jack burst out laughing. "Hell, she encouraged it. If he was getting laid elsewhere, he wasn't bothering her. Besides, she had her own stable of men."

Weber shook his head. "I just don't understand rich people. My wife would cut off my balls if I even looked twice at a woman."

Jack nodded. "You're right, the problem is you don't understand rich people. My parents were never in love, as I take it you are with your wife. The Ashworth name goes back to the founders of this country, and beyond. My ancestors helped fund the revolution. My father marrying Suzanne Cook was no coincidence. Her parents were equally as wealthy as my father's. Together, they were an unrivaled power couple."

"So, you're saying your parents had an arranged marriage?" Weber shook his head, again. "That's hard to believe in this day and age."

Jack's grin was sarcastic. "They made it work, at least once. I'm living proof of that."

"Just to clarify, you have no other living siblings?" Schultz asked, pen poised over his small notebook.

"No." He debated telling them his father's secret, then decided, what the hell. "After I was born, my mother informed my father that she was never going to go through childbirth again. He needed to make do with one heir. There would never be a spare. He was also welcome to fuck anyone he wanted but she would remain his wife, mother of his only child. The next day, my father went out and got a vasectomy and my mother moved into the east wing of the house. My entire life they had separate bedrooms. They also led separate lives privately. Publicly was a completely different story. They both had multiple affairs over the years, so if you're looking for a jilted lover, that's going to be a long list."

Detective Weber rubbed his hands over his face. "Thanks for letting us be there for the reading of the will the other day. Your mother would've been proud of their funeral."

"I couldn't disobey my mother's wishes in death any more than I could during her life," Jack admitted.

"So, Mr. Ashworth, what are you going to do with all those billions?" Detective Schultz held his gaze. "Quit your job and buy a Caribbean island?"

"I enjoy my job. What I do is important and I'm uniquely qualified for it." Jack knew he sounded snobbish but he didn't care. "I was born wealthy and decided to serve my country as a foreign service officer before moving to Homeland Security. My parents were never happy with my decision. I didn't care then, and I don't care now."

Jack had enough. He stood. "Gentlemen, it's been a long day. I intend to return to work tomorrow, which starts very early in the morning." He moved toward the front door. "Next time, please call me first before coming over. I can assure you, if I'm entertaining, I won't answer the door." On that cue, he swung the front door open.

"Thank you for your time, Mr. Ashworth. Next time, we'll call." Schultz waved as he trotted down the steps.

"Thanks for the insight." Under his breath, Weber added, "Rich people are really fucked-up."

Jack closed the door and turned the deadbolt. "Detective, you have no idea." He poured himself three fingers of his favorite libation and went to the sitting room off his bedroom. He collapsed in his recliner, propping his feet up.

Excitement about seeing Katlin the next day, vicariously watching her work, filled his mind…and his dreams.

The first thing Jack did when he sat down at his desk was to log into his most-secret part of the system. Then, he hunted until he found Katlin. They had her working in the audio-video department. They kept the rooms down there darkened but her face was illuminated with the light of her computer screen. She looked at the reel.

How perfect. Katlin was his angel.

When he started to get hard, he stroked himself, his hand hidden under his desk. He was about to step into his private bathroom and take care of his erection when the intercom buzzer jolted him out of his fantasy.

"Mr. Ashworth, Agent Chernakov is here as requested."

Jack smiled. Perfect timing. "Send her in."

Nikkole closed the door behind her and Jack pushed the button on his desk to lock it.

"I have something to talk to you about, but first, I need you." When he stood, her eyes fell directly to his cock.

She smiled and licked her lips. "It would be my pleasure to help you in your time of need." Her smile said *yes, whatever you want.*

He debated as she approached him. Did he want her on her knees, or bent over the desk? He glanced at Katlin, sitting in the dark, watching a video.

"Desk."

Nikkole stopped a few feet from him. "How about both?"

Oh, Christ. "Even better."

She dropped to her knees and all he saw was the top of her blond hair. Jack closed his eyes as she took him into her mouth. He ran his fingers through her silken strands, holding her head as she took him deep. He wanted to come inside her sweet tight channel, not her mouth.

When he pulled out, she knew exactly what to do. She hiked up her skirt and leaned over the desk while he pulled on a condom. With her face down, blond hair splayed over his desk hiding her face, he almost came the minute he entered her.

With her hand trapped under her body, Nikkole worked her clit until she convulsed around his cock, milking every last drop out of him.

He left her to right herself as he disposed of the condom in his private bathroom. He returned to his desk and pulled out a legal document.

"I told you that I had something more special for you than joining the Black Swan team." He tapped the papers. "As you know, my parents passed away. I am the only Ashworth heir…right now. Nikkole, I would like you to have my baby."

The woman exploded from the chair, sprinted around his desk, and threw herself into his lap. She had her arms around his neck kissing his face.

"Oh, Jack. Of course I'll marry you. We'll have as many

kids as you want. I'll sign any kind of a prenuptial agreement you want."

Standing, he set Nikkole several feet away from him. "You misunderstand. I want you to have my baby. That's all." He tapped the paperwork. "This is a standard surrogate contract. All your medical bills dealing with the baby will be covered. I'll provide you with a house or condo, your choice, and cover all your living expenses until the baby is born. You may continue working as long as it doesn't endanger the baby, or quit as soon as you sign the contract. You need to understand this clearly—you can never tell anyone, ever, that the baby is mine. You'll be paid one hundred thousand dollars, which is twice the standard rate. Do you have any questions?"

"I wouldn't take your money. I'd want my baby. We would share him, or her, but I wouldn't let you just take our child." Nikkole sounded firm on this point but she didn't understand.

"The baby wouldn't be any part yours. I have fertilized embryos that would be implanted into you via in vitro fertilization." He tapped the papers again. "All I'm asking of you is to carry my child through to birth. I want to rent your womb for forty weeks. You'll be well-compensated. I'll take my child at birth and you'll never have to be bothered with it again."

Nikkole's gaze was unreadable.

"Why don't you take this contract and review it? There are certain areas I'm willing to negotiate. The fact that the baby is mine, and only mine, at birth, isn't one of them." He picked up the contract and slid it into a brown envelope then handed it to her. "I'll give you twenty-four hours." He reconsidered. "No, make it forty-eight. When you're ready, I can have my attorney come here and finalize all the documents."

She snatched the packet from his hand. "I'll think about it and let you know."

Jack pushed the unlock button as she approached the door.

That went well, he thought as he sat down and pulled up the camera on Katlin. She would insist on being the mother to their baby, Jack was sure of it.

CHAPTER 24

As Katlin sat down at the desk in the soundproof room, she glanced around the small space with black egg carton foam on the walls, thick black carpet, and three large video screens on the black cork-covered desk. Everything in the room was meant to mute interior and exterior noises and eliminate light.

Katlin hated this fucking room.

Week two, day two of her light-duty and she was ready to kill somebody. She would take two weeks and two days in the desert heat over this personal torture, anytime. At least in the desert, there was sunshine.

Her first day back to work, she left the darkened room and walked in the sunshine for a full hour during lunch. Fighting her body's desire to nap in the afternoon in the complete darkness had proven useless. Thankfully, they'd given her six-hour days, so she'd crash the minute she made it into the bedroom at Guardian.

Although she missed Alex fiercely, she was glad he didn't know how weak she still was.

By day three, she took breaks every two and a half hours

and simply sat in the atriums that separated the wings of the building.

She craved sunlight.

Glancing at her watch, she had two hours and seventeen minutes before she could see the sun again. She needed to get to work. As she opened files, she wondered who she could talk to about the definition of light-duty. Someone must believe that term meant sitting on her ass for hours staring at video screens of potential candidates to see if they did stupid shit and shouldn't be hired.

Boring.

The familiar five-knock rhythm came at the door announcing the audiovisual department director. He didn't wait for Katlin to say anything because it couldn't be heard outside the door, anyway.

He barged in, way too chipper for eight o'clock. She needed more coffee. "Good morning, Special Agent Callahan."

Katlin didn't bother to correct him. Very few people at Homeland Security knew she was actually a Navy lieutenant commander, not an agent, special or any other kind. "Good morning, Director Burke. What I can do for you?"

"I'm working on something special and I thought you might want to watch. I don't get to do this kind of work very often and I'm using it as a training session for some of the newer members of my department." He held the door open wide. "Since you're a field agent, I want you to keep this capability in mind in case you ever want to use it. I have a very talented staff, but most people don't understand all the things we can do."

Katlin popped out of her chair. She'd do anything to get out of that room. Following the director to one of the seminar training rooms, she took a seat near the front out of habit.

"What I'm going to demonstrate today is how we take existing footage and change the people's faces and replace the voices." With a few clicks and drags of files, he filled a giant screen suspended from the ceiling. "We're going to take the facial images from this woman and patch them into this video. The agent who ordered this wants her contact to believe that his wife is cheating."

"So she could seduce him?" asked a man a few seats back.

"I have no idea, and that information is above your security level," the director chastised. "Now, I haven't used this video in years so I'm going to run through it and count how many places I need to insert her face. I want you to note that sometimes we must replace both faces and even the background. Those processes involve even more layers."

When the video started to roll, Katlin wanted to throw up. She recognized every second of it. It was different but the same. The man walking naked across the bedroom wasn't Ty. The woman with open arms was not his lieutenant jg's wife. That bedroom looked more like a hotel room than military housing at Virginia Beach.

But is was the same video.

"Where did the original footage come from?" the woman three seats down asked.

The director chuckled. "They both used to be agents. He was married, she worked for him. As you know, direct report fraternization is against the rules. When their affair was brought to the attention of their superiors, the directorate needed video proof in order to charge them. By the way, neither still works here. He transferred to another agency and she's a stay-at-home mom for their three kids. They got a happy ending."

"His wife didn't." Katlin thought she'd said the words quietly enough until the women behind her agreed.

"Not necessarily," the woman who'd originally asked the question interjected. "She got rid of the cheating fucker. Who's to say he's not fucking someone in his office again, or has a side piece? Once a cheater, always a cheater."

"True that." Said one of the women behind her.

Katlin needed air.

She left the small auditorium-style room and walked into the closest quiet atrium. She sucked in a long breath of warm D.C. air and tilted her head back so her face could absorb the heat of the sun. She closed her eyes and just breathed, calming her racing heart. She moved to one of the always-empty benches.

It had been a lie…and she believed it.

Ty had sworn that wasn't him…and it hadn't been.

She had divorce papers drawn up based on the lie. True, Ty had cheated on her many times, and that video had shown one more. But it hadn't been real.

Who would do such an evil thing to her? She hadn't completed the sentence in her mind before she knew the answer.

Jack.

She needed proof to add to her file. She should also give a copy to General Standish and her Uncle Tom. Although she had a high security clearance within Homeland, Jack would have buried any kind of connection he had between the video and himself.

She needed Lei Lu. That woman had crawled all through their computer system.

Katlin quickly pulled out her phone, shielded communications with the encryption software Lei Lu had added to all her team's devices, and sent a text to Lei Lu.

Minutes later, she got a group picture of her team and Black Swan Team Two with the caption: *Home in three hours. Shower. Nap. Chilled wine. Pizza. Men. Not necessarily in that order. See you soon.*

The happiness that filled Katlin couldn't be described. She'd get to see her team after work. She couldn't remember when she'd seen them last and that bothered her.

Katlin had texts and pictures all afternoon from her team members. She went straight to her condo on DuPont Circle rather than going to Guardian Security. She needed to see her friends.

When the team first moved to D.C., Katlin had bought the large five-bedroom condominium with enough space for everyone. Then Tori bought the unit two doors down and Marcus moved in with her. In between them was Rafe and Harper with baby Skylar and their live-in nanny, Maggie. Although Lei Lu had bought a condo in Crystal City, her parents seem to occupy the place more than she did, so her computer genius friend and teammate could often be found in the room next to Grace. After Nita married Daniel, she'd never stayed in the condo again.

As the doors opened on the top floor, it was obvious the party was in progress. She was instantly mobbed by her team, individual hugs turned into a huge group huddle.

Damn. She missed these women…and their men who seemed to be congregating in the kitchen.

"Katlin, beer? Wine?" Griffin called out as soon as he lifted his head out of the refrigerator. "Shakespeare is tending bar, creating all kinds of interesting concoctions." The former college football player shook his head. "I'm never going to get used to calling him Henry. He doesn't look like Henry or act like anyone with that name. As far as I'm concerned, he's Shakespeare."

"Fine by me. You called me Henry, I'm not sure I'd answer," the surfer-looking dude next to Lei Lu expertly shook the bar shaker.

"Thanks. My stomach has been a little sensitive lately. I'll just take a ginger ale." When several of her friends raised an eyebrow, she added, "I may have some wine later." That seemed to appease everyone.

Stepping into the large living room, she was thrilled to see Kayla Scarlatto, the leader of Black Swan Team Two, chatting with Marcus and Tori. Kira Frost, Team Two's medic, was watching videos on Nita's phone, most likely of baby Bella. The nurse practitioner had cared for Katlin's sick niece in Costa Rica while the teams were on a mission in Nicaragua.

Mia McCormick and Ashlin Cartwright, who Katlin didn't know much about, chatted with Grace, and Daniel broke away from the group as soon as he saw her.

After a loving hug, Daniel kept his arm around Katlin. "I don't want you to panic because there are a lot of people here. I think you know everybody."

She beamed back at him and started in the kitchen identifying people by name. "I think I know everybody here."

Male voices echoed in the hall as she and Daniel moved toward the door.

"Alex." Katlin slipped from her brother's grasp and flung herself into Alex's arms. "I thought you left for Miami?"

Alex crashed his mouth on hers. "I couldn't leave you at a time like this." His gaze swept the room. "When I called Griffin to tell him I was headed down, he informed me he was headed to D.C. to meet Grace since the team was returning. He mentioned Team Two would be here, so I brought along some of the off-duty men in case some of them wanted to go clubbing later." He grinned. "I'm quite sure all of your teammates are headed to a private evening and wouldn't be interested in showing the younger women Washington's nightlife."

Katlin kissed him again. "You're right about that." She then remembered her discovery that day. She'd intended to talk to him about it during their nightly conversation.

"What's the matter? Your whole mood changed." Alex pulled her chin up until their eyes met. "Can you tell me?"

"You might be the only one who understands." She grabbed Alex's hand and dragged him through the crowd into her bedroom. After closing the door, she sat on the edge of her bed. Fighting back tears, she swallowed hard over the lump in her throat.

"I told you I was working with audiovisual," she started. When he nodded, she closed her eyes. "The video…the one Homeland gave me warning me that Ty's affair could affect my security clearance…" She squeezed her eyes shut, trying to hold back the tears. "It was a lie. The AV department created that video." A tear escaped down her cheek. "Ty swore it wasn't him, and I didn't believe him. My last words to him…I was screaming at him. I called him a cheating liar." She huffed in a breath and tried to sniff back more tears. "I was divorcing him based on a lie."

Alex pulled her to his chest and the tears flowed. She couldn't stop them.

"I was a terrible wife to Ty."

Alex grabbed her shoulders and pulled her away from him. "You were no such thing. You were a better wife to him than he was a husband to you. Okay, so he might not have cheated *that* time, but we both know he was a serial cheater. You cannot blame yourself for his actions."

"But I…I yelled at him. Those were my last words to him." She drew in a ragged breath. "Then he died."

Alex cuddled her to him. "Babe. Whether the two of you had argued or not, Ty would still be gone. You had nothing to do with his death. His SEAL team was ambushed. It was as though the terrorists knew they were coming. Shit like that happened all the time over there. It's been done and over with for a long time. There's nothing we can do to change it."

Nothing we can do. The words finally sank in. Oh, there certainly was something that she could do. She could find out who ordered that fake video to be created.

Standing, Katlin wiped the tears off her cheeks, then strode into the bathroom and spent the next several minutes with cool washcloths on her face and eyes.

"I know that determined look." Alex stared at her in the mirror. He wrapped his arms around her just below her breasts. "What you thinking?"

Squeezing the water out of the washcloth, she hung it to dry. "I'm going to ask Lee Lu if she would research the video files and find out who requested that it would be made and shown to me. I'm pretty sure it's going to be Jack. It's just one more piece of proof."

He turned her to look at him. "Do that. But not tonight. We've had weeks together, alone. They left while you were still unconscious. Give them at least twenty-four hours with their men, especially Lei Lu. Her relationship with Henry is so new."

Katlin dropped her head to Alex's chest. "I am so fucking self-centered. I hadn't even thought about them." She lifted her head and kissed him. "This is one of the reasons I love you."

Alex just stared at her. One heartbeat. Two. Five. Ten.
He blinked.
"I wasn't sure I'd ever hear those words again." He cupped her face in his hands. "They said you might not

remember me…but you did." He gave her a quick kiss. "They said you might not remember our past." He kissed her again and her response was automatic, kissing him back.

Alex's eyes were bright in the low light of the bedroom as he blinked several times. "I didn't know if you would still love me, the way I love you. I love you so much, Katlin Callahan."

Their kiss was sweet and tender. They both kept it that way. There was no need for heat. This was not a prelude to sex. It was an affirmation of love.

Katlin broke the kiss and touched her forehead to his. "I love you, Alex, and I will forever."

"I've waited months to hear you say that again." They lifted their heads in unison until their lips met. "My love for you has no end." He gave her a quick kiss. "Say it again."

"I love you, Alex." As she kissed him again, the party seemed to roar outside the door.

"Everyone wanted to see you tonight before they went their separate ways." He kissed her one more time. "You need to socialize, but I'm going to keep an eye on you. I don't think you got your nap." He handed her a glass of ginger ale. "Stomach still upset?"

Katlin shrugged. "It comes and goes."

He took her hand and led her to the couch, seating her right beside him.

"Nita, Daniel," Katlin yelled loud enough to be heard above the crowd. When her brother and sister-in-law came over and sat on the huge ottoman in front of them, Katlin leaned up and gave Nita the biggest, longest hug. "I can't thank you enough for checking my medical file that night. If he'd…"

"We didn't let that happen." Daniel's voice was stern. "And Aunt Ava made sure that the secretary himself guaranteed your safety now that you're back at work. Jack hasn't bothered you, has he?"

Katlin shook her head. "No. Wasn't even there for my first week. He was on bereavement leave and dealing with his parents' murder."

"Are you talking about John and Suzanne Ashworth?" Henry and Lei Lu turned her attention to Katlin.

"Yes, Jack Ashworth is our boss," Katlin explained.

"My parents and grandfather flew down from New York for the funeral." Henry grimaced. "Grandpa Hank said it was practically a Who's Who on the New York City Social Register. It was nice to see them for a few hours. I can only handle Mother and Father in small doses. Suzanne was a few years older, but she and Mother attended Vassar at the same time. My father said more than half of their classmates showed up. I guess there was a great deal of speculation as to which designer's dress she was buried in since it was a closed casket. I'm just thankful Mother met her friends for drinks and supper. Father ran into several men he knew from work, so he ended up at some private club. Grandpa Hank and I had a great supper together before they took their jet back to New York." He glanced at Lei Lu. "By the way, Grandpa Hank wants us to take him skydiving for his next birthday."

Lei Lu shrugged. "We can do that."

"I read about that murder." Piper Knight shuddered. "They were both shot through the heart in their bedrooms, and yes, that was plural. The article I read said they'd had separate bedrooms since their son was born. I couldn't go fifty years without sex."

Ashlin Cartwright laughed so hard she almost spilled her drink. "You couldn't go fifty days without sex."

"Not true." Piper protested. "We've been gone longer than fifty days."

"Okay, I amend my statement." Ashlin set her glass down. "You couldn't go fifty days without sex if there were available men."

"I'm available if you need help proving that she's right." One of the Guardian men that Alex brought offered.

"Do you think the funeral was the reason that our transfer to Homeland Security has been delayed?" Kayla Scarlatto seemed to have changed the subject on purpose given the glance she gave her teammates.

"When did that happen?" Tori leaned forward from her seat on the couch.

"Just in the last week, I guess." Kayla gave an exaggerated shrug. "I asked Major General Burkhoff when she was out visiting us if we should start looking for a place to live in D.C. She told me I should hold off on shopping for real estate, that our orders may change."

"So, does that mean that we're going to continue to stay at the BOQ at Quantico?" Mia McCormick asked.

"That's the plan for right now." Kayla stood. "So, it looks like we're going to be relatively close, just not working for the same boss." She hesitated before asking, "Is Jack Ashworth planning on quitting? He is a billionaire now."

Katlin scoffed. "He was born a billionaire and never had to work to begin with. Jack works because he chooses to. I can see that changing, unfortunately. There's probably something else in play. Perhaps the State Department has decided they want their own all-female special operations group."

"Or the CIA," Ashlin offered.

Everyone in the room looked at Katlin. "Uncle Tom hasn't said anything to me about it and I'm sure he would."

"Who is Uncle Tom?" Mia asked.

Katlin glanced at her brother. "Our uncle is Tom Gillpatrick, the Deputy Director of the CIA."

"It must be nice having a powerful family," Kira noted.

"It's come in handy a few times," Katlin admitted, then yawned.

"That's my cue to get my fiancée into bed." Alex stood, pulling Katlin up with him. "She still requires a lot of sleep and she has to go to work in the morning. I'm quite sure everyone else gets a day off."

"Thank God," Piper said as she started picking up empty glasses. The other women from Team Two joined her.

"I distinctly heard somebody mention earlier about cruising some of the clubs tonight." Piper looked at the Guardian men Alex had brought. "Is that invitation still open?"

"Most definitely." "Absolutely." "You bet." Affirmatives filled the air.

"The limo should be here in a few minutes." Alex's voice carried. "You need a designated driver and I want somebody to be able to get the women back to Quantico."

"Yes, sir." "Thank you, Alex."

Katlin knew they would have a great time and be safe.

"I'm taking the day off to spend with my wife." Daniel pulled Nita into his arms and gave her a kiss before they headed to the door.

"I'm not going in tomorrow, either," Marcus said as he towed Tori across the room to follow them out.

"Have I shown you my suite in this condo?" Lei Lu stood and held out her hand for Henry.

"Does this mean I don't have to drive all the way back to Crystal City?" Henry smiled.

"That's exactly what that means." Lei Lu's smile was inviting and more than a little salacious.

"Hey, Lei Lu, can I ask a big favor of you?" Katlin moved to her friend and quickly explained what she needed.

"If that fucking bastard ordered that video to be made, I'll find out." Lei Lu looked up at Henry. "Tomorrow. Probably in the afternoon."

Katlin looked around the now-clean apartment. "Thank God I work with wonderful women."

"Want to stay here tonight?" Alex offered.

"Yes, if you don't mind. I missed my afternoon nap and now I'm exhausted." Katlin turned out the lights after Alex checked the locks on the door.

As they settled under the sheets, Katlin apologized, "I'm sorry, Alex. Can you just hold me tonight?"

"Sure," he said as he snuggled in behind her. "I love you, but that doesn't mean I need to make love to you every night."

She rolled over to face him. "And that's another thing I love about you." She kissed him before she set it again. "I love you, and I always will."

Katlin fell asleep surrounded by love, but her last thought was dreading going to work the next day back in that fucking black box.

CHAPTER 25

THANK GOD ALEX KNEW HER WELL...AND LOVED HER. BY the time she'd stepped out of the shower, there was a cup of coffee waiting next to the bathroom sink.

"You look tired, babe." Alex stood behind her, capturing her eyes in the mirror as she applied makeup. He kissed her neck next to the mandatory tight bun of hair. "I thought you went back to sleep after the nightmare."

She smiled at him as she smoothed in her foundation. Unsure if she was pale because she'd thrown up that morning or if she'd spent so much time inside lately that she'd lost any coloration. "I did, but my stomach was upset again this morning. I'm worried that perhaps I went back to work too soon."

"Isn't your next appointment with Dr. Tobias at the end of the week?"

"Yeah. I'll talk to him about it then." She sucked in a deep breath and applied a little more blush. "Are you sure you have time to drop me off this morning?"

"Babe. I'm the boss. For you, I make time." He kissed her neck once again. "How about we run up to the Smith

Mountain Lake house for the weekend? The whole team and significant others. You've been away from them too long and you need some girl time. I feel like cooking on the grill, waterskiing, cruising around the lake looking at the stars."

"Alex, that's a wonderful idea." She finished the last of her makeup, turning to him with hope. "Would you mind setting that up? I hate making personal calls from work because I know I'm being watched every minute and my calls aren't private."

He smiled and gave her a peck on the lips. "Sure. Now, I'm starving and Griffin is cooking breakfast. Let's go."

When Katlin touched her still queasy stomach, Alex suggested a bagel with her second cup of coffee.

As they stepped out into the common area, she was verbally attacked by Lei Lu.

"You're not going to believe what I found." Her friend dragged her over to the dining table and indicated the chair next to where she'd been sitting, laptop open.

"I've got you covered." Alex took her empty mug and headed to the kitchen. "Deal with that."

"Okay, show me what you've got." Katlin sat down. "Please tell me you found where Jack ordered the video."

"Oh, sister of my heart, that took me all of ten minutes. Then I found the good stuff on him. How does murder-for-hire sound? And I'm not sure what other laws he broke since he hired a terrorist to kill military men."

Everyone in the open concept area stopped and stared at the two of them sitting at the large dining table.

"Are you kidding me?" Grace scooted over to them, still in her pajamas, and took the chair on the other side of Lei Lu.

"Sweetheart, my fucking genius. Please tell me this is not going to get you arrested." Henry moved behind the three women and was quickly joined by Griffin and Alex.

Lei Lu patted Henry's hand which was on her shoulder. "You should know by now, I'm better than they are. I didn't leave any trace." She turned to Katlin. "How you can legally retrieve this information, I'm not sure, but I can give you its location on Homeland's system."

"We'll figure that out, just tell me what the hell you have." Katlin knew she sounded rude, but wanted her friend to move on.

When Lei Lu glanced first at Alex then held her hand over hers, Katlin knew she wasn't going to like the next words.

"Jack had Ty killed." Lei Lu squeezed her hand tight. "Stay with me." Using her mouse, she highlighted several lines of code. "This is where Jack hunted for, and found, a double agent in Afghanistan." A few clicks later, she highlighted more lines. "This is where he transferred one-hundred thousand U.S. dollars to that terrorist." One click later, she highlighted again and looked up at Alex. "And this is where he gave the man the coordinates of your rendezvous point and mission objective."

But her teammate wasn't done. Lei Lu clicked to the next screen. "Days later, Jack's assassin came back for more money. In this communication, our terrorist claims he lost nearly a quarter-million dollars because he couldn't take the heads of the SEALs proving to the Taliban that he and his band of mercenaries took out a whole SEAL team. He demanded more money and Jack paid him."

"Now, see this line of numbers? That was the Cayman Island account they used to do business. His terrorist wasn't very smart. He never moved the money into a personal account. But Jack did. Three days later, this account was emptied. It took me about half an hour this morning to follow the money, but guess where it ended up?"

"In an account with Jack Ashworth's name on it." Griffin offered.

"No, but it did pass through one of his accounts." Lei Lu stared at Katlin.

"Oh, please, don't tell me he put it in one of my accounts." Fuck. That would make Katlin look as though she had her husband killed. She already carried around enough guilt for falsely accusing him of an affair hours before he left on that mission.

Lei Lu grinned knowingly. "He put the money into the foundation that you created for the children of Tyler's SEAL team."

Katlin's stomach roiled.

"Excuse me." She bolted from the table and just made it into her bathroom in time before she started throwing up again. She was thankful her hair was pulled tight at the nape of her neck. She wasn't sure she'd have the strength to hold it out of the way.

Katlin didn't know how to feel about that money. She'd created it for the children and now it was covered in the blood of their fathers. On the other hand, it was also an excellent place for it but she would never thank Jack for the donation.

Alex kneeled, handing her a cool washcloth and a bottle of cold water. Another reason she loved this man. He took wonderful care of her.

Standing, she first rinsed her mouth then moved to the sink and brushed her teeth before gargling with mouthwash. When she finally looked at Alex, he was pale.

Oh, fuck. He'd been there, in the firefight that followed the ambush of Ty's team. Katlin wrapped her arms around him. Alex had just been told his best friend had been murdered...by Jack.

Most likely because of Jack's obsession with her.

"I'm so sorry, Alex." She repeated the words over and over again as she rubbed her hand up and down his back.

"I'm going to kill that fucker." Alex said in a low growl.

"That's always an option but I'd rather not visit you in jail. Let's put him in prison for treason."

"Ye of little faith. I'd never be caught." Alex threw his arm around her as they joined their friends in the dining room.

Two hours later, Katlin's head was still swimming with everything Lei Lu had revealed that morning. All the compiled information had been sent to General Standish and her Uncle Tom. Hopefully, there was enough there for Jack to be convicted of something that would put him away for years.

As she started the third set of videos for the day, someone cracked the door open and slid in. When Katlin raised her eyes to greet the newcomer, her doppelgänger was the last person she expected to see.

"Ni—"

The woman who looked more like her every day put her finger over her closed mouth and shook her head then pointed to a camera in the corner as she crouched down. Her fingers flew over her phone.

Nikkole finally stood. "There, I disabled the audio and video in here. We only have a few minutes." Her eyes scanned Katlin up and down. "I heard a rumor that Jack Ashworth tried to implant embryos that he'd fertilized into you. Is it true?"

Katlin took a deep breath and let out a slow, controlled sigh. She hated rumors, especially when this one was true. At this point, Katlin didn't give a shit if people knew what Jack had tried to do to her. "Yes. While I was in a medically induced coma. Several years ago, I had reproductive problems and had my eggs harvested. They were supposedly stolen and sold on the black market. Jack found them, bought them, hell, for all I know he could've stolen them. But they were my eggs, fertilized by Jack, that he tried to have implanted in me. Why do you ask?"

"Is it possible there are more of your eggs out there?"

Her question made Katlin sit up in the chair. "Guardian Security backtracked the ones he was going to use to the fertility clinic and retrieved what was left."

"But there could be more of your fertilized eggs out there, right?" Nikkole kept pressing the issue.

"Yes, it's possible," Katlin admitted.

"Fuck." Nikkole started to pace the small space. "I knew that motherfucker would fuck me over. It's always been you."

Katlin slowly moved her hand toward the small of her back where her pistol was available for easy access.

"Nikkole, tell me what fucking Jack did to you this time?" Katlin didn't want the woman's anger targeted at her. Did she dare share with Jack's known fuck-buddy? On the other hand, perhaps Nikkole could be handy.

When the other woman whipped around and slapped her hands on the desk, glaring at Katlin with eyes identical to her own, Katlin slipped the gun out of its holster. The sound of Nikkole's rapid breathing was absorbed by the small room.

"Take a deep breath, Nikkole, and talk to me. I might be able to help you. There are a lot of things happening in the background around here. Maybe you can help us, too."

She blinked. Then Nikkole let out a heavy sigh. "Katlin, I think Jack still has more of your eggs."

Katlin stood at that declaration. "What gave you that idea?"

Nicole stepped back and leaned against the wall as though she needed support. "He offered me a hundred thousand dollars to rent my womb long enough to have his baby." Her jaw quivered. "Then he was going to take my baby away from me. I could never see it again. He said no part of that baby was mine. He already had growing embryos that they'd put into me."

She lifted off the wall and started pacing again. "Oh, but he was making me one hell of a deal. I can have a house or condo the whole time I was pregnant. He'd cover all my expenses." She stopped in front of the desk and sneered. "I could keep working here as long as I wanted unless it affected the baby. Or, I can quit as soon as I sign the contract." She threw her hands up in the air. "Did I tell you one of the best parts? I could never tell anyone that I was carrying Jack Ashworth's baby."

She looked away blinking. "I'm such a fucking fool. When he first asked me, I thought he was asking me to marry him." She wiped away the tears streaking her cheeks. "I would have, you know. Married him. I'd do anything for him." She ran her hand in front of her body from her head down toward the floor. "I've already done more for that man than any woman should be asked to do. And what do I get for it? The privilege of carrying *your* baby."

Katlin felt like she'd been punched in the gut. She collapsed into the chair. "No. No!" She flew around to the opposite side of the desk and took Nikkole by the shoulders. "We can't let him do this. We cannot let Jack get away with this."

Katlin dropped her hands and started pacing the same track Nikkole had made. "What can we do? How are we going to stop him?" Katlin stopped in front of Nikkole. "And I'm talking about stopping him, forever. You mentioned the contract. Was it something in writing, or was it just going to be a verbal agreement?"

Blond hair went flying as Nikkole shook her head. "Oh,

no. He had a ten-page contract drawn up with my name already filled in."

Katlin smiled at her mirror image. "Nikkole, don't fuck with me. Are you willing to help me take Jack Ashworth down?"

"Absolutely. That man has shoved me to the lowest level possible for the last time. What do you need from me?"

"We need to go to lunch, with my favorite aunt and uncle." Katlin didn't want the woman out of her sight until a plan was solidified. She didn't trust Nikkole Chernakov one inch.

CHAPTER 26

KATLIN SAT IN THE FBI COMMAND CENTER VAN TWO BLOCKS from the Pennsylvania fertility clinic where Nikkole was being prepped for in vitro fertilization. Katlin wanted to be there when Jack was taken into custody, if nothing more than for questioning. She would take her satisfaction in watching Jack surrounded by federal agents as they walked him to a waiting SUV. She'd been assured that he could not return to his post as Director of Operations.

Everyone from the Secretary of Homeland Security to the head of the FBI task force and the Chief of Naval Operations wanted to talk to Jack Ashworth. The problem was, he hadn't been to work since the day Katlin and Nikkole had their conversation. According to Jack's boss, he'd emailed that he was taking a few extra days beyond his bereavement leave to settle his parents' estate. Although he'd been seen leaving his Georgetown home, he'd lost his tail each time. He was, after all, a trained agent.

Everyone felt sure Jack would be there when his babies were implanted into Nikkole.

But as the procedure time passed, Jack hadn't shown.

Two hours later, a tearful Nikkole walked out of the clinic, her uterus as empty as it was when she'd entered.

Katlin popped out the back of the van and embraced Nikkole in a hug. "What's the matter?"

"I want the baby." The other woman dropped her head to Katlin's shoulder.

"Me, too," Katlin admitted.

"But I don't want Jack's," Nikkole said half-crying, half-laughing.

"Neither do I." Katlin wasn't sure if her own tears were for the embryos containing her DNA that were thawing inside that facility that would never see life, or if they were tears of laughter that neither woman wanted anything to do with Jack Ashworth's babies.

"I hate Jack Ashworth. He didn't even care enough about me to be here when they were going to implant his babies into me." Her tears streaked her pretty makeup-free face.

"He's such an inconsiderate asshole," Katlin agreed. With her arm around Nikkole, they headed to the Guardian limousine that pulled to the curb.

"You know you can still go the IVF route with an anonymous sperm donor." Katlin settled herself in the back of the large, comfortable vehicle.

Katlin picked up the original conversation. "There are several fertility clinics around Washington D.C.. Millions of professional women are single mothers these days."

Nikkole smiled at her. "I don't need a place like that for a sperm donor. Have you seen me? I'm beautiful. This whole process has taught me how to get pregnant, and getting a handsome and intelligent man into bed isn't a problem for me. Now, I just have to decide if I'm more interested in being a Homeland Security agent or a mother."

"Or both," they said at the same time, then high-fived.

They rode in silence for a few minutes, Nikkole staring out the window. "I think I'm going to take a couple days off. I don't want to take the chance of running into Jack, not that he's been around lately. I need some time to myself."

"That sounds like a good plan." Katlin still didn't trust Nikkole and wondered if she'd told him of their plans. It was too late if she had. Eventually, the FBI would catch up with him. Maybe by then, the authorities would have solidified all the charges.

Nikkole turned her attention to the interior of the limo. Katlin was used to riding around in a limousine but by the way Nikkole seemed to absorb everything around her, Katlin would bet the agent hadn't ridden in many. She'd probably be bored with the new experience by the time they reached D.C. It was a long ride home. Her eyes lit up when she discovered the bar.

"Now that I'm not pregnant, or going to be anytime soon, how about a drink?" Nikkole opened the bar and pulled out two wineglasses, pouring each of them a drink. They toasted to not being pregnant by Jack, but the wine didn't sit well with Katlin so she set it aside after the first sip.

She discussed her sensitive stomach with Dr. Tobias and he said that wasn't unusual. He suggested that she stay away from spicy food, alcohol, and soda. He also limited her to one cup of coffee a day. That was the hardest recommendation to follow. Katlin loved her morning coffee.

When she reported to work the next day, she had an email saying she'd been taken off light duty. Thank God. No more black box. No one seemed to know who was in charge of Section 7 but her team was ordered to Quantico, acting as the enemy against new lieutenants at The Basic School.

That afternoon when Alex picked her up, he was all smiles. "Tuesday morning before the sun rises."

"Okay, I'm game. What happens Tuesday morning before the sun rises? I'll probably just be crawling into my bed at the officer's barracks at Quantico. Our whole team is headed to Virginia. We're supposed to report there tomorrow, by the way."

Alex reached over and grabbed her hand. "Then I guess we'd better take advantage of every minute between now and then. I'm quite sure you're in need of a nap." He moved her hand over to his crotch. "I'm fully capable of tiring you out."

"No sex until you tell me what's going to happen Tuesday." She loved to tease Alex.

"Well, then I guess you're going to miss Jack's arrest."

"No. I want to be there." Katlin sounded a little whiny, but she'd really wanted to see Jack in handcuffs.

Alex's smile was sassy. "I got an invitation to watch". He shrugged. "I have to stand across the street but at least I get to see him take the perp walk."

"They were able to bring formal charges against him?" Katlin turned in the front seat as Alex slipped in and out of traffic.

"Yes. Misappropriation of government funds. He used Homeland Security money to pay the terrorist." He gave her a shit-eating grin. "They are still working on murder for hire and a few others, but they have him cold on the misappropriation. He won't be allowed to post bail because he's too much of a flight risk."

"Take pictures," she demanded.

Five days later, Alex stood across the street in the dark of night wearing similar black camouflage to the special operators from the FBI. His buddy had allowed him to watch and listen through their communication system, but from a distance. Leaning against the Guardian SUV, arms crossed over his Kevlar-covered chest, he heard when Jack's Georgetown home had been surrounded.

Shit was about to get real.

Two men in standard FBI suits rang the doorbell. There was no answer. No lights came on inside the large house.

They tried one more time.

No answer. No lights.

Several men carrying a door breacher moved in behind the suits.

"Why don't you try the knob before you go busting it down?" somebody suggested over the comm.

To everyone's surprise, the door wasn't locked. Neither was the back door. Men rushed in. Alex heard "Clear" multiple times as the team determined each room to be uninhabited.

Alex's friend exited the front door, flipped his assault rifle to his back, and took off his helmet. "There's nothing in there," he announced.

"No trace of Ashworth?" One of the suits asked.

Alex's friend chuckled. "No. When I told you there's nothing in there, I meant absolutely nothing." He turned around and flicked on the lights. "Go see for yourself. The place is empty. Are you sure we've got the right house?"

"Absolutely." Suit number two headed through the door.

Alex was sure, too. He'd been inside that house, more than once. It had been filled with antiques. A grown man couldn't take more than two steps without bumping into something fragile and expensive.

As lights flicked on throughout the house, Alex could see from his post that the place truly was empty.

Men still milled around as the sky started to lighten.

A woman in her mid-sixties wearing a blue suit with a red tie at her throat clicked up the sidewalk carrying a sign.

"Excuse me," she called as soon as she was within hearing distance. "Is there a problem with Mr. Ashworth's house?"

One of the suits eyed the woman up and down. "Do you know where I can find Jack Ashworth?"

"I would imagine he's already on an island in the Caribbean." She looked around at all the men in black SWAT gear. "If they got those floors dirty, you're going to pay to have them cleaned again. They were such a mess after the movers left, but Mr. Ashworth left me plenty of money to get the house in shape. My cleaning crew worked for two days straight just so we can get this house up for sale today."

The second suit threw his hands in the air. "So much for any evidence."

The first suit pinned her with a stare. "When was the last time you saw Jack Ashworth?"

"Never. Everything we did was via email and courier. Mr. Ashworth is a very busy man, too busy to meet with me in person. He needed to finish up the last few days before retiring." She waved her hand. "I work with a lot of government executives this way. They're transferred somewhere else, to another country, whatever, and want their home sold quickly." She lifted her chin. "I'm known in certain circles for getting the job done on time." She looked around the front yard and pushed the sign into the soft grass where it could be seen from each direction.

"Ma'am, I have a few more questions." Suit number one took out his phone and started making notes. "What makes you think Jack Ashworth is on a Caribbean island?"

She looked at him as though he were stupid. "He said he was going to go to the Caribbean and enjoy some time in the sun. He was tired of cold D.C. winters." She pointed to the house. "He's such a wonderful man. He had me send all the beautiful antique furniture that filled this house, and his parents', over to that high-end auction house in Alexandria. He's donating the proceeds to a charity for military children."

"What about the profits from the houses?" The detective tilted his head as though listening carefully.

"That money goes into his account in the Caribbean." She looked at him through squinted eyes. "What agency did you tell me you're from? I think I need to see a badge."

Alex had seen and heard enough. He walked across the street to thank his FBI special operations friend and return the communications unit.

"Can you believe this?" His friend's gaze swept the area from the real estate agent being quizzed by the suit to the empty house.

"Oh, yeah." As Alex walked away, he wondered if Jack really was on a Caribbean island, or if his body was someplace where it could never be found. If Jack was dead, Alex was the only person he was absolutely sure was innocent of the crime. Although he thought about it way too many times.

Alex was able to get a hold of Katlin later that afternoon, just before they were heading out for night maneuvers. "The house was completely empty."

"That doesn't surprise me. We heard through the grapevine that his letter of resignation was on the Secretary's desk when he arrived to work this morning. Jack probably moved to some island in the Caribbean that doesn't have extradition to the United States. Too many people knew he was going down. Somebody told him and he decided to cut his losses and run." Kat sounded as though she really didn't care. "I hate to cut this short, but our ride's here. Thanks for calling. I love you."

Alex got a text on Thursday afternoon that Katlin's team had been released for a long weekend and they were all headed to the condo.

Katlin, her team, and all their men were sprawled around the seating area, most on their second or third drink.

Nita scanned the crowd, then asked, "Am I the only one who thinks Jack is really dead?"

"Everything document-wise is easy to fake." Lei Lu sipped her wine and settled into Henry's chest.

"I'd certainly want to get rid of the house that my parents were murdered in as quickly as I could." Grace shuddered.

"That would've been one of the easiest things for him to do," Henry noted. "Jack was an only child, so he immediately inherited everything. There was no one to contest the will so everything becomes his."

"If Jack was moving, wouldn't he want to keep some of the contents of his house for his new place?" Griffin took a long pull on his beer.

"No." Katlin immediately spoke up. "When our parents passed away, they had five storage facilities filled with things they had picked up all over the world that had meaning to them, but we could care less."

"I had no use for anything they'd purchased twenty years ago when living in South America," Daniel added. "I personally didn't need any reminders of that continent. I spent enough of my life there and in Central America."

"Hell, I lived there and didn't even want that shit." Katlin slowly shook her head. "We ended up giving stuff away to anybody who would take it and then sent the rest to an auction house. Jack wouldn't need any of his furniture in the Caribbean. I was only there once for a Christmas open house and if I remember right, the house was filled with 16th-century French furniture. I remember thinking it seemed extremely feminine."

"And fragile," Tori added. "Not to mention small. I ended up standing because I couldn't fit on any of those tiny chairs. My knees would've been under my chin."

"That shit never would've held up in the Caribbean," Henry noted.

"Well, if he's dead, he wouldn't need any furniture in the Caribbean. This could all be somebody's way of redirecting attention." Alex tipped his bottle and emptied it before standing and heading to the kitchen.

"It is quite neat and tidy, isn't it?" Griffin redirected his attention to Alex. "Could you pick up a fresh beer for me, too?"

At the kitchen door, he asked, "Anyone else want anything while I'm up?" When the orders were yelled, Katlin got up to help him bring them back.

Nita shrugged. "He could be dead. We make people disappear all the time. Cleanup is one of the first areas you work in when you're hired at homeland. Every one of us went through it."

"I've never bought or sold property," Grace said as she held out her glass and Katlin filled it with wine. "But don't you have to sign papers? Wouldn't the real estate agent have seen Jack then?"

Katlin shook her head. "I've sold at least ten pieces of property and never met with the real estate listing agent. I try to not even talk to them on the phone. To be honest, I hate buying property because the agent has to be with you as you walk through the house. When I can, I do everything via email. They'll FedEx or courier over the papers and I sign what I can then send them right back."

"There. Jack had to sign the listing papers, so he had to be alive at that point." Grace bounced up and down, so happy with herself.

Tori took a pen from her pocket and wrote something on a napkin, then handed the pen to Grace. "Sign your name on that napkin." When Grace held it up, Tori held hers beside it. They were identical. "Do you want to see me sign Jack's name now? We took a class in forgery."

"Well, darn it." The edges of Grace's mouth turned down.

The dog stirred. "Nobody called you." Katlin petted Damnit who closed his eyes and went back to sleep.

"Doesn't that back and forth paperwork take time?" Grace asked.

Henry chuckled. "Money makes things happen very quickly. When my aunt and uncle were killed in a plane crash in Africa, my cousin had their house cleared out, painted, refurnished, and he'd moved in with his latest girlfriend before their bodies made it back to the United States."

"So, what you're telling me is that hypothetically, if one of you had killed Jack, disposing of the furniture and the houses, setting up his supposed exit to the Caribbean, and creating his letter of resignation would be easy.

"Yes." All five women said at the same time.

"The hardest part would be killing Jack," Grace suggested.

Katlin scoffed. No, it wouldn't. I wouldn't have any problem putting a bullet in that fucker."

"Wouldn't be hard to dispose of the body, either." Tori sipped her wine. "I'd dress him like a bum and dump him in a slum."

"Good idea," Katlin agreed. "But I would take him to Philadelphia, or maybe New York. He'd never be recognized there."

"Nobody would be looking for him." Nita waved her hand as though to shoo away that thought. "Everybody in D.C. would believe that he was working on his tan in the Caribbean."

"Or, his killer could take him to the Caribbean. That would get him out of the country, his passport recorded elsewhere." Lei Lu grinned. "There's a lot of ocean out there. Kill them on the boat and throw him overboard."

"You'd want to tie the anchor to him," Tori added to the scenario. "The last thing you'd want is for his body to show up."

"We were all on Grand Turk and saw how quickly a body decays underwater and how fast the fish began to feast." Nita pointed out.

"Or, you could put him in your trunk and take him down to the Georgia or Florida swamps," Tori suggested. "Gators would make quick work of the body."

Marcus leaned forward and looked at his girlfriend then at the men in the room. "Is it just me or are these women truly frightening?"

The other men chuckled. Everyone except Marcus had been, or was currently, special operations. Alex believed that SpecOps people truly thought differently than the average person.

"Playing devil's advocate," Griffin grinned fiendishly. "If Jack is dead, who killed him?"

"I don't really care. I'd just like to give her, or him, my sincere thanks." Katlin stood up. "I'm going to take a bio break. Don't talk about anything important until I get back."

Before Katlin got to her room, the other four women had stood and were headed to their own bathrooms.

With the women gone, Marcus looked at Alex with a

serious expression. "Do you think they did it?" He asked quietly.

Alex shook his head. "I believe that our women have too much honor. Yes. They kill on every mission. Those are sanctioned assassinations. If Katlin let her emotions rule her actions, I have no doubt that she could pull the trigger on Jack. She hates that man. But she's so much better now than she was right after she awakened from the coma. I expect she'll be on the next mission."

Katlin was yawning as she walked back into the common area. "Along the same morbid lines, did Jack kill his parents?"

"No." Came a chorus of agreement from everyone.

"Grandpa Hank and I talked about this." Henry repositioned Lei Lu on his lap. "Jack's parents may have been very powerful politically, but they were terrible people. For every person they put into power, there was at least one, and usually many, whose hopes and dreams they'd crushed. That's what makes them politicians."

"My family has been in politics for generations, and I can tell you with firsthand knowledge, they play dirty." Griffin nodded his head.

"Then there's all the affairs they both had." Tori loved the celebrity rags. "Hell hath no fury like a woman scorned."

"If it had been a scorned woman, she would've shot his balls off." Nita held up her glass in a toast.

Daniel stood. "And on that note, I'm taking my wife home."

Half an hour later as Alex and Katlin got into bed, he had to know.

Before he could ask, Katlin leaned in so their faces were mere inches apart. "I didn't kill Jack, and neither did anyone on my team, but I hope he's dead." She gave him a small kiss.

"But if he is indeed dead, I have a pretty damn good idea who did it."

"I didn't kill him either." Alex kissed her then pulled back. "But I thought about it."

Katlin smiled. "I love you for wanting to kill him for me."

Alex pulled her warm body to his. "I'd do anything for you…because I love you."

The end.

If you've enjoyed *Unending Love,* please tell others what you liked about this book by leaving a review on your retailer's site.

You may also wish to consider other books by KaLyn Cooper…

Black Swan Series
Military active duty women secretly trained in Special Operations and the men who dare to capture the heart of a Woman Warrior.

Unconventional Beginnings Prequel (Black Swan novella #0.5) ~ He's dead. But they can't allow it to affect her. She's too important.
Download FREE https://dl.bookfunnel.com/uec4utb66d

Unrelenting Love: Lady Hawk (Katlin) & Alex (Black Swan novel #1) ~ Women in special operations? Never… Until he sleeps with the most lethal woman in the world.

Noel's Puppy Power: Bailey & Tanner (A Sweet Christmas Black Swan novella #1.5) ~ He's better at communicating with animals than women, but as an amputee she knows firsthand it's the internal scars that can be most difficult to heal.

Uncaged Love: Harper & Rafe (Black Swan novel #2) ~ The jungle isn't the only thing that's hot while escaping from a Colombian cartel.

Unexpected Love: Lady Eagle (Grace) & Griffin (Black Swan novel #3) ~ He never believed in love, but he never expected to find her.

Challenging Love: Katlin & Alex (A Black Swan novella #3.5) ~ A new relationship can be fragile when outsiders are determined to challenge that love.

Unguarded Love: Lady Harrier (Nita) & Daniel (Black Swan novel #4) ~ She couldn't lose another sick baby…then he brought her his dying daughter.

Choosing Love: Grace & Griffin (A Black Swan novella #4.5) ~ Hard choices have to be made when parents interfere in a growing relationship.

Unbeatable Love: Lady Falcon (Tori) & Marcus (Black Swan novel #5) ~ Scarred outside and in, why would his beautiful friend ever want more with him?

Unmatched Love: Lady Kite (Lei Lu) & Henry (Black Swan novel #6) ~ Scarred outside and in, why would his beautiful friend ever want more with him?

Unending Love: Lady Falcon (Tori) & Marcus (Black Swan novel #7) ~ Their life together is not over. He has to believe it…or it will be.

Guardian Elite Series

Former special operators, these men work for Guardian Security (from the Black Swan Series) protecting families in their homes and executives on the road, but they can't always protect their hearts.

Double Jeopardy (Novella #1 Guardian Elite series crossover with Hildie McQueen's Indulgences series) ~ Guarding a billionaire and his wife isn't easy when you can't keep your eyes off your bikini wearing, gun carrying partner who is lethal in stilettos.

Justice for Gwen (Novella #2 Guardian Elite series crossover with Susan Stoker's Special Forces World) ~ She's not what she seems. Neither is he. But the terrorist threat is real. So is the desire that smolders between them.

Rescuing Melina (Novella #3 Guardian Elite series crossover with Susan Stoker's Special Forces World) ~ When Jacin awoke stateside, he remembered nothing about his escape from the Colombian cartel or his torture. He was sure of only one thing, his love of Melina, his handler. When she disappears, neither bruises nor the CIA will keep him from rescuing her.

Snow SEAL (Novella #4 Guardian Elite series crossover with Elle James Brotherhood Protectors World) ~ Terrorists want her…but so does he. The chase isn't the only thing that heats up when the flint of the former SEAL strikes against the steel of the woman warrior.

Securing Willow (Novella #5 Guardian Elite series crossover with Susan Stoker's Special Forces World) ~ Guarding her wasn't his job, but he couldn't let her die…even before she stole his heart. When he discovers the temptingly beautiful foreign service officer is being threatened, his protective instincts take over.

SEAL in a Storm (Novel #5 is part of the Suspense Sisters new wave of connected books, Silver SEALs featuring a seasoned hero and heroine, second chances, and edge of your seat suspense.) ~ With a hurricane bearing down on the tiny island, they only have days to find and rescue ten kidnapped young girls and their chaperones…and keep their hands off each other.

Cancun Series
Follow the Girard family —along with their friends, former SEALs and active duty female Navy pilots—as they hunt Mayan antiquities, terrorists and Mexican cartels in what most would call paradise. Tropical nights aren't the only thing HOT in Cancun.

Christmas in Cancun (Cancun Series Book #1) ~ Can the former SEAL keep his libido in check and his family safe when the quest for ancient Mayan idols turns murderous?

Conquered in Cancun (Cancun Series Novella #1.5) ~ A helicopter pilot's second chance at love walks into a Cancun nightclub, but she's a jet fighter pilot with reinforced walls around her heart.

Captivated in Cancun (Cancun Series Book #2) ~ His job is tracking down terrorists so he's not interested in a family. She wants him short-term, then needs him when their worlds collide.

Claimed by a SEAL (Cancun Series crossover Novella #2.5 with Cat Johnson's Hot SEALs) ~ How far will the Homeland Security agent go to assure mission success when forced undercover for a second time with an irresistible SEAL?

Never Series

The mission brought the five of them together, disaster nearly tore them apart, a mystery and killer reunited them forever.

A Love Never Forgotten (Never Series novel #1) ~ Dreams or nightmares. Truth or lies. He can't tell them apart. Then he discovers the woman who has haunted his dreams is real. Is she his future? Or his past?

A Promise Never Forgotten (Never Series novel #2) ~ As a Marine Lieutenant Colonel, he could take on any mission and succeed. Raising his two godchildren…with her…just might kill him.

A Moment Never Forgotten (Never Series novel #3) ~ The moment he realized she was in serious danger…he couldn't protect her.

ABOUT THE AUTHOR

KaLyn Cooper is a USA Today Bestselling author whose romances blend fact and fiction with blazing heat and heart-pounding suspense. Life as a military wife has shown KaLyn the world, and thirty years in PR taught her that fact can be stranger than fiction. She leaves it up to the reader to separate truth from imagination. She, her husband, and Little Bear (Alaskan Malamute) live in Tennessee on a micro-plantation filled with gardens, cattle, and quail. When she's not writing, she's at the shooting range or paddling on the river.

For the latest on works in progress and future releases, check out

KaLyn Cooper's website www.KaLynCooper.com
http://www.kalyncooper.com/

Follow **KaLyn Cooper on Facebook** for promotions and giveaways
https://www.facebook.com/KaLynCooper1Author/

Sign up for exclusive promotions and special offers only available in **KaLyn's newsletter** https://kalyncooper.com/kalyn-cooper-newsletter

www.ingramcontent.com/pod-product-compliance
Lightning Source LLC
Chambersburg PA
CBHW051532050726
47595CB00002B/459